Afraid of the Light

Douglas Kennedy's previous thirteen novels include the critically acclaimed bestsellers *The Big Picture*, *The Pursuit of Happiness*, *The Moment*, and *The Great Wide Open*. He is also the author of three highly praised travel books. *The Big Picture* was filmed with Romain Duris and Catherine Deneuve; *The Woman in the Fifth* with Ethan Hawke and Kristin Scott Thomas.

His work has been translated into twenty-two languages. In 2007 he was awarded the French decoration of Chevalier de l'Ordre des Arts et des Lettres, and in 2009 the inaugural Grand Prix de Figaro. Born in Manhattan in 1955, he has two children and currently lives in Maine, but continues to loiter with intent in Paris, Berlin, London and his hometown of New York.

Praise for AFRAID OF THE LIGHT

'I can't recommend this more highly . . . one of my books of the year'
Phil Williams, *Times Radio*

'A pulse-racing thriller centred on hot-button debates over U.S. reproductive rights . . . Kennedy's action-packed storyline puts a punch spin on the traditional narrative of male later-life crisis'
Daily Mail

'The story burns slowly, catching fire midway through and speeds up to an exciting climax'
Irish Independent

'A wily plot'
Mail on Sunday

Also available by Douglas Kennedy

Fiction

The Dead Heart
The Big Picture
The Job
The Pursuit of Happiness
A Special Relationship
State of the Union
Temptation
The Woman in the Fifth
Leaving the World
The Moment
Five Days
The Heat of Betrayal
The Great Wide Open
Isabelle in the Afternoon

Non-fiction

Beyond the Pyramids
In God's Country
Chasing Mammon

Douglas Kennedy

Afraid of the Light

PENGUIN BOOKS

PENGUIN BOOKS

UK | USA | Canada | Ireland | Australia
India | New Zealand | South Africa

Penguin Books is part of the Penguin Random House group of companies
whose addresses can be found at global.penguinrandomhouse.com

First published by Hutchinson 2021
Published in Penguin Books 2022
001

Typeset by Jouve (UK), Milton Keynes

Printed and bound in Great Britain by Clays Ltd, Elcograf S.p.A.

The authorised representative in the EEA is Penguin Random House Ireland,
Morrison Chambers, 32 Nassau Street, Dublin D02 YH68

A CIP catalogue record for this book is available from the British Library

ISBN: 978–1–529–15692–8
ISBN: 978–1–529–15693–5 (export)

www.greenpenguin.co.uk

Penguin Random House is committed to a
sustainable future for our business, our readers
and our planet. This book is made from Forest
Stewardship Council® certified paper.

for Antony Harwood

my agent and friend for a mere twenty-eight years

'We can easily forgive a child who is afraid of the dark; the real tragedy of life is when men are afraid of the light.'

– Plato

one

'WHERE WE GOIN'?'

The voice belonged to my first fare of the afternoon. I'd picked him up at one of those big nothing office buildings on Wilshire, just on the edge of Westwood. A fast ride, two miles, to another faceless office building in Century City. I looked him over in my rearview. The guy was around fifty. Bad tan suit. Bulky – around two sixty and, like me, not happy about all the fleshiness he was carrying around with him. A sweaty guy – and not just because the mercury was punching three figures with killer humidity.

'I asked you: where we goin'?'

His tone was low-level aggressive, a *time-is-money* type who believes that the loudest voice in the room wins.

'We're going to the address you gave me,' I said, thinking: one of the rules of this game is that you frequently pick up people who hate the lives they're living.

'But surely you fucking well know that going east on Wilshire at this time on a Friday –'

'According to my GPS Wilshire Boulevard was supposed to be clear right up to West Pico,' I said, wondering if an accident had just leapt into our path. 'Let me see if the GPS is showing me another way out of this.'

'Fuck your GPS. Don't you know the city? Have you never read a fucking map? Or did you just recently show up in this town and land this loser job?'

My instinct was to tell Mr Nasty to go have sex with himself. I knew that making such a statement might result in an email against me … and one which could end my only possible source of income right now. So I sucked down my fury and maintained a polite conversational tone. Saying:

'I was actually born here, sir. A true Angeleno. I've spent much of my life stuck in traffic.'

'But you still steered us into some serious shithole constipation …'

'The reason why there has been this sudden build-up of traffic –'

'– is because you don't know how to do your job and because, like every loser behind the wheel, you only listen to where your fucking GPS tells you to go.'

Silence. I found myself tensing after that second 'loser' slap across the face; his immediate sense of superiority being his way of telling me: *I may be nowhere in this world, but I am at least three ladder rungs higher from nowhere than you.*

Count to ten.

It's a strategy I use every day – to keep my own quiet rage in check as I do a job that I don't want to be doing.

But as my career options have flatlined – and the only other work possibilities are minimum-wage nightmares (like stacking shelves at Walmart or doing an eight-hour buried-alive shift in an Amazon warehouse) – sitting behind the wheel of this car still strikes me as less of a mind-fuck option. Even with a guy like this one in the back seat.

'Now as you will see on the right, sir, the reason we've run into such traffic is because that Triumph chopper went under the wheels of that Jeep Cherokee … and the driver of the bike looks kind of dead to me.'

Big Boy looked up from his phone and stared out at the body beneath those Detroit-made wheels. He finally said:

'He's not getting to wherever he was going.'

'Time is never on our side,' I said.

'So now you're not just an Uber sad sack, but a philosopher.'

'What kind of work do you do?'

'What business is that of yours?'

'Just making conversation,' I said.

'Say I don't want conversation?'

Silence again. We were crawling by the scene of the crime. Cops everywhere. Two ambulance guys covering the dead biker with a sheet while a third colleague came out with a fold-up metal stretcher. Meanwhile the driver of that new-model Cherokee – I figured him around twenty, all skinny and tanned with Daddy money behind him – had just finished blowing into the breathalyser held for him by a woman cop. The kid looked like he knew that his future was cooked.

'Sales,' the big guy said. 'I'm in sales.'

Just as I figured.

'What kind of sales?'

'Fiber optics.'

'No kidding,' I said.

'No kidding what?'

'You into optical transport? Baseband video?'

'How do you know that shit?'

'Ever heard of Auerbach?'

'They're our competitors,' the guy said, aggression gone from his voice. 'You know them?'

'Yeah, I knew them ... for twenty-seven years. Regional sales director for SoCal. Petrochemical production and distribution was my game. Flames sensors. Transducers and transmitters. Custom-engineered electro thermocouples.'

'That's fucking weird. 'Cause I cover just about the same territory – only my beat is Nevada, Idaho, Wyoming, Montana.'

'Who with?'

'Crandall Industries.'

'Yeah, you were chasing the same client base as us.'

'Twenty-seven years you tell me?' he asked.

'Twenty-seven years.'

'Then what happened?'

'A downturn,' I said. 'A bad streak. Three big strikeouts.'

'And they just let you go?'

I glanced in the rearview. Saw the way that his lips were all scrunched up. I wanted to ask: *is the reason you play the obnoxious shithead because, like me seventeen months ago, you too are having a losing streak?* But I have a 'never step out of line' face that I show to the world; a face that parents and priests forced me to wear from a young age. I still wear it for all public transactions. Especially those that take place in my seven-year-old cream-colored Prius. In Uber World once a complaint is made against you then you are in the wrong. Which means: when dark thoughts show up at a moment like this I've to keep them locked down inside my throat. Instead saying: 'Yeah, they just let me go.'

'I'm sorry,' he said.

Well, how about that? A moment of shared humanity. A moment that arose not from any kind of actual compassion, but his own fear that he too might end up behind the wheel like me.

The traffic began to move.

'You gonna get me there on time?' he asked.

'According to the GPS … two minutes before your appointment.'

'You said four minutes before.'

'Things change,' I said.

'Tell me about it.'

He said nothing during those final minutes in my back seat. When he got out he also said nothing. When I later looked back on my app to see if the guy had tipped me … zilch, zip.

A rule of thumb in my game:

Guys who hate their lives never tip.

two

PICKUP NUMBER TWO of the afternoon was all talk. She got into the car in mid-conversation. Her telephone spiel was super-clipped, super-fast. An exchange finished within the ten seconds it took her to close the passenger door and me to pull out into traffic. Machine-gun talk: 'We don't make a habit of losing.' End of call. She hit another number. On she went: 'We don't got a gun to our head … you do.'

A check in the rearview. The talker was in her mid-forties. With a hard face. Jet-black hair with gray streaks. No warmth in the immediate vicinity. Fatigued, disappointed by so much – but still up for a fight. And for saying things like '*Don't got*'.

My dad talked that way. 'I don't got the time for this, sonny boy.' Never the name he gave me: Brendan. Never the 'Brennie' that my mom called me. Sonny boy. That was Dad. Always keeping me at an emotional distance. Always letting me know: *I ain't there.*

Dad. No formal education … but he prided himself on reading the *LA Times* cover to cover every day. 'Don't got the smarts to do Electrical Engineering like sonny boy here.' But Dad still had smarts – even if his grammar was a little left field from time to time. The woman in my back seat also had smarts and a far higher degree of education than my father. But the 'don't got' was a hint of origins as no-frills and basic as my own. We've all got our way of making it through the day. Hers was 'no mercy' repartee.

'You expect compassion? Really? That's the word you want to use here: *compassion*? You? Asking for lenience, commiseration? You? Maybe you'd like me to throw in "grace" and "benevolence" as part of the package . . . which, I got to tell you, is going to land on your doorstep on the 12th of Never.'

Did I see in the rearview a flash of a killer smile behind the killer patter? Did that 'I crush ants like you' instinct keep down all the loneliness going on inside her?

We were now hitting the intersection of Beverly and Wilshire. Pulling up in front of a big-deal building with about eight high-end law firms occupying all its square footage. I stopped outside its chrome-and-glass frontage. Ms Machine Gun Talk kept doing just that: talking. *Rat-tat-tat.* I braked. I shifted into park. She slid across the seat, her menace monologue still carrying on. She opened the door. She put her legs onto the pavement. She volted herself up, forward motion propelling her toward the corporate doors facing her.

'Have a nice . . .' I said just as her left hand remembered to slam the door behind her.

But Ms Machine Gun Talk was gone from the car, gone from my story.

Pickup number three was coming out of the same building. A bookish guy, late thirties. Black jeans. A black T-shirt. Black Adidas sneakers. Too cool for school black glasses. A black leather backpack over one shoulder, an Apple Book under his arm.

'How's it going?' he asked.

A guy doing nice. A climate change from my last two fares.

'Going okay,' I said. 'Just ending my first hour.'

'With how many more to go?'

But his phone rang. He actually said 'Excuse me' and was into a conversation straightaway.

You do my sort of work you eavesdrop. You pick up the details and clues that, put together, start to form a picture of all that is going on in a life outside of this car. You try to work out their story. From what I was hearing, this was a dude under pressure. An agent asking for a rewrite on four episodes. A kid not sleeping. Cash-flow fears. I knew the address that popped up on my screen. Dropped someone off there before. It was a street right off Vermont in Los Feliz. Full of little cottages which went for the low seven figures.

'It's going to be okay,' he was saying. 'I'm calling UTA right after and Lucy will get me ... Yeah, yeah, I know all about the car payment ...'

Oh man, not just money worries. Badass debt. He'd bought into the system as most of us had done: the mortgaged house, a family, the leased car, the credit card liabilities ... while simultaneously telling himself that he was going to sidestep all the compromises and limitations that big grown-up responsibilities bring to the table. Whereas the truth of the matter was: we buy in because we tell ourselves that *not* to buy in is not to do what we were raised to do – which is to buy in. My story like so many others.

I liked this guy. Someone with the smarts to be paid for writing ... but vulnerable. Especially as, from what I heard, he was a new dad. And when you have kids ... man, are you endlessly vulnerable.

His phone call ended. I heard him do a few breathing exercises – something to calm down the worry within. Then he was dialing another number.

'Lucy Zimmerman, please ... Zach Godfrey here ... Yeah, I very much am her client ... Sure I can hold ...'

His face scrunched up. Being told to wait showed his lower status on the totem pole. The fact that the receptionist didn't recognize his name ... not good. He kept the phone to his ear, he shut his eyes, he sank back into the seat. Asking me:

'Could you please put on a little music? KUSC?'

'You got it, sir.'

I clicked the radio into life. KUSC was number 4 on my presets. The classical station. Something old and violin-heavy came on.

'Thank you,' he said. 'Are you always so decent?'

'Try to be, sir.'

'You like the work?'

'It's … work,' I said.

'I hear you. Working for Uber is working for The Man, right? But don't think that's a reproach. We all, on some level, work for The Man these days.'

'I appreciate your point of view,' I said, 'and agree with it. But I need to explain something to you. When it comes to "working for Uber" …'

Someone was now back in his ear.

'Hold that thought,' he told me, then started his phone call.

'Lucy? … Yeah, yeah … So listen … You know all about that already? And do you think … ?'

I wanted to tune further into his talk but I noticed a big long swathe of red on the GPS – a hint of traffic trouble up ahead on Melrose. Should I leave this jam and zigzag around a lot of twisty back streets – heading down to Beverly, eventually getting to S Western Avenue, then turning north? Following that route would give us the appearance of moving forward and getting somewhere but which would end up taking as much time as driving into the slowdown up ahead on Melrose – one of the big old-school boulevards that are the real arteries of the city. The guy didn't seem to be in a hurry. I was hoping that he'd finish up his call before we reached his address. Because there was something I wanted to tell him before we parted company in front of 179 Melbourne Ave.

You don't work for Uber.

Nobody works for Uber.

But you do drive for Uber.

You might not be their actual employee …

But you are their captive.

Because they hold all the cards – and you have to abide by all their rules. You also have to be driving about seventy hours a week to earn some modestly acceptable money – which is about thirty hours too many. Mathematically that works out to an extra six hours on a normal workday to keep yourself just about afloat.

So, again, I don't work for Uber. But I still have to pay lip service to their rules and restrictions. Just as I know: if I didn't take an interest in everyone I pick up, if I didn't play surface detective and try to figure them out in the few minutes that they are with me, the job would be beyond punishing. My life for many hours a day is letting a screen on a smartphone direct me around this crazy sprawl that I call home. Wanting to put together a storyline, a police dossier, on each of my pickups … well, it chews up the clock, right?

Mr Writer finished his call with:

'Surely you can convince them to come up with a little more. What they're offering now … Okay, you don't have to remind me that my stock out here isn't the highest right now. Still, they can look at that series of mine … So what if it was back in 2014? … Fine, fine, understood, other clients … Yeah, sure, and yeah, know you'll do your best, and sorry if I … Right, right … You too.'

I heard him doing another long intake/outtake of breath, then muttering 'shit, shit, shit' to himself. The delay on Melrose still had us only a mile east along the route.

'Looks like we might be here for a while.'

'Home is going nowhere. Home can wait for me.'

To which I wanted to say:

'Don't I know that one.'

But I said nothing.

three

It wasn't always like this.

I have a degree in Electrical Engineering. And a career in sales.

Did I ever like the work?

It was a living. It was, for a while, not a bad living.

But did I ever really like the work?

There was a moment ... a summer thirty-four years ago ... when just out of Cal State I spent three months climbing electrical poles in that high country near Sequoia. All those crazy tall redwoods and being at an altitude of 8,000 feet and watching snow white out the horizon in May. Then there was this discovery of oxygen. Pure uncorrupted oxygen. After my twenty-two previous years in Los Angeles – where several hundred thousand internal combustion engines define the daily air quality – I was having my first proper encounter with ozone. And I was out in the wild, far away from city and family: that bungalow-bland corner of North Hollywood which hasn't changed much over the past thirty years. Dad himself grew up in South Central LA. A couple of streets of prole Irish America right near some badass ghettos. Hispanic, black ghettos. A place where being a white guy was decidedly no-go. And where – as Dad never tired of telling me – if you kept to certain rules you could also sidestep trouble.

Dad liked to play the Paddy card. Though he also loved singing the 'I was born on Mean Streets' blues the fact is: no one in his family was ever busted by the cops. All of his three sisters – one of whom became a Carmelite in Nevada (yes, they actually have a convent near Vegas) – were classic 'good girls' … blue-collar shorthand for not getting caught peddling themselves down a dark alleyway. And to the best of my knowledge there were no gang warfare moments where the tough Irish boys got into a rumble – in pure 1950s teen movie style – with the local Hispanic gang on some dirty boulevard.

My parents grew up three streets away from each other. Florence Riordan met Patrick Sheehan at the local high school. They were both the kids of emigrant parents. Their families had arrived from County Limerick and County Louth respectively at the kick-off of the last century. Their grandparents started out on the East Coast, then their parents headed west to the alleged golden land. Mother and Father were both born in Good Samaritan Hospital in South Central. Neither of them ever left this corner of the city. Dad trained as an electrician and got a job as a 'cable and lights guy' (his turn of phrase) at Paramount. He stayed in the same job for forty-one years.

Mom stayed at home with her three children. I was the last in the pecking order. We all did what was expected of us. We pushed ourselves into the middle class. There was a brother who was an accountant. He died of cancer ten years back. A quiet, decent man. We were close – even if Sean steered far away from any displays of emotion. But at life's darker moments we were always in each other's corner. Our sister, Helen, became a senior ER nurse. She went east for work and now lives in a retirement community on the Delaware shore. Like Sean, like everyone in our family, she too was raised to be respectful, reserved. She has a retired cop husband and no kids. We talk a few times a year on the phone. It's always a reasonable chat – even if, truth be told, we don't have much to say to each other.

And then there's me: the electrical engineer turned salesman.

Why did I study Electrical Engineering? Because my father told me to. He was the guy helping light up stars at Paramount. 'It's a good living, kid,' he told me. 'But you can make an even better living if you get your college degree.' That wasn't a suggestion; that was an order. I was going to college. As a kid I showed some facility for math and taking apart and putting stuff together. As a teenager I had no damn idea what I wanted to do in life – except drive the clapped-out 1970s mustard-yellow Dodge Dart

Swinger that I bought for $725 after eighteen months of an afterschool job disemboweling old jalopies in a wrecking yard down the street from us. How I loved that idiot car. It took me to and from Cal State every day as I pursued that degree in Electrical Engineering to please Dad. I had no real interest in Electrical Engineering. I had no real interest in anything except the Los Angeles Dodgers and my Dodge Dart. Back then Dad would often complain that I was just Mister Blah. Middling grades. Middling interest in the world around me. Middling curiosity in current affairs or even the issues menacing the 'hood. Mister Blah. Dad's name for me. And one which really got up my nose – because I knew it to be true. I had a minor talent when it came to getting a busted radio to work again and a dad who wanted to brag to his fellow cable and lights guys at the studio that even his less than sparky youngest child was advancing in the world by doing Electrical Engineering at an okay college. I knew Cal State was as middling as my grades – but I didn't have the academic muscle to find some better niche in the U Cal system. Still, Dad was pleased. Naturally he expected me to live at home – and abide, without an argument, by his midnight curfew rule (1 a.m. on the weekends after I turned twenty-one). Just as he informed me from the get-go that if I didn't maintain a minimum B average I was going to be responsible for the $1275 per annum that it cost him to send me to Cal State in 1980. I did all that was expected for me – and even managed a B+ average. Only twice in four years did I breach his curfew – and Dad let it ride. Because he knew I was playing the game, buckling down, doing his bidding. Why did I do what was demanded of me? Truth be told I couldn't figure out what else to do with myself.

But then, as I was entering the final semester of my senior year, some Career Guidance dude told me that the State of California was running a program trying to rewire the electrical grid for the Sierra Nevadas – specifically the sparse communities in and around Sequoia National Park. They were looking for young electricians wanting to do a spell up in the mountains. When I said that that sounded rather cool – a chance to run away from everything and everyone for a while and do time in the Great Outdoors – Mr Career Counselor had one question for me:

'How do you handle heights?'

I came to handle them pretty damn well. What I couldn't handle (initially anyway) was my dad's dismay that I was taking on such a blue-collar job after four years of college. When I explained that I was doing it for the adventure he got even more outraged.

'Adventure is for the rich boys. For you, for me, life is about advancement and meeting our responsibilities.'

But I had no responsibilities back then. Nor was I looking to accumulate them. So I suffered Dad's sulks. I took the job and discovered that I could scale a forty-foot electrical pole without much in the way of vertigo. Once up there I was able to wield all my equipment and maintain my equilibrium. Of course I was trained into this work by the foreman on the project: a guy who went by the name of Chet and came from Comanche stock and called me 'college boy' and laughed at me being 'the Irish guy trying to get atop the totem pole'. He also let me know that I was the first 'white kid' he'd ever had on his crew, as the majority of 'pole climbers' (as he called us) were Native Americans – "'cause we all have a head for heights and danger'.

I lived in a bunkhouse with 'the rest of the tribe'. I learned how to drink cheap vodka. I developed a liking for Viceroy cigarettes which turned into a habit (and now, thirty-three years on, remains a total dependence). I met a woman who worked in a local bar named Bernadette. She was almost thirty-five; a one-time croupier in Vegas until her guy Wayne (who dealt blackjack) was discovered trying to cheat the house – and got a bullet in the back of the head for his stupidity.

'Rule number one of Vegas croupier life,' Bernadette told me, 'never cheat the house. Because you're cheating the Mob – and the Mob only have one answer for people dumb or crazy enough to try to rip them off.'

Wayne found that out big time. Especially as he denied any wrongdoing. Bernadette herself got roughed up a bit – until she told the Mob that Wacky Wayne (her name for him) had a storage unit around two hundred miles from Vegas in the capital of Nevada, Carson City.

'Once they discovered much of the money he'd cheated them out of they told me that, as a thank you, they weren't going to cut my tits off (as they had threatened to do). They also let me know that I had twenty-four hours to get out of Vegas and never come back. As long as I never showed my face in their world again, they were going to let me keep my life. That was ten years ago. I was broke. I was frightened. I needed work. I had a cousin who ran a bar up here in Sequoia. He offered me a job. Time flies when you've fled the Mob and you have no idea what to do with your life. Ten years on I'm still pouring shots and living in the same trailer I found the week I arrived from Vegas. Still … in you walked two weeks ago and I found myself thinking: now that's a lovely young guy and someone who believes in being nice and decent with me. And treating me not like the potential fast fuck behind the bar, but a person … which is why you should meet me at my trailer around a half-hour after we close up at one tonight.'

That's how it started. Because we were in the smallest of communities – and because Bernadette feared she was going to get severe shit from everyone for taking up with 'the new boy in town' (as she sometimes called me) – she wanted to keep 'us' quiet. When I pointed out that I was a legal adult she gave me a light kiss on my lips and said:

'They're still gonna call me a cradle robber.'

Bernadette would only see me three nights a week – and exclusively in her trailer. Thanks to her not only did I learn much about sex (and how to make it more than just sex), but also about the way that passion stays passionate if you're not doing the day-to-day thing with the person with whom you think you love. And after just a few days I was certain that I was in love with Bernadette. Just as she was certain that what we had here was nothing more than a very pleasant moment in our lives.

I so loved this 'moment' with Bernadette, so loved the pole-climbing work that I extended my initial three-month contract twice over. I was making $180 a week. I had free room and board on top of that. I spent six bucks a day on smokes and a couple of drinks. I saved the rest. At the end of nine months I had $5400. Enough to put a down payment on a small house in North Hollywood. Which is what Papa insisted I do. Just as he insisted that I leave my high-altitude work and return to the real world and start my career – and stop acting like life could be fun. Why did I buy into this program? Perhaps because I've always felt the pull of authority over me. When I am having one of those four-in-the-morning moments of looking at myself in the mirror – and wondering how it all turned out this way – I plead guilty to the fact: at those crucial moments in young adult life when I could have broken free, I played the 'keep Dad quiet' card. Maybe because I've never been brilliant about standing up for what I want. And, in turn, that could be linked to another uncomfortable truth: I've never had the big grand passion that fuels a career, a love, a sense of life as an evolving adventure. I knew I was being talked into playing it safe. I allowed myself to be led down that path. Because I really didn't know what else I should be doing with myself.

Could it be that, like so many of my fellow citizens, I kowtow because I can't figure out a different storyline? I knew that I never satisfied my very critical father – but I still followed his directives about what I should do with my life. Just as all those years as an altar boy and being told to respect the ultimate authority of the priest – especially as God was always sitting in judgment on us all – did indoctrinate in me the belief that I really did have to do what I was told … even if today I understand that those telling me how to live my life didn't have my best interests at heart and really had no idea about the world beyond their narrow, limited experience of it all. Only now – starting to crowd sixty and realizing that time just isn't on my side – am I beginning to think: why this lack of imagination when it came to dodging risk, danger?

Still, all those years ago, I made the bad call and did what my father demanded. I packed up my life in Sequoia. The wrench of saying goodbye to Bernadette was huge. She knew I was in love with her. She told me on our last night together that the reason I was getting emotional was because I was just seeing her for six hours a week of passion and companionship – and that we had no day-to-day life.

'When you do start making that day-to-day life with someone you're going to find out just how boring it can be ... even though everyone's going to convince you to do the day-to-day. Because they've all entrapped themselves ... and why should you escape?'

On the long bus ride back to LA I knew that I was about to let myself be talked into a life I didn't want ... but also didn't know how to sidestep.

Bing. A new fare. Westwood. Fuck. It was now 3.33 p.m. That moment when LA becomes as blocked and coagulated as that artery to my left ventricle that needed a stent ... and which I was able to have taken care of when I still had company health insurance. Silver Lake to Westwood was going to be forty minutes at this time. I wanted a fare somewhat closer. But I saw that the Westwood client was heading south to Van Nuys. A fare that would be worth $31. So it was worth the long trek in traffic.

I am a fifty-six-year-old man working sixty- to seventy-hour weeks and making on average eleven dollars an hour. I am expendable. I have a family to support, bills to pay. Eleven dollars an hour is just above minimum wage. Better known as: nothing.

But earning nothing these days is better than earning absolutely nothing.

four

A LUCKY BREAK. Driving down Sunset I got a job picking up a woman at a spa in Silver Lake. The spa was called The Now. Located in a stretch of Sunset where everything smells like tech and television money. Boutiques where a shirt costs $250. Vintage furniture shops with all this original mid-century stuff at crazed prices. A tattoo parlor which caters to cash-heavy hipsters who think nothing of adding indelible after indelible image to their skin. The usual upscale coffee joints where everyone has a flat white and a piercing and a MacBook with a screenplay they are never going to get produced. And this spa – all white and Zen design – where you can get your muscles de-stressed by paying one hundred dollars for forty-five minutes.

I need a cigarette at least once an hour. This involves stopping and finding some corner of wherever I am at a given moment where I will not be called out as a walking health violation for smoking. Despite the perma-smog, the dense car fumes intermingling with the endless blue above, being seen with a lit cigarette on a sidewalk in LA can land you in a shitstorm of self-righteousness. Lighting up near any sort of outdoor cafe or restaurant is also a serious no-no. Even smoking across the street from a playground is something akin to a hanging offense.

So I tend to choose side streets and vacant lots in which to suck down my hourly American Spirit (since they stopped making Viceroys some years ago). I tell myself that this brand is less lethal than the non-organic brands, though my daughter Klara recently sent me links to about six articles saying that American Spirit were as dangerous as any other cigarette. 'It's a dumb habit, Poppa, and I don't want you to die.' Klara. My precious little girl. My tough-minded, super-smart daughter. Twenty-four. Always up front with her opinions. An original take on everything from the moment she started in middle school. Always in trouble with teachers for not playing by the rules – and questioning the system all the time. Always in trouble with her mother for not being the good little convent schoolgirl that she'd groomed her to be. Always knowing she could come to me with her questions, doubts, rages ... and I would not just hear her out, but also didn't take it the wrong way when she exploded in my direction. Maybe because, after a life of jumping out of the way of conflict, disagreement, I was often amazed and simultaneously unnerved by Klara's ability to wade into an argument and fight her corner; her ferocious sense of right versus wrong; her refusal to be cowed by what she called 'the system'. Recently I found myself wondering: did I so admire her independence because that was something I could never find in myself?

The Now Spa. 3329 Sunset. A hard place to loiter – as cops moved you off if you waited outside this address for more than thirty seconds … and the fine was $315 if the guy in uniform decided to be a prick and give you a ticket. $315. That was sometimes all I earned in a week. So you had to park around the corner, a residential street with a high-end candle shop – $68 for some French hunk of scented wax – and some designer chocolate joint with its beautifully handwritten cards next to artful cubed piles of their product, telling you about cacao percentages and the ginger they used and how it had been harvested for them in some Peruvian rainforest.

How did I know this shit? This was the task that Klara set me when I started being an Uber guy. 'Become super interested about all that crosses your path,' she'd told me. 'Look around you. Listen to people. Everyone has a story. And in LA almost everybody also has *attitude*.'

'You're not supposed to smoke near a place that sells food.'

The voice belonged to a young woman, early twenties, short leather skirt, cool Ray-Ban sunglasses, a bottle of San Pellegrino in her free hand.

'Sorry,' I said, dropping the cigarette on the ground while wondering if a shop selling overpriced chocolate qualified as a place where people ate.

'Now you're littering,' she said.

I reached down and picked up the butt.

'Are you Angelique?'

'That's right. But I don't want to ride with someone who smokes.'

'I wasn't smoking in the car.'

'But once I'm in the car I'll smell it on you.'

I glanced at my watch, thinking about the pickup awaiting me in Westwood.

'If you want to cancel …'

'Can't cancel. Got a class. Late as is. But I want you to crank up the air con as high as it can go so I don't have to smell your bad habit.'

'No problem,' I said, getting into the car. She followed, sliding across the back seat. I turned on the ignition. I set the air conditioning to 10. I pulled into Sunset, watching the GPS, looking at the route ahead and the red-lined bottlenecks to come. The 101 South to the I-10 West to the 405 North to Sunset Boulevard. ETA: forty minutes from now. I had forty-one minutes to get to my next pickup and I really didn't want to lose the second fare. In the rearview I could see my current fare on her iPhone, messaging at crazed speed.

'What are you looking at?' she snapped.

'Just looking behind me.'

'I saw your eyes move toward me.'

'You were mistaken.'

'No, I wasn't. Keep your eyes off me. Unless you want a complaint against you.'

Her tone was dangerous. And someone with whom a further argument on this subject might turn very wrong for me. Best to say nothing more. Best to use the side mirrors to look behind me. Best to hope that the entire incident would blow over. She wasn't finished.

'You know you've got an empty Chick-fil-A bag under the seat here?' she said.

I was about to look at her in my rearview but stopped myself.

'Had no idea. Must have been an earlier passenger.'

'You know they're homophobic shits, Chick-fil-A.'

'I don't eat there.'

'And you didn't see someone getting in with their redneck fried chicken shit?'

I thought back to three fares ago: the chatty guy from Ohio who told me he was in town for a sales conference and that he was leaving his wife for a woman he met at his church. I thought I smelled food coming from the shopping bag he had with him. But as he didn't eat in the back seat I said nothing. He was even decent about me asking if I could pull into the Shell station on Melrose and have a quick bathroom break (which I don't like doing with a fare in the back seat unless it's a genuine moment of urinary urgency … which it was a few hours ago). The guy must have finished his Chick-fil-A while I was taking a leak, then shoved the box under the front passenger seat. My bad call: my far-too-fast inspection of the back of the Prius after Mr Toledo left. And now …

'If I had seen someone eating I would have told them to stop.'

'You're just saying that to get on the good side of me. And because you know that if I reported you to Uber with a dirty car … or mentioned that big dent on your fender …'

Fuck. She saw that. Happened yesterday when I stopped to drop someone off at a cafe on the corner of Abbot Kinney and Venice Boulevard. I parked in their lot. Got out for a coffee and a smoke. Must have strolled twenty–thirty yards from the restaurant, just to get some blood circulating in my legs and suck down my American Spirit of the hour. When I got back I found the Prius's rear bumper severely dented. Sonofabitch. About five hundred bucks in damage – and if I claimed it off insurance it would fuck up my deductible and call attention to me as a risk. Because some clown went into me a year ago on the corner of 5th and Broadway downtown. A FedEx driver who was texting while driving. An insurance notch against me – even though they knew it was not my fault.

This new fender bender was something I did not need on my plate. Especially as money was beyond tight right now – and five hundred minimum to get it beaten out and repainted was $499 over my current budget. Yeah, I knew a guy two streets down – Reuben the Dent Dude – who could probably do it for $150 under the table. But that was still too big an outlay. The last two weeks I managed to clear around $480 a week – and the way I figured it, we could just about keep our life afloat for $850 a week – and that was bare minimum living. On Uber I got paid around 80 cents a mile in LA County, 73 cents outside the city limits. Driving to a job earned me nothing. I paid for the first ten minutes of waiting for a pickup. I got bonuses for drives over an hour, to the airport ... and I got to keep all tips. But that was if and when people tipped me. Uber is not tipping-friendly. It hinted, but it didn't insist, that users should tip the driver 15 to 20 percent extra on top of the fare. For those of us behind the wheel Uber insisted that your car was under ten years old and that it was in perfect mechanical and physical condition. As they didn't have inspectors out there on the road, they couldn't really check up on you to see if you were playing by the rules. But if a client called in and said, 'He's driving a car with a dented fender,' you were no longer driving with Uber. Which is why – as much as I wanted to say something to this spoiled, angry child in my back seat (oozing what my Klara liked to call 'the furious entitlement of my generation') – I knew that a comment pointing out her brattishness could be like pulling a pin out of a hand grenade and holding it close to my face. Uber came down on drivers who breached the rules. Just as Uber monitored you to ensure that you didn't drive more than twelve hours in a day. Because they allegedly didn't want their drivers engaging in dangerous behavior by extending their time on the road into excessive hours. There was a way around this no more than twelve-hours in a day rule. Go offline for two hours. Have a nap somewhere. Turn your phone on again. Go back to work.

I'd done sixteen-hour days – with three seventy-five-minute pauses during that lengthy shift. On a really good week I'd been able to clear as much as $790. But that was working day and night and getting lucky with long-distance fares and tips.

Uber economics. All the anxious calculations I made on the back of an envelope at home late at night. Say I picked up a trip to LAX from downtown. That would cost the passenger about $40, I'd net around $32, the rest going to Uber. But if the passenger added 20 percent – that's eight bucks – then that would make up the deduction. However, the majority of people who took Ubers never tipped. And I'd find myself some weeks working sixty hours and only earning $465 because I was only getting short $7 and $8 trips. Kids going to the mall from their house. Gym runs. Late-night staggers from bars when the car has been left behind to avoid an inevitable DUI. Shopping trips to the local supermarket. Etc. Etc. Etc. If I got two of these an hour I could hit the $15 per hour goal that I liked to set myself. But it was more likely that two of these came along every ninety minutes. What I was also calculating was gas – which I have to pay for – and insurance and everything else to do with the vehicle, like upkeep. When I drove for twelve hours I was probably using over $40 worth of gas – around a tank and a half for my Prius. My insurance is $58 a month. Twelve times $12 (a normal hourly yield) is $144. I lose $40 for the gas. $624 for the week. Just under $2500 for the month less $58. And the car needs a service ($350) every 10,000 miles. I drive 1200 miles easily every week. 4800 miles a month. That's like driving to the East Coast then turning around and getting back as far west as Santa Fe. Only in my case I was doing all that driving in one town and going nowhere. And I was driving an eight-year-old Prius and would have to replace it in two years to keep it under the ten-year Uber rule. How I was going to do that was beyond me. Our little house was paid off. I had little in the way of debt. But my wife Agnieska hadn't worked for over fifteen years. It was me and me alone who had to make our monthly nut.

I accepted this as part of the deal. According to the code that I was raised with: the man picks up the tab.

Even if the woman is working, even if she has a career, the responsibility for keeping the roof over everyone's head comes down to the man. Klara has often joked that, in that corner of the San Fernando Valley where I was raised, all the big social movements of the sixties and seventies had passed us by. My response was:

'Maybe it was just my family who never moved beyond the 1950s.'

'Maybe your church had a hand in that as well,' Klara shot back.

Your church. As Klara well knew – because we talked openly about such things – it was never really *my church*. Yes, I was very much raised to be a serious Catholic. Yes, my parents maintained until the end of their lives that the priest's word was law. Yes, my mother was a daily communicant. Yes, I was still married to a woman who had not only become a daily communicant but a serious Catholic militant after tragedy scorched our lives. As for me . . . I stopped going to Mass some years back. Especially when things in my marriage started going wrong. Just as I started struggling with the idea that all I was raised to believe – especially when it came to the Paradise awaiting us all as long as we played by the rules during our messy time here – was Divine Truth. My friend Todor once told me that, to borrow a line from the Book of Psalms, our life on earth was a true 'Vale of Tears'. He said that when

I was reeling from the nightmare that had upended our lives. He also said that, after a 'personal catastrophe', it wasn't unusual to have a crisis of faith. It was understandable that I was angry at God. Todor advised me to pray hard to the Holy Spirit to help Him guide me back to belief. I've known Todor for over fifty years. We met in third grade in the local public school down the road from our homes in the Valley. From the outset we were pals – especially as we both had emigrant backgrounds, stern but responsible fathers and stay-at-home tough-cookie mothers. Over the years we truly watched each other's backs – even if our paths very much diverged when he announced in our last year of high school that he was seriously considering becoming a priest. The Holy Spirit had spoken to him. As it did to my mother and father and later my wife … yet somehow sidestepped me at a moment when I truly needed faith.

Somehow a corner can be turned … tomorrow is another day … Climb ev'ry mountain, forge ev'ry stream …

One of the things ingrained into the vast majority of Americans is the idea that things going wrong is a personal flaw; that we are all capable of picking ourselves up and dusting ourselves off and starting all over again. Even if we secretly know that beginning again at a late age is a tough call we want to nonetheless buy into the belief that everything is still possible. That's another American self-delusion … but maybe a necessary one. Otherwise how the hell do you get up in the morning?

In the aftermath of losing my sales executive position I applied for jobs. I went through every employment agency in LA … the ones that would deign to look at my résumé. No sales work. No corporate work. 'You're crowding the big Six-O,' one young placement guy told me. 'There just isn't a niche I can land you in – outside of stuff just a few dollars above the minimum wage.' I thought about retraining as an electrician – but was told by friends in the business that I needed at least two or three years to build up a client base … and any of the big 'electricians on call' companies were not going to look at someone who hadn't done any electrical work since his time atop those high-wire poles in Sequoia National Park over thirty-five years ago. Uber was the fastest way for me to start earning again – and to do so with the minimum of interference from bosses.

To become an Uber driver, you don't deal with a management team or do an interview or have an inspector drop by to check out you and your vehicle. To become an Uber driver you download their app. You fill in the online application. You have to take a photo of your driver's license and send it to Uber. Ditto the state inspection certificate for your car. You have to take photos of your vehicle and make certain that one of them has the vehicle's license plate. You have to take photos of yourself – which Uber uses for facial recognition purposes. You have to nominate a phone that will be exclusively your Uber phone – and which will verify your facial recognition and will also monitor the number of hours you are driving on a given day. Only this phone will be allowed by Uber for you to get your rides. You set up a payment method with Uber to get your money at the end of the week. I had my earnings for the week paid directly into my bank account. You could also get paid via an instant Uber cash card – but Uber charged you a fee for doing this. Just as all billed hours ran according to the Uber clock: from Monday at 04h01 in the morning until the following Monday at 0h400. If you had a ride that started at 03h30 Monday but ended at 04h03 you wouldn't see the money from that fare for another week. You couldn't really complain about any of this, as there is no Uber office to complain to. Yes, there was a help line for drivers – but it took around thirty minutes to get through to an actual human. Though none of their phone people will tell you this it's obvious that their call center is far away in some sweaty corner of the Philippines . . . and everyone is very cheerful and never in any way helpful.

But God forbid that you should get a complaint against you – or if a passenger reported that you had a damaged vehicle (and a bent fender qualified) – then you could lose your right to drive with Uber. You would be black-listed. You would be out. And you could find yourself stacking shelves at Walmart and living even closer to the edge of all-American poverty. Which so many of us danced around every day.

So what could I do in the face of this young woman thinking that a rearview mirror glance was a come-on and the fast-food bag left behind by a previous client was an excuse to get me into considerable trouble?

'I am so sorry about the bag,' I said. 'If you give it to me –'

'You're still trying to get on the good side of me. I don't like your attitude. So maybe I will report you.'

'Then you will be taking away the only source of income I have.'

Silence. I avoided monitoring her reaction to my statement in the rearview. When I checked the mirror before changing lanes I saw that she was stretched out across the seat with big Bose headphones on her ears, a sulky look on her face. The traffic started to move. The GPS told me I would reach the edge of the UCLA campus at 5.27 p.m. Luck came my way. We made it there by 5.26 p.m. My passenger pulled the headphones off her ears and glanced at her iPhone.

'You actually got me here four minutes before my five-thirty.'

Then she was out the door and gone. As she walked away I saw that she had the Chick-fil-A bag in her hand and dumped it into a campus trash basket.

Was this her way of telling me that she took on board what I told her? Is that why she acknowledged (without a thank you) the fact that I got her to her class on time? I checked my watch; I checked my GPS for the next pickup. I was four minutes away and not scheduled to arrive for eight minutes. I turned off the ignition, I got out of my car. I felt shaky. I felt vulnerable. I felt small ... and needed a break from the endless confinement of the driver's seat. I wondered: is this my destiny for years to come? Day after day of traffic and automobile hustling and dealing with people who often looked on me as a nobody; their momentary chauffeur to be ignored or abused and hardly ever tipped or thanked for his work? 'Gotta keep food on the table,' my dad used to say when he had to miss one of my Little League games to work an overtime shift. That was my daily catechism; the way I told myself that doing this job was worth the sixty- to seventy-hour weeks. Because it kept food on the table and 80 percent of our bills paid. But I had no time for life now. I worked. I slept. I took one day off every two weeks and fretted about losing the hundred bucks (if I was lucky and worked to the max) that I might have reaped for the day. I had to drive nine hours to make what that young woman just spent for sixty minutes of kneading her tensed muscles. I hated myself when I thought this way. I was giving in to envy and the sense that life had dealt me a bad hand. Which is why – lighting up my third American Spirit of my shift – I thought back to myself atop one of those electrical poles with no responsibility to anyone but myself; the view from on high of massive trees and snow-dappled peaks and little in the way of human interference in the vista ahead. My sole obligation was to get down off that pole without causing harm to myself. I could have told Papa: 'I'm staying atop of this pole ... I'm making my life elsewhere and the way I want to do it.' Instead I buckled. Electrical Engineering. Why did I ever end up doing that?

'Hey, fella, why are you trying to get yourself into trouble?'

The voice belonged to a UCLA campus cop. A big guy, Irish face, name-tagged O'Shaughnessy, walking toward me, looking seriously pissed off. Immediately I dropped the cigarette to the ground and stubbed it out with my shoe.

'We are a non-smoking campus,' he told me. 'And we also especially don't like folks who smoke and litter – so how about picking up that butt?'

I did as ordered. I told him I was sorry.

'I could fine you $280 for what you just did. I could take down your license and have your car banned from

UCLA. I could cause you all sorts of shit. But you look like someone who doesn't need such grief. Can you give me your word that you will never be so stupid again?'

'I won't be stupid again.'

'Smart guy,' he said. Then with the curtest of nods he walked off. I shouted thanks after him. He didn't turn around.

I drove off. I gripped the wheel, trying to maintain calm. I was anything but calm … but still grateful for this flash of decency in a hard town. The GPS told me I had two minutes to my next ride. I couldn't afford to be late. I couldn't afford …

five

The address was on the west side of Santa Monica Boulevard. A nice, calm residential area. 1710 Malcolm Avenue was a white apartment building. Probably built in the early 1960s. A little drive in front of it where I could park for a moment and wait for my ride to show up. I checked the GPS. Going to an address far from here. On Van Nuys Boulevard in Van Nuys. A straight shot up the 405. 12.8 miles – but with the usual rush-hour traffic we were looking at a thirty-five-minute trip.

Be right there came the text from the pickup. One of the standard lines that Uber provides for its passengers to send to the driver to let them know of their progress. I was still feeling jumpy from that encounter with the UCLA cop. I experienced something new: a trembling of the hands, a shortness of breath. Panic. I told myself*: but you managed to walk away from both incidents without complaints to Uber.* I needed a good night's sleep. Ever since starting as an Uber driver five hours had been the norm. Frequently the best I could do. My wife Agnieska slept nine–ten hours a night. Unlike me she did so without medication. I'd started needing the sleeping pills when I was tossed under the bus by the Human Resources guys in the company that I gave far too many years to. They'd been told by Head Office to 'trim' the sales force by forty-two. I was one of their chosen victims, I got six months' salary and a year's health insurance – and that was the extent of their benevolence. When I spent the next half-year scrambling for new sales jobs and none came my way, the sleeplessness started.

A knock on my passenger-door window. I snapped out of my reverie. I hit a button. The glass lowered down. I was now facing a woman in her late sixties or thereabouts, with silver hair, a thin, angular face, very pale complexion. Someone who dressed simply (a plain cream-colored dress), who didn't do the LA bling thing. She carried a large dark blue canvas holdall with that morning's editions of the *New York Times* and the *LA Times*.

'Brendan?'

I glanced at the screen.

'Elise?'

She nodded and got in.

'And how are you today?' she asked.

'I'm good. And you?'

'As good as one can be – given the way of the world right now.'

'I hear you, ma'am. We're heading to Van Nuys, right?'

'That is right, sir.'

She settled back into the seat. I pulled out into the road. She asked me to tune in to the local NPR station – 'so we can get all the bad news of the day'.

I did as asked. I got us out onto the highway. As indicated on my GPS the traffic was classic mid-afternoon-on-the-405-going-north crap. I asked my fare:

'You in a hurry?'

She glanced at her watch.

'The appointment is at six-thirty. Which means I have to be there for six. A little earlier if you could do that ...'

I glanced at the GPS. Our ETA was: 6.01 p.m.

'It'll be touch and go,' I said. 'I'll do my best.'

'I'm sure you will.'

A small smile on her lips as she said that, then she turned to her newspapers. On the radio there was a news report about an anti-immigrant rally near the Mexican border and a senator from Texas saying we were in danger of being overrun by 'people we don't want. People who don't speak our language, who don't understand our values, who want to take away our jobs, who endanger our communities.'

The woman put down her newspaper, her face scrunched up.

'What an idiot,' she said. 'Maybe we should be listening to nothing,' she said.

'Nothing is something we can do,' I said, hitting the off button.

I saw her acknowledge this with a nod. I felt uneasy glancing at her in the rearview mirror. I kept trying to look ahead, not wanting a repeat of that girl earlier.

Elise turned back to her newspapers. When she looked up to ask how we were doing, she saw me glance at her in the mirror. She smiled. A tight smile. But a smile. I was relieved. I looked at the GPS.

'A half-mile and we are free of this,' I told her.

The GPS never lies. Three minutes later we stopped crawling. I pushed the pedal down. We reached 70 mph. I told her:

'I am determined to get you to your appointment by 6 p.m.'

'That is most kind of you, Brendan.'

The road ahead was free and clear. We were at the exit for Victory Boulevard in Van Nuys by 5.54 p.m. Four minutes later I was pulling into a strip mall.

'Where can I drop you, ma'am?' I asked.

'Over in that corner,' she said, pointing to a unit caught in between a dry cleaner's and a pawn shop. I pulled up to its entrance. There was a heavily reinforced door with a code pad to its side.

'This the place?' I asked, wondering what might be behind that steel door.

'This is the place,' she said. 'Nice riding with you, Brendan. And thank you for getting me here on time.'

'All part of the service, ma'am.'

She left. She walked to the door. She consulted her cell phone. She punched in a number on the keypad, glancing back and forth from its collection of numbers to her phone. The door opened. She went inside, shutting the door immediately behind her.

I put the car into gear and checked my GPS. No one was demanding me right now. I decided to take a thirty-minute break. There was a little luncheonette place in a far corner of the strip mall. It looked cheap. It was cheap. They did a decent Spanish omelet. $3.99 including toast and home fries. The one-dollar bottomless coffee was just about drinkable. I could get out of there for six bucks including a 20 percent tip. And I wouldn't need to eat again until I got home around one this morning.

I ate my food. I drank three cups of coffee. I got a text from my wife, telling me that she didn't know my schedule today – but she herself would be at a meeting of her 'group' tonight and that she would leave some chicken in the fridge for me if I wanted to eat something when I got home. *Her group*. A group I increasingly didn't trust – though Agnieska would never hear a word against them. *Her* group. Why are 'groups' often so extreme? I asked for the check. I reached for my cell phone. I went to the

Uber app. I clicked the button informing the computer running us all that I was back on duty and ready to drive. *Bing.* I had an immediate fare awaiting me two streets from here just off Victory Boulevard all the way to LAX. Another big fare: $42. It was my lucky day.

I laid six dollars down on the check that the waitress had left on my table. I headed out, walking to my car, just as a motorcyclist drove up in front of the place where I'd dropped off my last ride. He had his visor down over his face. I watched as he said a few words into the speaker by the door. I saw the door electronically pop open. The courier put his foot in the door. Then reaching into his backpack I saw him remove a bottle with a rag stuffed into its neck. He shook it once. He reached into his pocket. He pulled out a lighter. He ignited the rag. He hurled the bottle into the hallway. He jumped on his bike, gunned the motor and shot off into the street. All this took maybe five seconds tops. I heard myself yelling at him:

'What the fuck ...'

But my voice was drowned out as the entrance to the building exploded into flames.

six

There was a UPS van parked right outside, the uniformed delivery guy just getting back into his vehicle when the motorcycle courier slammed his lit Molotov into that building. As it detonated with a loud terrifying blast he froze behind the wheel for a moment, then hit the gas and shot off into traffic. I too froze. I thought of the woman I'd dropped off half an hour earlier. She might still be inside. I charged toward the doorway. But right before reaching it there was a second detonation – as if the fire had ignited something flammable inside. There was now a wall of fire in front of me, making it impossible to get in through the entrance. The heat was ferocious. I backed off, yelling to the people who had come out of the coffee shop to dial 911. I dashed down a side alleyway to a back entrance surrounded by garbage cans and a metal gate that was locked shut. I could hear screaming from inside as I desperately tried to pull the gate open. Then the door behind this gate flew forward and a big guy – armed with keys and a taser – was in front of me. He raised his gun, screaming:

'Freeze, motherfucker.'

'I dropped someone off here –' I screamed back.

‘Get your fucking hands up.’

He kept the gun trained on me as he handed the keys to a woman and pointed at the lock. She scrambled to get it open as behind her I saw two women in hospital gowns and several doctors and nurses in scrubs desperate to get out of the now burning building. As she sprung the lock and threw open the gate, they rushed out.

‘Call the cops,’ he shouted. ‘Tell ’em I got the asshole who firebombed us.’

‘I’m an Uber driver. I was just trying to –’

‘Shut the fuck up,’ he yelled as the woman ran over and caught me in the stomach with her fistful of keys. I doubled over. She grabbed me by the hair and slapped me across the face, screaming at me, calling me a fascist, a terrorist. I was in such pain I couldn’t get words out of my mouth, let alone protect myself from her assault. A man in scrubs was now grabbing one of my arms, shoving it up behind my back, marching me toward a wall, telling me he was going to beat the shit out of me before the cops got here.

And then a woman nearby started screaming at them both.

‘What are you doing?’

‘He’s the asshole who firebombed us,’ the guy in scrubs yelled.

‘That’s the man who brought me here!’

Elise.

'Then why is he still here?' screamed the other woman.

I managed to say:

'Having some food … taking a break … saw the guy throw the Molotov … came running … too much fire … ran to the back …'

I started to buckle.

'Let him go now!' Elise said.

He let me go. Elise turned on them.

'You're as bad as they are, doing this to a bystander just trying to help us!'

She now had her hand on my shoulder.

'Where's your car?' she asked.

'In the front.' I felt as if I was about to fall to my knees, the wind knocked out of me, the slaps across the face still stinging, fear of being pounded into pulp still shooting through me.

'We're getting him to his car,' Elise told the guy in scrubs.

'Fuck, fuck, fuck,' the guy suddenly screamed as flames jumped out from everywhere. With Elise he started guiding me down the alleyway. It was impossible to move forward, fire now engulfing this passageway. There was no air. Just the stink of burning brick, burning wood, burning flesh. The roar of fire engines and cop cars was deafening. Back we went. The guy with the taser was still in front of this rear door, trying to get the last of everyone out. Some women were still in hospital gowns, running away in shock. Then a fireball of flames burst forth through one of the nearby windows. It engulfed the taser guy. The man in scrubs dropped me and ran toward his colleague – as his shirt was on fire and he was howling with agony. Elise dashed to him as well. I staggered over to a garbage can, leaning against it for support, then saw that there was a hose attached to a faucet in the nearest exterior wall. I grabbed it. I hit the faucet with my foot. Bingo. A rush of water. I managed to aim the hose toward the man on fire. It drenched the flames. He pitched forward in agony, hitting the pavement. I fell to my knees. Elise somehow managed to hoist me up.

'Are you okay?' she asked, leaning me against the nearby garbage can.

'I'm …'

I didn't know what to say. Especially as there were cop cars racing into this back alley, their sirens drowning out all other sounds. At that moment the entire upper windows of the clinic blew out. Flames melting the frames, then exploding. An ambulance pulled up. The scrubs guy raced over, pointing madly at the burnt man on the ground.

Cops were now everywhere, their movements frantic, disorganized, lost in the chaos of the fire.

'Get the fuck out of here,' one of the cops yelled at me and Elise. 'Run!'

I was still winded from the punch to the stomach, my eyes stinging from the slap to the face. Elise yelled back at the cop:

'I have to be with my people here.'

Another explosion from the top floor of the building.

'You're both out of here now,' the cop yelled, then ran off. Elise wanted to follow him, but when the roof suddenly blew off we both started running toward the street.

'I've got to get my car out of here,' I said.

'You're in no condition to drive.'

'That car is my life. No car, no money. And if the fire spreads –'

'You have insurance. You are injured. You can't –'

'I'm fucking driving,' I yelled at her. 'I'll get you home.'

'I can't leave ...' she yelled back.

But the shock was now slamming into her. I got my arm around Elise just before she fell forward. I got her upright and started leading her towards my car. It was at the back – a lucky break, as the cops had already cordoned off the front half of the lot. When we reached it she said:

'You don't have to drive us,'

'I'm driving us. Get in.'

She got into the passenger seat.

'In the back,' I said.

'Why can't I sit here?'

'Uber rules. In the back ... *please.*'

She got out of the front. She got into the back seat. I hit the ignition button. We drove off. Once we were back on the 405 she leaned forward.

'Are you sure you're all right?'

I ignored the question, asking:

'What kind of clinic is that place?'

'It's an abortion clinic.'

I said nothing for a few moments. Then:

'Was that the first attack like this?'

'Yes. We've had threats – the usual crazies. We didn't think ...'

Silence. I gripped the steering wheel. I felt a surge of anger, of fear. It sucker-punched me. Out of nowhere I now had an attack of the shakes. My entire body was overtaken by an extended shudder, my eyes fogging up as they became awash in tears. I gripped the wheel harder. I felt unable to see ahead. I began to swerve. A car horn blasted me.

'You need to pull over,' Elise said.

'I'm okay,' I said.

Silence again. I kept my eyes focused on the road in front of me. We were going against the usual rush-hour madness. I got lucky with the traffic. We were off the 405 in twelve minutes. I glanced several times into the rearview. My passenger was fighting hard to maintain calm as well.

'Are you all right, ma'am?'

'You can call me Elise. And no, I am not all right.'

She was close to tears now and I could see she had shut her eyes. She took several steadying breaths. We were now in the back streets of Westwood, moments away from her apartment.

'You're nearly home,' I told her, wanting to reassure her.

She opened her eyes.

'It's Brendan, yes?'

I nodded.

'And this number – 646 555 9479 – that's your cell ... if I need to contact you?'

I nodded again, thinking: don't contact me again.

I pulled up in front of 1710 Malcolm Avenue.

'You won't be paid for this trip, will you?' she asked.

'Don't worry about it,' I said, knowing that because of all that went down I'd lost that big airport fare. The ride probably complained to Uber and that might be a strike against me. I just wanted to go home, to close the door and sit in the dark and try to get all this out of my head – which I also knew just would not happen. Just as I told myself: if you lose today's driving you will be $100 short. My monthly car insurance payment of $58 was due next week. I had no choice but to somehow keep on the road.

I braked slowly. I shifted into park. Elise reached into her bag. She pulled out a small wad of money.

'Please take this,' she said, pushing it all into my hand.

'You don't have to,' I said.

'Yes, I do. And thank you. Take care.'

She was out the car and gone. I looked down at the money. I began to count it. One hundred and eighty dollars. Crazy. When I was a kid my dad often told me: 'Fucking someone over is the American way . . . but not our way.' That idea lodged in my head and never went away – the idea that you should never take advantage of someone else, especially if someone was being foolishly generous to you. It made me want to run after her and give all the cash back. But then I was hit with another attack of the shakes. When it subsided I shoved the money in my pocket. I stepped out of the car. I fired up a cigarette, the lighter trembling in my hand. After that one-eighty bonus I could take the rest of the evening off. But that would mean going home and having to face Agnieska. Which, after all that had happened, was something I was going to dodge. I reached for my phone. I hit the Uber app, informing the faceless computer that somewhere controls my life behind the wheel that I was ready for my next ride.

Bing.

A pickup in Westwood Village, heading to Santa Monica.

I got into the car. I went back to work.

seven

I WORKED THAT night until 3.47 a.m. I knew the precise moment because Uber twice texted me with the warning that I was getting dangerously near the twelve-hour mark – after which I could not collect any further rides for another twelve hours. But staying in the car right now felt safer than being outside of it. I only headed home when I knew that my wife would be fast asleep. After all that had gone down, facing Agnieska right now … not possible.

Home. A bungalow, constructed in the 1950s, on a back street of similar houses. Off-white brick. Concrete steps. A low wrought-iron fence telling the outside world: Private Property … though truth be told if anyone wanted to break in they could do so with ease … and would then be disappointed with how there was so little to steal.

Inside this little world of mine was furniture inherited from my in-laws. They had a garage full of old stuff after they moved to Anaheim in the seventies. They pushed it on us. We had little money at the time. We accepted it. We never changed it. Even when I was making decent money we never spent much on nice decor. We'd both been raised in simple surroundings, never into 'stuff' or the sort of things that hinted at an interest in style. I made decent, but not great money. So too did Agnieska – until she couldn't work anymore. What savings I had ensured that we could cover ourselves for a while on one income and that Klara got through college without debt. So the house has never had much in the way of improvements. When the plaster began to crack two years ago, I got a decorator friend to hide these fractures with chip paper painted cream. There's a kitchen with seventeen-year-old appliances. There's a TV in the living room. Family photos. One from a family outing at Disneyland fifteen years ago when Klara was nine years old and we all looked very happy standing next to a life-sized Donald Duck. There is a crucifix, but I told Agnieska that Sacred Heart lamps and portraits of her favorite saints had no place in the rooms we shared. They cover the walls in her bedroom.

We stopped sleeping together years ago. My bedroom has nothing on the walls. It is simply furnished. A double bed. A chest of drawers. A beat-up mahogany table on which I left tonight (as always) my wallet, money clip, car keys. I needed to sleep but I found myself still wired, still thrown by the day's events. I got out of my clothes. I put on a pajama bottom and a T-shirt. I went out to the kitchen and opened the refrigerator and took out a bottle of Corona. I unlocked the back door off the kitchen and stepped outside and lit up a cigarette and took several long pulls off the beer. I kept replaying in my mind the moment when that security guard exploded into flames. The victim of an attack by someone who thought he was justified firebombing the personnel of a clinic performing a procedure that was totally legal. But in his mind the doctors and everyone else inside there deserved to be murdered. Because they, in turn, were engaged in the very act of murder.

I sucked down my cigarette. I lit another. I felt a further attack of the shakes coming on. Not just because I couldn't get that burning security guard out of my head. It was also due to the very subject of abortion – and how it had become my wife's absolute obsession. What she called 'the monstrosity of killing an unborn child'.

It's a subject that has, on a certain level, taken over her life ... and has caused an immense rift between us. I am not fanatically pro-choice. As a Catholic I would try to argue someone out of ending a pregnancy. But abortion is still legal in this country – and as I am someone who believes the law *is* the law I certainly wouldn't advocate violent protests or worse against the men and women who carry out this procedure. Agnieska, on the other hand, has become something of a radicalized fanatic when it comes to being what she and her fellow militants call being 'pro-life' ... and trust me it gives me no pleasure to call my wife a fanatic.

When we first got together Agnieska was hardly an extremist. Yes, she too had been raised a serious Catholic – but was, like me, flexible when it came to many of the Church's more inflexible teachings. She privately questioned the chastity vow that priests and nuns had to take, wondering if it went against 'basic human nature'. Though she only agreed to start sleeping with me when it was clear we were 'serious' about marriage and a future family, she did go on the pill once we began to fall into bed on a very regular and happy basis. She knew I was a lot more ambivalent about the Church than she was, but she never pushed me to rekindle my faith. We were young. We were happy together. If I wanted to sleep in most Sundays early on in our marriage she didn't insist that I was at her side taking Communion together ... though she did ask that I show up at Mass once a month just to keep up the 'usual appearances' in our community.

We grew up a few streets from each other. She was two years my junior, so we knew nothing of each other at school. And her parents – tough-assed emigrants from Gdansk – took Mass at an all-in-Polish church deep in the Valley. As such we didn't meet cute while preparing for our First Communion. That came many years later when I was in my late twenties. The circumstances were anything but romantic – as I opened my mouth in a dentist's office and Agnieska reached inside with a sharp instrument to scrape the plaque off my teeth. Her first words to me – after the usual 'Good morning' and 'When did I have my last cleaning?' – were:

'You're not flossing your teeth, are you?'

Back then Agnieska was a dental hygienist. I was twenty-eight, working in the sales division of a big electrical cable company, living in a small house around a ten-minute drive down back streets to the house where I grew up and which my parents still called home. I'd landed a starting position in the company around a month after coming down off the poles high above Sequoia. I didn't think I'd like sales – but Dad knew some honcho in the LA sales division of the company because of all the cable they bought for the studio where he was now the senior electrician in charge of purchasing. He pushed me to meet the sales division guy – who seemed to like me and offered to start me off as his assistant with the idea that I could, in that classic American way, work my way up the corporate ladder. I told Dad that I'd rather start working at Paramount as an electrician. He wouldn't hear of it. 'Why d'you think I sent you to college?' he asked, then answered the question for me: 'To stop you from ending up like me.' Since coming back to LA I'd been living at home, I wanted out of home. The sales division guy was offering me a starting salary of $28K a year – not bad in the nineties. The money I'd saved paid for a downpayment on the little house not far from my parents' place. The salary allowed me to easily cover the mortgage and buy a blue 1975 Mustang that was, back then, my dream car. Two years into the job I was promoted to be one of three assistant sales managers. My dad kept asking me why I didn't seem to have a girlfriend. I told him work was keeping me too busy for such things. The truth was: every second weekend I'd drive up to Sequoia to see Bernadette. That kept me happy – and in no need of someone in LA. Then Bernadette's bar got bought by some businessman from Sacramento. He was in his late fifties. Well off. Widowed. Lonely.

'He's a pretty nice guy ... and he's offering me security,' she told me when I saw her for what she said was going to be the absolute last time. 'I'm now almost forty and still tending bar and still living in a trailer. Is he in any way interesting? A Q-tip is more interesting. But I'm going to get to live a nice life in exchange for being there for him. That's the deal ... and I'm taking it.'

I understood Bernadette's reasoning behind this decision. It saddened me. Of course I wished her well. Six weeks after she broke it off I was at the dentist's for my annual checkup and cleaning. Agnieska asked me to open wide, criticized my lack of flossing and ...

I got her phone number at the end of what was a rather painful cleaning. That happened during a fast exchange as I got out of the dental chair, during which we discovered that we'd grown up in the same neighborhood, gone to the same high school and had so many other local points in common.

Life works that way, doesn't it? Agnieska was subbing for my usual hygienist that day. I was still feeling a little bruised about saying goodbye to Bernadette for what was now the last time – and was beginning to think that, as I was now in my late twenties, I should really try to find someone with whom to build all that we are told to build. Agnieska had just ended something with an army guy who had become increasingly paranoiac and angry (well, he had survived his tank being hit by one of Saddam Hussein's shells during the fight to liberate Kuwait). She was single and looking. I was single and looking. Timing is everything. So too a shared program. Were we in love? We certainly told ourselves we were. We genuinely did get along. As my father told me in his old-school way:

'She's perfect wife material. You shouldn't hesitate here.'

As always I followed Dad's stern advice. Two years after we met we were married by my old friend Todor in Agnieska's home parish. The Mustang got traded in for a more sensible 1993 Subaru Legacy station wagon. And in the summer of 1995 Agnieska gave birth to our first child: a boy whom she insisted on naming Karol (the original first name of Pope John Paul II). A son! Agnieska very much wanted a boy – and was happily obsessed with everything to do with him. I was pleased too. But Agnieska said that she wanted to take at least a year off from her work to look after Karol. I couldn't argue against that. Karol rarely slept more than three hours. As such sex became a rare event owing to baby insomnia and Agnieska complaining about being exhausted all the time – though I was putting in twelve-hour days on the sales front to make up for the loss of my wife's income … and doing so on little sleep thanks to Karol's colic. Full admission: I started to seriously wonder why I'd bought into a domestic life that I privately knew wasn't for me.

Todor could sense my … what was the big word he used to describe how I was feeling? … *ambivalence*. We'd have a weekly beer in a local dive bar. Back then he was a parish priest up I-5 in Santa Clarita: a place he described to me as 'early nowhere' and where (as he also noted) 'drama of any sort – outside of people being unhappy with the routine of their lives or dying too young from something unfair – was seriously lacking'. Privately he told me that, as he too was now over thirty, he had to bide his time and excel in every parish he was offered … but he had his eyes on bigger prizes: like a tough inner-city parish or somewhere really monied and influential like Brentwood. A third beer (with shots of Jameson on the side) and he would occasionally admit his own worries about having 'bought into a system that provides lifetime and eternal security in exchange for so much'. Whereas other moments he would profess the wonder of his faith and how he was determined to ascend the Vatican ladder, determined to become a bishop by forty-five.

I heard out Todor's uncertainties alongside his almost ecstatic flashes of conviction. I offered little in the way of advice. That is not my style ... and Todor didn't want it. As he himself admitted, the priest in him preferred giving counsel rather than receiving it. When it came to my own doubts about having dug myself into all the responsibilities of marriage, Todor was both understanding and smart.

'You yourself had reached a point in your life when you felt the need to reject the loneliness that I know you felt and create a life with someone else. And you did tell me repeatedly early on how right Agnieska was for you – especially as you all but grew up together in the same way. All couples go through a big bump when the first child arrives. It is a huge change of life – and the biggest responsibility either of you will ever have. But all the love you felt at the outset will come back, Brendan. Especially when little Karol finally starts sleeping.'

That night happened four weeks later. On the day that Karol was nine months old. We all went to bed that night around ten, Karol quickly asleep in his cot near our bed. For the first time in many months Agnieska allowed me to make love to her. It was good. That sense of desire we once had for each other was now rekindling again. We held each other afterwards. I fell asleep thinking: this is going to be okay. When I next opened my eyes it was seven in the morning. Karol had not cried once during the night.

One minute later my wife was holding our baby in her arms and screaming. Because Karol was no longer breathing. Because our son was dead.

The ambulance and the police were at our little house five minutes later. Agnieska was so crazed with grief that the ambulance men insisted she be taken to the psychiatric hospital. I was asked to go with the police to the local precinct and I was politely kept there as they waited to hear from the medical examiner about the cause of death. Six hours later the call came from the coroner: Karol had succumbed to SIDS – sudden infant death syndrome. I was put on the phone with the doctor who had done the autopsy. He tried to assure me that the name of the syndrome said it all: it was sudden and came out of nowhere … and there was no exact reason why such a monstrous thing happened to an innocent baby. 'What can I say, sir,' the doctor said, 'except that it's a bit like the Angel of Death showed up out of nowhere and took your son away.'

The cops were kind. Our families were kind. Todor was especially kind – sitting with me every night for the two weeks that Agnieska spent in the psychiatric ward. I wanted to sit with her all day. The doctors would only allow me an hour with her every morning and early evening. She was on suicide watch. Todor came along several evenings and always asked for a half-hour alone with my wife. I never asked him what went on during those private moments between them – but when she emerged from the hospital at the end of that terrible time she did start going to Mass daily. She did tell me on several occasions that Todor had brought her back from the absolute brink; that she had blamed herself for Karol's death. And that she would carry this tragedy with her forever.

With Agnieska, with our family and friends, and at Mass every Sunday (which my wife now insisted that we attend together), I put on a brave front, especially in front of my father – who would have called me a sissy for buckling under the desperate grief that I felt within. Todor kept me steady. But inside I felt beyond torn up. I threw myself into work, having six consecutive banner-sales quarters. My wife went back to cleaning teeth. The silence at home in the evening was often terrible. For months

Agnieska wouldn't even let me hold her. Todor stepped in when I blurted out one night that 'intimacy' had vanished from our lives; that we had become strangers to each other; that I didn't know how to help her because (truth be told) I also didn't know how to help myself.

Todor's counseling brought Agnieska back to my bed (she had, in the immediate aftermath of returning home from the hospital, started sleeping in our guest bedroom ... and stayed there for many months). Though we started having sex again – as Agnieska became very determined to get pregnant as soon as possible – passion had gone south in the wake of our son's death. I blamed myself for not being as engaged as I could have been with her in the terrible months after. I started traveling around California and nearby states like Nevada and Arizona for my work. There were moments when I told myself: now that we don't have a child binding us together I could end things and escape a marriage that I knew was not what I wanted. Todor sensed this and kept steering me away from shirking the vow I'd made in front of God ... and the fact that 'if you abandon this very good woman, whose suffering is still immense, you will never forgive yourself'. I stayed put. But I am sure that Agnieska sensed my uncertainty at the time – and that must have increased her sense of loneliness (for which I still, many years on, blame myself). It took her over two years to conceive again – and though we were both elated by the birth of our daughter Klara, neither of us had attended properly to our marriage. The gulf that arrived after tragedy sideswiped us quietly widened with each passing year. Agnieska was a loving mother to Klara, but also hyper-vigilant about everything to do with her. As our daughter got older she felt increasingly crowded by her. Agnieska, in turn, became more and more critical of Klara (especially when, as a teenager, she started to express ideas that Agnieska found radical and decidedly anti-Church). My wife also began to silently resent the fact that Klara and I were so close.

'You're such a daddy's girl,' she would tell her whenever they clashed. 'And Daddy lets you get away with everything.'

I wasn't that lenient with my daughter. She was raised to be polite and to work hard at school. But it's true that I did encourage her to think for herself and to be as independent as possible. Which, in turn, ran contrary with everything to do with her mother and her ever-increasing belief in the sanctity of faith.

That faith came in for a further testing when, three years after Klara's birth, Agnieska fell pregnant again … only to miscarry ten weeks later. It was too early to tell whether she was carrying a boy or girl. This time she did not descend into the terrible grief that accompanied Karol's death. This time her initial sorrow was quickly replaced by a steely resolve.

'It's God's will,' she told me when I found myself in freefall after losing another child. 'Your lack of faith is allowing God to punish us in this way. You have brought this all down on us. Because God knows that you have fled Him.'

eight

YOU HAVE BROUGHT *this all down on us. Because God knows that you have fled Him.*

I tried to write that comment off as part of the anguish that Agnieska was going through. But it pushed me away further. It also added to the guilt I was already feeling about retreating into my work and focusing all my energy and love on Klara – which, in turn, pushed her mother away even more. Then one day she came home from work and informed me that she'd had a panic attack while cleaning a patient's teeth, causing him to bleed. The dentist had immediately suspended her from his practice – and she informed me there and then that her days as a hygienist had ended. No longer could she face looking into someone's mouth again. From this moment on she was going to devote herself to the Church. While I tried to be supportive – and mentioned that losing the second salary was going to impact our standard of living – her response was a simple one:

'"In sickness and in health … for better and for worse …"'

It was difficult arguing my way out of that one. Even Todor counseled me that – after all she had suffered – 'the important pastoral work she was doing was crucial to her well-being'.

Todor informed me of this around the same time that he had finally been, parish-wise, bumped upwards. No, he hadn't achieved the loftier heights he was aiming for in the Church. The Archbishop of Los Angeles found him a little too ambitious for his liking. The fact that he was born in Sofia and brought over to the States as a baby made him come across to His Eminence as an emigrant on the make (as Todor learned from certain insiders in the Church). Especially as this archbishop was an old-school Irish American with a wildly anti-Communist bias who even regarded John Paul II with suspicion because he came from the Socialist East – and also took pleasure in holding back far too outwardly ambitious priests. So Todor was blocked from advancing further up the hierarchy until His Eminence died in his sleep one night. A few years later his successor was impressed by the anti-abortion work that Todor was doing in the Valley and decided to give him the posh parish he always craved: Beverly Hills.

Once there he quickly began to consolidate his reputation as a priest who could rub shoulders with the rich and was also key in sponsoring youth programs that saw his parishioners putting their hands in their pockets to help fund inner-city charities. Todor got a lot of publicity for creating a controversial one called Angels Assist. It helped pregnant young women who didn't want to become mothers. It allowed them to give birth in a 'protected environment' (Todor's words) and then hand away their child for adoption to good Catholic families.

Todor came across in press interviews and public forums as someone who could convey what was essentially a rigid stance on the sanctity of the unborn child without sounding like a crazy. His was a sane, rational, persuasive pro-life voice. To many pro-choice campaigners Todor was the smooth-talking mouthpiece for the reactionary Catholic right. Certainly that was Klara's take on the man she had grown up considering almost an uncle – but whose openly expressed desire to see the overturning of Roe versus Wade had turned him into what my then seventeen-year-old daughter called 'an enemy of women'. The very fact that her mother had been, for many years, seriously involved in his Angels Assist work also made Klara consider Todor to be even more destructive. Especially as, a few years ago, Todor introduced Agnieska to a fellow daily communicant named Teresa. She was in her late forties; a one-time obstetrics nurse who'd been fired from her job at Cedars-Sinai Medical Center after trying to convince a young woman not to terminate her pregnancy, cornering her minutes before the procedure, telling her that 'murder was murder ... even if the baby wasn't yet born'. This caused a shitstorm of repercussions. It also resulted in her being blacklisted from every medical facility in Southern California. To the pro-life brigade Teresa – with her creepy saintly smile – was a martyr. Their very own Joan of Arc.

Am I sounding a little sour here? Maybe. Because I began to resent having my wife host meetings of her fellow pro-lifers. And having to put up bail four times when Agnieska was arrested for blocking clinics. Or approaching women entering Planned Parenthood up in Los Feliz with red roses and telling them there was another choice awaiting them with Angels Assist. Maybe as well it was the ongoing memory of a Sunday when my wife convinced me to go to Mass with her a week or so after she had been arrested with Teresa for lying down in front of an abortion clinic in Reseda and refusing to move when the cops tried to talk them into leaving. During the service I did take Communion with my wife and afterwards waited while she popped into the confessional to be cleansed of her sins. When it finished, Agnieska told me that we were invited to a lunch at Teresa's house. I said that I didn't want to go; that I had to start work at four and ...

But Agnieska told me it would mean the world to her if I would stop by for just an hour. I could see the subtext of her request: she wanted to show her church girlfriends that all was good between us after her recent arrest.

So after Mass I drove us to Teresa's house in Boyle Heights. She was always dressed up in severe black suits, as if she was about to give evidence at a trial. Her husband had died of cancer five years ago when he was eighty-five. She'd never been able to have children. Nor did they find a way of adopting – which, given her ultra-Catholic credentials, surprised me. She herself was almost forty when she married her husband – a man many decades her senior. A first marriage – and a late one. My wife noted that the state and even Catholic charities were dubious about placing children with older parents. And Teresa refused to adopt directly from an agency in Central or South America 'because you can never know his or her actual parentage and you could be buying into a whole genetic nightmare'. She made this statement when over at our house around five years ago on the occasion of Klara's nineteenth birthday. My daughter – who wasn't fully radicalized yet – heard Teresa's pronouncement and later asked me:

'How can she be so Catholic and so cruel?'

I wanted to reply: sometimes the two go together. But this was not the sort of thing you told a kid. Instead I said:

'She's just a little severe, that's all.'

'You can't say anything really hard about others, can you?'

To which I could only reply:

'There is enough hardness in the world already.'

Considered now, especially in light of the way that Teresa became my wife's aggressive mentor in pro-life activism – and the way she was vehement about how everyone who worked in what she called 'the abortion industry' was 'nothing less than a murderer' – I couldn't help but agree with my daughter: I tend to soft-pedal my true feelings about anyone difficult. And Teresa was certainly difficult. Still, as a gesture of marital goodwill, I agreed to go with Agnieska to her house. A place furnished with deep pile carpets, cream-colored leather furniture, gold taps in the bathrooms, not to mention all the crucifixes and sacred heart lamps and framed pictures of the Apostles that decorated her walls. There were about nine other people at this post-Mass lunch. Teresa greeted me with a dismissive nod of the head and the comment:

'Well, the dead do walk and eventually come to their spiritual senses. Welcome to the Fight.'

I was the only guy in the room. I didn't last long. Because, after making small talk around the buffet of chicken parts and pasta and tuna salads and green beans, Teresa began to address the crowd. Telling them that her overnight 'imprisonment' with her 'sister of the cross', Agnieska, hadn't intimidated her. Rather it had ingrained in her the belief that hers was 'the right crusade against the forces of progressive evil who think nothing about infiltrating the minds of our young girls with the belief that "My Body, My Choice" is a credo they can believe in'. Just as she also said: 'Thank God that we now have a Supreme Court who will soon consign Roe v Wade to the compost heap of history, and who will hopefully rule against state funding for wicked organizations like Planned Parenthood – groups determined to ruin the lives of a whole new generation of young women'.

There was huge applause for this outburst that coincided with Agnieska suddenly kneeling down and saying a decade of the rosary. I started moving toward the door, thinking that a fast escape was called for. But before I edged out Teresa was back center stage, shouting at everyone present and the larger world beyond:

'Contraception as we know it is nothing less than an assault on all women! The pill, the IUD, it's pumping women full of chemicals and allowing men to take no shared responsibility for the act of conception. Women are being poisoned everywhere by chemical contraception. The use of a spermicide must also be outlawed. And we now have highly sophisticated rhythm methods – like the Creighton Method – which is natural, which fits in with Church teaching, and which stops women from being infiltrated by drugs that play havoc with their reproductive cycles and are known to be carcinogenic. This is what should be taught in high schools today: the fact that when you take a contraceptive pill or allow an evil coil to be inserted in your uterus you are increasing the possibilities of an early horrible death by cancer.'

That was the moment I fled.

Once outside I lit up a cigarette and tried to banish from my memory the sight of my wife kneeling down with her black-as-death rosary beads as her fellow womb-obsessives spat forth vile words that made me wonder: so when did my wife join the Christian wing of the Taliban?

I fished out my cell phone and sent Agnieska a text.

Had to go. Off now on my shift.

I figured that one of her fellow crusader friends would give her a lift home. I knew that had I waited until the end of Teresa's rant I would be in a seriously angry place. Not just because I so disagreed with the extreme nature of her opinions, but also because they struck me as so imbalanced and not based in reality. But something I discovered early on with my wife, her priest, Teresa and all their pro-life cohorts: any time you try to argue another approach to this issue you get slapped down with their fierce arguments. You cannot get them to ever budge from their point of view. There is no give whatsoever – and even the slightest whiff of a question about the complexities of conception will land you with the accusation that you are in favor of the most heinous crimes against a biological mass that has yet to become a thinking, feeling creature. Once I asked Agnieska if she herself remembered her time in her mother's womb, if she was truly aware of anything before she was squeezed out into the world. Her reaction was explosive.

'Don't tell me you are siding with them! Don't tell me that my husband endorses the killing of –'

'I am just asking you if you were aware of anything when you were being carried by your mama for nine months.'

'I don't remember anything until I was about four years old. So if someone had come along and killed me before I had "memories" of my life, would that justify the murder?'

I could have said:

'A fetus at twelve, sixteen, twenty-four weeks doesn't have a name, doesn't have a personality, doesn't have attachments . . .'

To do so, however, would have been to open myself up to even further accusations. I stayed silent. Agnieska pounced on that.

'When our beautiful third baby was born dead you saw him –'

'Maybe it was a "she". It was too early to tell.'

'And you wonder why we are now so far apart?' she said, fury in her voice. 'You lost a son, then a second one arrived in this world stillborn … but you never saw him as a real person.'

'I didn't say that. You are twisting my words.'

'And you now have embryonic blood on your hands.'

That conversation was six months ago – and was followed by my dinner with Todor. Having heard from my wife that I was not taking the hard line against abortion, he suggested we have tacos and beers in our local taqueria and began to make me feel morally reprehensible … with a smile on his face throughout.

'I'm not coming down on one side or another,' I told him. 'I am just asking some questions. To be accused of being in favor of killing babies …'

His response was perfectly reasonable, perfectly measured.

'But, Brendan … say you had been born German in the 1920s. Say you had grown up in the town of Dachau which is just a tram ride away from the center of Munich. Say you knew that, from 1942 onwards, there was a concentration camp on the outskirts of your hometown where they were exterminating Jews because they were Jews. Say you knew that, because of the totalitarian nature of Nazism, you couldn't speak up against the Holocaust. Would you, after the camp was liberated and so much of Germany was rightfully destroyed to bring Hitler to an end, still have felt good about yourself for saying nothing?'

I remember gripping my beer bottle hard as he said all this. Wanting to explode in rage at the absurdity of his argument. How can you compare the Nazis with a legally sanctioned procedure for ending a pregnancy? How can you equate personal choice with state-sanctioned killing? And why does this subject become such a monumental issue with people raging at each other and hurling accusations that are beyond vicious and extreme?

But trying to have reasoned arguments with Agnieska and her activist sorority – as well as my very intelligent and now ultra-conservative priest friend – was impossible. The one simple lesson I had come to learn from all these back-and-forths on this subject was: this is an argument best stayed away from if you wanted a quiet life.

I wanted a quiet life. I simply answered Todor's abortion/Dachau analogy with the following lame response:

'Maybe you have a point here.'

'I respect a man who can change his mind on one of the key issues of our time,' he said, a self-satisfied smile telling me all I needed to know.

That conversation – which took place a few months ago – started bouncing around my head again tonight as I stubbed out my third cigarette in a row. Todor was now something of a celebrity; the anti-abortion star of the Los Angeles diocese. The fact that his Angels Assist charity was being largely funded by one of the biggest financial hotshots in town had meant I was seeing less of my old friend. A quiet but evident gulf had grown even further between us since my wife had become a militant while working as a full-time volunteer for Angels Assist. When I brought up my concerns early on about her growing fanaticism Todor told me that I should be pleased she was doing God's work. And that 'civil disobedience' against the murder of unborn children was justified.

Civil disobedience. Again I saw that man on the motorcycle – his identity hidden by that shiny black helmet with its frosted visor pulled down – throwing the lit Molotov cocktail into the abortion clinic, and the man with the taser catching fire just minutes later. Again I was hit with another shudder that seized my entire body. It took a good minute to subside. I wiped my eyes, I tried taking a few steadying breaths, then I went inside and put the empty beer bottle into the garbage can we use for recycling. I stopped in the bathroom for five minutes. I went to my little room and I climbed into bed. I closed my eyes. The exhaustion of the day caught up with me. I slept.

When I woke it was just before eleven. Nearly six straight hours out of the world. Something of a recent record for me – even though I knew that it was still not enough. I showered and dressed and then came down the hall. Agnieska was dressed and ready for church work. She'd already been to our local gym, as she did every morning. I smiled as I came in. She smiled back.

'You look like you just did an hour of hard exercise,' I said, noting how she was getting more toned and fit all the time.

'You should join me,' she said.

I immediately put a hand on my ever-growing gut. She saw that and touched my hand.

'I had one of those too, remember. If you get with the program ...'

'I know, I know,' I said, quietly cursing myself for my rundown shape.

She glanced at her watch, lifted her coffee cup and reached for the remote control. The local news filled the screen. It was the top of the hour and the lead story was about the bombing of the abortion clinic in Van Nuys. And then the anchorwoman said:

'This bombing is now being treated by the LAPD as a homicide as it resulted in the death of a security guard who worked at the clinic.' I stared blankly at the set, feeling myself in freefall. Even though I knew the guy with the taser couldn't have survived, hearing it confirmed on the television was beyond terrible. Would that image of him on fire – and me finding a hose and trying to extinguish the flames engulfing him – ever go away? Would I keep replaying it years from now?

I sat down at our little kitchen table, trying to steady myself. I wanted to tell my wife that I'd been there, that I'd seen that man die. Instead I stayed silent. I learned that the security guard killed was named Jose Fernandez; that he had a wife and two children, and that the police were looking for a motorcycle courier who threw 'the homemade bomb' that exploded in the clinic's front doorway. There was also an interview with the head of the Well Woman Clinic, a Dr Mary Morgenstern – who looked shell-shocked and simultaneously defiant. She talked about 'those who scream that they are pro-life yet engage in an act of domestic terrorism and kill a husband and a father who was simply doing his job and protecting patients and the staff and doctors who work at this clinic'.

I swallowed hard and found myself thinking: in the chaos of yesterday I should have told the cops about seeing the motorcycle courier. But I didn't get his license number. I didn't see his face as his helmet visor was deliberately pulled down. But then there was an interview onscreen with the manager of the coffee shop. He said:

'I saw the guy on a chopper speak into the security phone at the clinic – so he must have told them that he had a package for them or something. The door opened electronically and this guy lit up this rag in a bottle and slammed it into the entranceway. Then ... *bam!* This crazy explosion. Flames everywhere. Never seen anything like that before ...'

Well, at least the police had a statement from the other eyewitness. Nothing I could tell them would add to what Mr Coffee Shop told them. And that cop on the scene did order me to run. But I still felt guilt about not giving the police a statement.

'That poor man who died ...' Agnieska said. 'Why did he take that job? Of all places to work ...'

I could see her turn away, knowing full well that she was crossing over into that territory which was a minefield for us; that continued to drive us further apart. This morning, however, after all that had gone down, all that I'd witnessed, I found myself unable to ignore her, to stay silent.

'Maybe he didn't have a choice,' I said. 'Maybe it was the only job on offer.'

She looked at me in serious surprise, especially as my tone was edgy, challenging. But then her eyes narrowed, like a cat realizing she had prey in her sights. And she pounced – knowing full well what would follow. Knowing I was about to be trapped again in an argument I would never win ... but which I was now suddenly willing to wade right into.

'Maybe they paid him more to work at a place that kills babies,' she said.

I reached for a spoon on the kitchen table and found myself twisting it between my hands – an attempt to keep my anger under control. She saw this, saw the effect her words were having on me. She smiled.

'You really think they're paid more because they carry out legal abortions?' I asked.

'Of course they are,' she said, 'because they have all that extra money from the pro-choice brigade, all of whom are funding these clinics.'

'The reasons they have security guards there is because of the threats they receive. You don't hear of the pro-lifers being threatened by people who are in favor of abortion.'

'But the people leading the campaign against abortion aren't engaged in the murder of the innocent.'

'That security guard was certainly innocent,' I said.

'You choose to work in an abortion clinic ...'

'What? The fact that you work there means you deserve to be killed? Like that doctor shot in Nebraska by your pro-life friends?'

'They are not my friends ...'

'Yeah, they are.'

'I would never condone violence. I would never engage in violence. Killing doctors is wrong. But working at an abortion clinic is now a risky job. And why are you bending that spoon out of shape?'

I looked down and saw that I had indeed twisted the spoon into a sort of circular sculpture. Nearly snapping it in half.

'Maybe I don't agree with you.'

'So you take it out on the spoon?'

'The spoon can handle the pain,' I said, tossing it down and reaching for my jacket, my phone, my car keys.

'You're running off because of what I said?' she asked, sounding thrown by the way our exchange had turned angry and how I was now walking out.

'That's it,' I said. 'I don't want to be around your extremism.'

'I'm hardly extreme. I am just saying –'

'I know what the hell you're saying – and I don't like it.'

'But you went with me last year to that pro-life rally.'

'Because you kept on insisting that I had to be there. Maybe I now don't think that "abortionists" – as you call them – are murderers. Maybe I think choice *is* choice – and a woman has a right to decide –'

Agnieska's eyes went wide – as if I had just jumped over to the dark side; what she saw as the immoral side.

'Tell me you don't really think that.'

My answer: I put on my jacket and headed to the door.

'You can't walk away from this,' she yelled.

'Yes, I can,' I shouted at her, not turning back.

'You get back here! There are things to say.'

I walked out the door.

I went to a local joint for breakfast. Eggs and sausage and two sides of white toast and too much coffee. I really should be eating better. I really should do the gym thing five days a week as I kept promising myself. I really needed comfort food right now. Part of me wanted to call Klara, tell her what had happened in Van Nuys yesterday, and how I had walked into it all. But I knew that when I explained the exchange that I'd just had with her mother ... well, the division between them was big enough already. I didn't want to widen it further. Klara spent up to ten hours a day as a social worker in a shelter for abused women. I knew that letting her know about all that I had witnessed would have enraged her – and have also made her go into one of her rants about her mother and how she was now 'aligned with the fascists who are trying to control our lives'. I certainly understood and appreciated her angry sentiments – but just couldn't face them right now.

I went to work. I drove twelve straight hours. And netted $163, tips included. I kept thinking of Elise and what her business was at that clinic. Was she a doctor? A senior nurse? Someone working for the social services? And how was she handling the blowback from it all; the trauma that kept catching me unawares all the time? Over the rest of the week I put in sixteen hours daily behind the wheel, taking a two-hour break somewhere during the course of this long shift. I worked six straight days – and had almost $1100 to show for such crazy hours. It paid for some essentials. Being out for all but a few hours late at night meant I could dodge any contact with my wife – which struck me as necessary right now. Especially as I couldn't get that burning man out of my head.

After ninety-two hours of work over six days I decided to take a twenty-hour break. I crashed in bed for a long stretch. When I woke it was just after twelve noon. Agnieska had left me a note saying that she was out 'on church business' ... whatever that meant. I made coffee. I turned on my phone. There was one text awaiting me. My lips tightened.

The text read:

Hi Brendan – could you please give me a call?

Instinct told me: don't call back.

I didn't call back.

But I did text her.

Hi Elise – how can I help?

Immediately she texted back:

Could you pick me up at home at 3.30? I will need to go to an address in Burbank. I will then need you to pick me up again at 8. Possible?

I texted back:

Possible. Send me the address we'll be heading to.

The address arrived a minute or so later.

916 Burbank Blvd.

I googled the address.

It was another abortion clinic.

nine

Risk is something to which I have an aversion. When you have played by cautious rules your entire life – and you fear what could happen if you stepped away from routine and put your foot into uncertain waters – the idea of going toward something weighed down with potential danger is not an easy one . . .

But here I was, driving toward Westwood. Knowing I was putting myself back into the story of all that happened last week at that clinic in Van Nuys. Knowing that I wanted to do just that . . . if just to learn more about that security guard who died and who continued to spook me. Perhaps because part of me kept thinking: the moments he spent confronting me might have cost him his life.

I also wondered: would lightning strike again? Would I be driving her right back into potential danger? Still, it had been reported on the radio that every abortion clinic in the Greater Los Angeles area had beefed up security in the wake of the Van Nuys attack. I tried to feel reassured by that. Just as another part of me now thought: fuck the fear.

But as I got closer to her address another question kept nagging at me: why did she call me directly? Why didn't she just order an Uber normally – and get whatever driver was assigned to her by the big computer in the sky?

That was my first question to her after we drove away from 1710 Malcolm Avenue.

'I called you,' she said, 'because, after all that happened, I felt immense guilt about dragging you into this literal inferno. Are you okay?'

'I'm here. Unlike that security guard. Was he a friend?'

'A colleague. Not someone I knew well – but Jose always struck me as a good guy. I went to see his widow a few days ago. Felicia. She's just twenty-eight, with two kids to now support and bring up alone. A boy and a girl, seven and five, who can't work out why their father was murdered. Felicia told me that Jose was working three jobs and managing to somehow cover their bills. He had no life insurance, no savings. And she had done bartending jobs – but with two young kids she can only work just a few hours a day. There's no way she can make next month's rent on their little house in Lakeview Terrace. I paid it straightaway – but in the long term the family is probably facing eviction unless we can get some sort of emergency fund together. Their prospects are bleak. I wish I had the money to pay their rent for a year.'

'I hear you.'

'I'm sure you do. How long have you been doing this?'

I told her – and answered all her questions about my past professional life selling fiber cable.

'From your tone it sounds like it was a job, not a passion.'

'It was a job.'

'Really?' she said. 'But surely there's something you love doing?'

'Do you love the work you do?'

'I never told you what I do,' she said.

'But I'm bringing you to another clinic, right?'

'How did you know I was going to another clinic?'

'The usual way we figure things out these days.'

In the rearview I could see her smile.

'Yet after you googled that you still decided to do this trip with me.'

I didn't respond. I asked:

'So ... are you a doctor?'

'Not at all. I'm a retired professor.'

'What did you teach?'

'French.'

'Wow, that's kind of unusual. Speaking French in LA ...'

'Well, there is a university down the road from here. And they do have a French department. I taught there for forty years.'

'You ever live in France?'

'For five years when I was in my twenties. Which was another time, another epoch. I did my doctorate there.'

'Why didn't you stay?'

'Fell back in love with someone from my college days. He lived out here. I wanted to be with him. I followed him back to Southern California. Got lucky when an opening came up at UCLA. Four decades later …'

'Where is your husband now?'

'In the great beyond, I'm afraid. He died two years ago.'

'I'm sorry.'

'So am I.'

A silence.

'You teach French at the clinics?' I asked.

Now Elise laughed.

'What a thought!' she said. 'I'm a volunteer.'

'Doing what?'

'I'm what's called a "doula". Someone who spends time with women who are about to have an abortion and don't have anyone with them for support.'

'That's like charity work?'

'As I said: it's volunteer work. I am not paid for it. I don't like the idea that it is "charity".'

'But teaching at UCLA … that's not charity,' I said. 'It's a good deal being a professor, right? Not many hours, right?'

In the back seat I could see Elise's face tighten.

'Just interested,' I said, hearing a strange edge come into my voice.

'Six hours of teaching a week, four months off a year.'

'And how much did you get paid for that?'

'Let's not go there ...'

'Why not? I'm not being envious or anything. Just never talked to a professor before. I don't know what you people get paid.'

'Why would that interest you?'

'Because everything interests me. And because I don't have much to do but drive all day. So ... if someone wants to talk to me – and most of my rides don't – well, I'm interested in what they are about.'

'What I *was* about isn't that interesting.'

'It is to me.'

'Why's that?'

'Because it's going to keep my mind off everything that happened a week ago ... and because I know I'm driving you to another abortion clinic, and that kind of weirds me out. I wonder what you're getting me into and whether I'm driving us back into trouble.'

'Let's drop this subject,' she said.

'I'm sorry,' I said, knowing that I had stupidly crossed a no-go line with her.

'But it's me who should be apologizing to you.'

'You know I've got a college degree,' I said, ignoring her last comment.

'In what?' she asked.

I told her.

'What college?'

I told her that too.

'I have a couple of colleagues who teach there,' she said.

'But not in Electrical Engineering, I bet. And as I didn't do French ...'

I heard that edge in my voice again. I found myself gripping the steering wheel even harder now. Just as I had a flash image of that poor guy, Jose Fernandez, with his taser in my face, then the fireball hitting him, sending him up in smoke.

Elise must have known what was going on. Because she said:

'Turn the car around, please.'

'I'm fine,' I said.

'No, you're not. Nor am I.'

'I'm getting you to your destination, your clinic.'

'I now want to go home.'

'No, you don't. You just think I'm acting strange.'

'I think you're more traumatized by –'

'Don't tell me how I'm feeling, don't tell me whether or not I can drive. I can drive. Do you get that? I can, I *will* drive.'

I slammed down on the accelerator and charged up the on ramp of the 405. Light traffic. Good. I was in the fast lane. I pushed the pedal to the metal. I hit the radio. The classical station. I cranked it up. The guy on the radio said that he was playing something by Beethoven. I know nothing about Beethoven outside of *dum-dum-dum-dum*. This was something different. But something just as loud. Good. I blasted it. I glanced in the rearview. Elise's eyes were wide, her lips tight. She saw my eyes taking in her reaction in the mirror. She remained silent, cold. She did not tell me to slow down. She did not tell me to lower the Beethoven. She said nothing when I screeched across three lanes to catch the turnoff for the 101 South. She said nothing when I broke all sorts of laws and hit a top speed of 88 mph in a 65 mph zone. I knew I was gambling with the little I had in this world. I knew that, if a cop stopped me, I was risking a big crippling fine and a bunch of badass points on my license … points that would get reported to Uber and might cost me big time. But careful, responsible me … bills get paid, the eternal fucking good boy me … suddenly I didn't give a shit. Suddenly I was doing the zig and the zag across the highway and shaving eight minutes off the original GPS estimated time. No one once honked or flipped me the bird or looked like I was some fucking kamikaze in this piece of crap Prius. And, roaring now off the 101 down Cahuenga, Beethoven right up to max, I found myself thinking: *I am invincible. Nothing can touch me. Life at this moment is not the grind I have to live day by day. I am all speed.*

Signs to Burbank Downtown. Signs to Burbank Boulevard. Another strip mall. My city: one big strip mall. I pulled into the parking lot. I scanned the storefronts. Health Central. That must be the one. I floored it one more time, then screeched to a halt in front of its steel-barred doorway. I checked the rearview. Elise had shut her eyes, as if she was awaiting the crash that would end it all. The Beethoven was still blaring. I braked. I cut the engine. I cut the music. Silence. A long pause. I saw Elise taking several steadying breaths. She opened her eyes. She looked as if she had just snapped out of a nightmare. Which might have been the truth. She opened her pocketbook. She pulled out another wad of cash. I said:

'I don't want your money.'

She ignored me, tossing the money onto the passenger seat beside me.

'Thank you for getting me here so fast,' she said. 'No need to wait.'

And she was out of the car, gone.

Immediately I had a stab of guilt, thinking: *you fucking madman*.

I gripped the steering wheel. I started to cry. It took me many minutes to calm down; to regain an equilibrium where I could focus again on the world in front of me. A strip mall with a yogurt joint, a donut joint, a thrift store joint. And the clinic, marked out as nothing more than a place you can go for your health … but which had triple bars on its windows and a reinforced steel front door, and where there was a guy out front with an assault rifle strapped across his big chest. I watched Elise head toward this establishment, her walk a little hesitant, as if something was about to again blow up in her face. She stopped, straightened her shoulders, becoming very purposeful. Very determined. Very don't look back.

But she did look back. I saw the way she regarded me. Not with anger or fury. More with concern. Borderline concern. Yet concern, nonetheless.

I nodded back. Telling her … well, I had no fucking idea what I was trying to tell her. But I watched as she pushed forward into the clinic. She punched some numbers into a keypad. The door opened. She moved inside it. The heavy steel door closed behind her. I reached over and retrieved all the money dropped in front of me. I counted it. Eighty dollars. Crazy. I pulled out my cell. I texted her.

Please come back and let me give you half of all this.

Pause. Silence.

I leaned against the steering wheel, suddenly letting go. Sobbing again. Uncontrollably. But within minutes I was back in control. Or something near to that. Within minutes I could put the car into drive and get the fuck out of here.

Five minutes later …

A *bing* on my phone.

A text.

From Elise.

Please pick me up at 8 tonight. Same address where you dropped me.

I looked at this text for a long time, thinking: she is even more twisted up than me.

But I still texted back:

Okay.

She then texted back a single word:

Courage.

ten

I HAD FIVE short trips after I dropped Elise off. Then an extended one: a woman staying at the Beverly Hills Hilton who wanted me to go to the Armani store on Rodeo Drive. Once in the car she then asked if I would bring her shop to shop. I told her that, after I deposited her at Armani, she could walk to most of the stores. But she insisted that she be driven to each and every one of them. I explained that to do this would be tricky. Stopping on Rodeo Drive meant dealing with the cops who wanted to keep traffic moving ... and who gave deference to the limo guys in their sharp suits with their over-monied clients. They also looked upon anyone behind the wheel of an Uber as trash. But I had done the Rodeo Drive run enough over the last year to know a couple of back alleys where I could loiter and hope some cop on the beat didn't tell me to move on. The Asian lady was around thirty-five. Thin as a needle. Dressed to impress anyone who was into designer labels. Big sunglasses on her clenched face. She told me she had an American cell number and would pay me a cool one hundred per hour if I was able to pick her up as soon as she finished in one shop and was ready to move on to the next boutique. We agreed a system: a text from her two minutes before she was outside a certain store.

'And you have to be there waiting for me – no delays allowed.'

'Will do, ma'am.'

'If I am waiting for you more than a minute I am deducting ten dollars. Understood?'

All too fucking well. Money can give certain people – in fact a lot of people – not just the illusion of power, but also the ability to insist on things that shouldn't be insisted on ... and actually make them come across as crass and mean. But this could be a $300 afternoon for me ... and no payment to be made to Uber. I swallowed hard and fought to keep my rage down.

'No worries, ma'am. I will make the deadline every time.'

We arrived at Armani. I went offline with Uber. Taking a break. I found an alleyway. I shut my eyes. Twenty-two minutes later ... *bing*. She came out accompanied by some tall slick dude with the flattest stomach in LA and a crisp black shirt open to the sternum. He was carrying three big shopping bags for her. Into the trunk they went, the dude turning up his nose at my cheap car.

'Off now to Vera Wang,' she said to me.

Twelve minutes there.

Bing.

Made it to Her Ladyship in eighty-eight seconds. One shopping bag. Off now to Ralph Lauren.

Six minutes there.

Bing.

A goddamn jam-up with a garbage truck blocking the alley. I slammed the horn four times. The asshole wouldn't move and was taking his sweet fucking time dumping bins on the back street. I leaned on the horn again. Guy blew me a kiss and gave me the finger.

I got out of my car. I shouted:

'Gonna lose a big fare if you block my way. You gotta help me here.'

He shrugged. Then thought about it. Then did the right thing. Got into his trash truck and moved it three feet to the left, allowing me to squeeze by. I nodded. I panicked. The time on my phone told me I had thirty-four seconds to make it, or I would lose ten bucks. I swerved around a corner, got back onto Rodeo. I was with her in thirty-one seconds. She had two bags this time. And a tight look on her face.

'Cutting it close,' she said, getting in the back seat after I had put her bags in the trunk.

'Where to next, ma'am?' I asked, all smiles.

We went to Louis Vuitton and Tiffany's and G-Star and Dolce & Gabbana. By the end of the afternoon there were seventeen bags in my trunk. It was 6.32 when we got back to the Beverly Hills Hilton. A doorman there found a trolley to bring in all her bags. She opened her purse – which no doubt cost $1,000 – and pulled out three crisp $100 bills. She handed them over.

'Thank you, ma'am.'

She left without a word. There was a knock on the window. A hotel security guy.

'Move it on, bud.'

I put the car into gear. I moved it on. I pulled over on a little side street off Wilshire. I had $380 in my pocket. And I had eighty minutes to get back to Burbank. The traffic was dense, constipated. I clicked on the Uber app. Surge hour. One and a half times the fare. I got lucky. A couple in a Holiday Inn Express on North Highland were heading to Burbank Airport. Bingo. $46 courtesy of the surge. I could just about get them to the departure drop-off and haul ass back to the clinic and make the 8 p.m. pickup deadline.

We made Burbank Airport at 7.42. I texted Elise, telling her I was en route. I texted her again when I was out front at eight sharp, The security door opened and she hurried out, getting into the back seat. She looked strained, exhausted. I asked:

'Home?'

She nodded. I reached into my shirt pocket. I handed her the eighty dollars she had given me this morning.

'Why are you giving me this?' she asked.

'Because it's too much and because I acted like a crazy today.'

'You're keeping the money.'

'I don't want it.'

'Yes, you do. Because you need it. And because you deserve it. Now take it back please.'

That schoolmarmish tone. It made me anxious. The voice of authority.

'Brendan – I'm insisting.'

I took back the money.

'That eighty covers both rides today,' I said.

'If you insist.'

'I insist.'

Silence. I put the car into gear. We hit the road. After we reached the highway she asked:

'Are you in a better place?'

'I got through thc day.'

'I'm glad to hear that.'

'Why did you text me back after I tried to kill us both?'

'Guilt. About all that you had driven into last week.'

'But I chose to drive into it. I chose to get involved.'

'Which makes me feel more guilty. "No good deed goes unpunished" and all that. I'm not surprised that it got to you. But I knew that, when you put the pedal down, you weren't trying to kill us. You drove very well. Just very fast.'

'Maybe I wanted to kill myself. Maybe you being in the back of the car stopped me'.

'I'm glad I was here then. But I also worry that asking you to drive me to another clinic sparked something.'

'I've thought about going over the edge for a while.'

'What's stopped you?'

'Fear of the dark.'

I glanced into the rearview after saying that. I saw Elise's face tense up, as if she was struggling not to cry.

'Did I say the wrong thing?' I asked, adding: 'Or am I just being too cheerful for you?'

She laughed. A laugh in spite of the sadness within. She opened her bag. She pulled out her Kleenex. She dabbed her eyes.

'Life has been just that bit too hard recently,' she said. 'Or more to the point: awful. I am not just talking about Jose. It is an appalling moment in the world. Or maybe I now am being too cheerful for you . . .'

I smiled. I asked:

'A hard day today?'

'Very hard. The young woman I was with during her abortion . . . she's twenty-four. A graduate student at USC. She'd been drugged and date-raped by a fellow student; a guy she'd known for over a year and thought was her friend. She went to the college authorities. They called the LAPD. He was held and questioned and let go

– because the cops decided that, as she had invited him back to her apartment, there would be a big question about whether she was sending out the wrong signal.'

Twenty-four. The same age as Klara.

No, no, steer away from that appalling thought. I asked:

'Did she tell the guy "no"? Because "no" really does mean "no".'

'As I said: he was her friend. She invited him back for a drink. They opened a bottle of wine. She went to the bathroom. He clearly poured something into her drink while she was out of the room. When she came back, two sips later she was down for the count. When she woke up hours later she was half naked – and she knew that he'd had sex with her. She was in such a traumatized state for the next few days that she didn't see anyone and spent much of the time thinking about killing herself. As she wasn't on any contraception, and was so devastated by what had happened, she only thought about taking the morning-after pill two days after the rape. It was too late.'

'How far along was she?'

'Ten weeks. And her parents are these real country club types from Scottsdale, Arizona – and very pro-life.'

'Did she have doubts?'

'No – she knew she had to go through with it … even though she very much wants children. But not at her age and not as the result of a rape. She was very resolute going in for the procedure. Afterwards, in the recovery area, the agony started. Not because she regretted having gone through with the abortion, but because the trauma of what happened to her sideswiped her. Absolute torment – and no family or truly close friends to turn to. I felt so terrible for her.'

'Where's she now?' I asked, thinking that if she was still in the clinic we could go back and bring her to her apartment.

'She left five minutes before me. I told her I was happy to get her home ... but she insisted that she wanted to be on her own. Though I felt that too was a bad idea I have no right, legal or moral, to tell the woman what to do. I did press home the point that I sensed she needed someone with her right now. But she insisted otherwise. And ...'

In the rearview I could see her fall back in her seat and shut her eyes, a small shudder overtaking her. Then she said:

'Sorry, sorry. I shouldn't be talking shop with you.'

'Why not? I like to listen. The work you do – it's pretty damn unusual ...'

'That's one way of looking at it,' she said.

'How many clinics do you visit every week?'

'Two or three. Recently I've been thinking about upping it to four, maybe five. If they need me. I've got time on my hands. And the work is something that means a great deal to those whom I'm there for. So … it's good work.'

'But if you're doing this four or five days a week the money you're spending on Ubers must mount up. I mean, three–four hundred bucks a week … that must be a lot for a retired professor. It has to put a dent in your pension. You do have a pension, right?'

'Yes, I have a pension. My late husband was a labor lawyer who didn't earn corporate attorney money – but was smart about putting enough aside for us to have a reasonable retirement. I am in no way rolling in money. But compared to most people in the world … as long as I remain relatively modest and careful, I will see out my life with no worries about falling into indigency.'

'Is that another way of saying you won't end up on the street?'

'Yes, it is.'

'Lucky you.'

'Yes, lucky me. Could you end up on the street?'

Pause. I chose my words carefully.

'As long as I keep doing this job we will stay under our roof.'

I wanted to get off the subject of me fast. I asked:

'Does the charity pay for the Ubers?'

'They cover the travel expenses for doulas who do this volunteer work. Either Ubers or gas and mileage if you drive. But my eyesight isn't what it once was – and I actually came to the conclusion after my husband died that driving in Los Angeles is one of life's ongoing nightmares. So here I am in your Uber. And I think we should get something to eat.'

'But I'll have you home in about twenty minutes.'

'I want to buy us dinner.'

I told her I had to work. She said:

'You have to eat, don't you?'

The truth was: I hadn't eaten since that morning. Now it was almost eight-thirty and we were coming into Westwood. And I had made big money (for Uber) today.

'I'll eat with you if you let me buy,' I said.

'But I'm the one who invited you. You can do the next meal …'

If there will ever be a next meal together.

I was tired. I was also very hungry.

'Ok then,' I said. 'Kind offer accepted.'

She told me to bring us to an Italian joint right near the Hammer Museum in the heart of Westwood. It was late by LA standards for dinner. There were a handful of people in this stone-and-vine place. What I imagine some villa on the Mediterranean might look like … not that I have been to Europe or anywhere else for that matter. Not that I even have a passport. The restaurant had style. So too did everyone dining there. But not the sort of bullshit monied style that I saw when dropping rides off at big-deal restaurants in Venice and Santa Monica and West Hollywood. Low-key relaxed style. I felt shabby, cheaply dressed. I went to the bathroom as soon as we arrived. I washed my hands and face over and over again, trying to somehow make myself like them out there. When I got back to the table and opened the menu I saw that a plate of pasta cost anywhere between eighteen and twenty-six dollars. My face must have been what they call in poker 'a tell', as Elise said:

'I can afford this. We deserve it. And please stop thinking that you somehow don't belong here.'

Could she read minds too?

I ordered some sort of fancy pasta with a meat sauce. I let Elise convince me to have a glass of red wine with it. I was beyond hungry. Fourteen hours without food will do that. I saw how easily she handled the waiter and how eating in a fancy place like this came naturally to her ... even though probably one of the qualities she liked about this place was that it was not fancy.

'I usually cook for myself most nights. I have a couple of friends I see from time to time. A dinner, maybe a concert at Royce Hall. Once a month I go downtown to hear the LA Phil. I have a subscription. And at least once a week a movie. A quiet life.'

'Children?'

'There's a daughter who lives in New York. We don't see much of each other. Her choice … though maybe I shouldn't speak my mind so much.'

'Just the one child?'

'I miscarried twice before my daughter was born, so Alison was kind of a miracle.'

'My daughter's a bit of a miracle too,' I said, explaining how we lost Karol when he was nine months old and it took over two years afterwards for Agnieska to fall pregnant again.

'The death of a child. That's beyond horrible. How did the two of you get over it?'

I stared down at the tablecloth.

'I don't think we ever did,' I said.

Our wine arrived. We silently raised our glasses. I took a small sip. The wine was good. I said:

'My wife believes she finally got pregnant again because she went to Lourdes.'

'Do you believe that?'

'Faith is something I want to have and can't seem to find. Still, when Klara was born and made it through childhood without being taken away from us …'

'How old is she now?'

'Twenty-four. Living here in LA. A social worker. Dealing with battered, abused women.'

'Important work.'

'Tough work. Like yours.'

She just shrugged and asked:

'Are the two of you close?'

'Very.'

'You must be a good father,' she said.

'You'd have to ask Klara that. But the thing is … who's to say if all those conversations my wife had with God, and traveling to France and rubbing statues' heads and saying the rosary in a place of miracles … who's to say it didn't help?'

Elise paused for a moment and sipped her wine.

'You're right: who's to say? I remember a line in a movie I once saw about chance and happenstance. Someone was talking about prayer. And saying: "Faith is the antithesis of proof." But it *is* faith. It works for a lot of people.'

'Not for you?'

'I was raised back east as an Episcopalian. Very WASP. Very thoughtful and liberal. The American branch of Anglicanism. The Queen's church.'

'Wow. I mean, that sounds kind of impressive. Praying to the same God as the Queen of England.'

'Well, I never thought of it that way. Episcopalians don't mind accepting that faith doesn't always provide definitive answers; that there's a lot of ambiguity in the heavens above. That doesn't play well with a lot of people. Because one of the big central things behind faith is the need for certainty … when, in fact, there is none in the world. Are there answers? The fundamentalists think so. The fellow who firebombed us last week thinks so. So too the people behind him – and there were definitely others behind him.'

She took another sip of her wine, then asked:

'Mind hearing a story?'

'I'm always up for a story.'

'Okay then … I have a cousin named Susan back east. Very much an evangelical, the whole works. Why did my cousin become Born Again? Her husband – a very successful, very angry lawyer who hated his job and hated even more this very cushioned suburban life he'd created for my cousin and their two children – got into a rage one night and stormed off. Their two little boys were at the Boy Scouts. He told my cousin he would pick them up. She thought that was a good thing; that he might cool off once he was with his children. He picked up Charlie and Jack. He started driving home up Interstate 95 between Fairfield and Westport in Connecticut. He put his pedal down on the floor of his Volvo. He reached 110 miles per hour. He deliberately crashed into the wall separating the highway from a big gas station. They were all killed instantly. My poor cousin went into what could be best described as freefall. Because as she confessed to me some days later – when she was being held in the wing of a big psychiatric hospital in Stamford after attempting to overdose – the last words she said to him, at the height of their fight, were: "Then why don't you just fucking kill yourself?" Understandably she fell apart thereafter. She'd had a small but successful accounting business. That completely went under in the turmoil that followed. She hit the bottle. She became dependent of all sorts of pharmaceuticals. She got done for DUI. She was a catastrophe. Four years after her husband did what he did – right about the time that she had to sell her house to stave off bankruptcy – one of her former accountancy associates brought her to this church in Fairfield which was into charismatic Christianity. At the end of the service everyone visiting the church that day for the first time was asked to stand up and tell the congregation a little bit about themselves. When it was Susan's turn the whole terrible story came pouring out. The crowd loved it. Tragedy, insane guilt, a cry for help from the abyss ... and she was surrounded by a couple hundred people who all believed in the power of on high to precipitate redemption. She fell on her knees, hysterical. She accepted Jesus as her Lord and Savior. She found a community who were going to pull her back into their version of Happy Life.'

She paused for a moment, her face scrunched up, as if she were displeased by something. Then:

'I want to apologize for that last comment. It sounded far too bitchy, a little mean. The truth is: becoming an evangelical Christian probably kept my cousin alive. Of course she got herself into AA. Went to intensive Bible classes and became beyond learned on all lessons to be learned from the Good Book. She rebuilt her business. She started giving inspirational motivational talks about overcoming the worst that life can throw at you. And, as I knew would happen, she met a fellow Born Againer. Ralph has a senior sales job for one of the evil Big Pharma companies, but comes across as the nicest, most concerned fellow you could run into … even if he is pushing Ambien on the masses. And there I go again, being all sardonic and snippy.'

'That's quite a story,' I said, my voice hushed, uneasy. She picked up on my discomfort.

'I'm not telling you this as a comment on how fast you drove earlier today. As I said before: I sensed you knew what you were doing, that you were showing all the classic signs of PTSD, and that you ultimately weren't trying to kill yourself.'

'But you still knew that one wrong move, or another car changing lanes suddenly, and we could have been involved in a terrible crash.'

She sipped her wine again.

'Maybe I was having one of those moments that I've been having ever since the clinic was firebombed and Jose was killed … where I find myself thinking: if I go now is that such a bad thing?'

I stared down into my wine glass. She had just said what I felt so often recently myself.

Our pastas arrived.

'Under the circumstances we won't say grace,' Elsie said. 'But I will wish you: bon appétit.'

'Bon appétit,' I repeated, trying out the French words.

'Your accent is good,' she said.

'You're just trying to be nice.'

'Is there anything wrong with that?'

I tasted the fancy spaghetti with the fancy meat sauce. It was pretty damn wonderful. I let the waiter grate a lot of fresh Parmesan over it. It became even better with all that cheese. Not a big serving – and I was used to big servings whenever Agnieska cooked. But this was spaghetti about as good as I had ever tasted.

'You approve?' Elise asked.

'I approve. Thank you.'

We ate. After a few mouthfuls of pasta I asked:

'Do you think your cousin will ever come to terms with what happened?'

'She tells me she's reached "closure" with it. Know what I think? That's her way of comforting herself. We only talk a few times a year. As my late husband used to say: "There are certain people who, even if they are family, are best to give a wide distance to. Because all they can ever do is get under your skin and make you feel uncomfortable."'

'Your husband was a smart man.'

'That he was. And he put up with my grumpiness. Especially in the face of human stupidity. I suppose if I have a central fault it's that I don't suffer fools ... and I don't know when to hold my tongue.'

'But he still thought the world of you?'

'Now that's a bit presumptuous.'

'So he thought you a jerk?'

She smiled.

'Sometimes, yes, I think he did. But only when I was in one of those moods where I was at odds with the world. He was a very patient man.'

'Were you a patient woman?'

'You ask a lot of questions.'

'When you drive a lot of people around ...'

'He was called Wilbur – a terrible name, I know, but he was stuck with it, because his very tyrannical father was Wilbur Sr. My husband had his complexities. We met when we were both undergraduates at Harvard ...'

'You really went to that place?'

'Radcliffe – that's what they called in my day Harvard for "young women". But yes, it was still Harvard. Wilbur was my first love. We met our second year there. We were together for the next three years. Wilbur got accepted at the law school. He wanted me to marry him. I got accepted into the doctoral program at the Sorbonne in Paris – so we had a problem. I decided to choose Paris over marriage … even though I could have stayed on at Harvard to do my PhD. Wilbur was stoic about it. But I could tell that I'd broken his heart. Still, it was the right call. I needed a sense of liberty. I needed to flee the regularity of American life for a while. I wasn't ready to be with one man for the rest of my life. Paris gave me many opportunities on all those fronts.'

'Yet you ended up together.'

'I had several boyfriends during those five years. Then, just before my sixth year in Paris, a letter arrived from Wilbur. He had finished law school two years earlier. He'd sidestepped an engagement to a highly connected Boston woman from one of those upper-crust families where everyone is beyond white, Anglo and Protestant. He'd found his way to Los Angeles and work in a law firm noted for its progressive politics and taking on the establishment. And he asked if he could pay me a visit in France. I said yes. And …'

Her eyes became full. I could see that all this talk of her late husband was leaving her raw.

'You must miss him a lot,' I said.

Her lips tightened. She shut her eyes, then opened her purse and took out a Kleenex and dabbed them.

'Only every hour on the hour … even if, like most marriages, there were periods when we drove each other mad. Still … a good man, Wilbur. Did I ever really see myself – the ultimate East Coast girl – becoming an Angeleno? Hardly. But I adapted … and even grew to like the idea of living under a near-perpetual dome of blue. And listen to me, talking, talking, talking … and all about my little self.'

'But it's interesting.'

'You are far too nice, Brendan.'

'As you said earlier: is there anything wrong with that? And your daughter? Alison, right … ?'

'She followed her parents to Harvard. But then, in an act of rebellion, she went to Wall Street and became a Master of the Universe. Mutual funds. A true believer in social Darwinism. She gives money to the Republican Party and even voted for Trump. We don't see much of each other – and she had a big political falling-out with her father a year before he died. Which was terribly sad … though, to Alison's credit, when he got hit with pancreatic cancer and was given just weeks to live, she did drop everything and came back to be with us in LA. Ran her high finance business from our modest living room …'

'Is that where she grew up?' I said.

'We once had a proper house not far from our apartment. But after Alison went east – almost fifteen years ago – and was clearly not coming back much we decided to downsize to an apartment. With a guest bedroom for her whenever she deigned to pay us a visit. Which wasn't often. Still … when her dad was not long for the world she was there for him.'

'Do you visit each other a couple of times a year?'

'Mothers and daughters do a funny tango – and we have always had a complicated dynamic. Not just because she considers me a rabid socialist and I look upon her as a heartless plutocrat, but also because we just don't really seem to like each other. Which is a terrible thing to admit. But sadly true.'

'I know all about that. My daughter Klara is the center of my life. But she and her mom … it's beyond terrible.'

'At least she has you. And you have her. And your wife …'

'That's beyond terrible too. We're married. But there's no marriage … if you get what I'm saying. And it's not just down to her. We're kind of … lost.'

Bing. A text arrived on my phone. I ignored it. Bad manners looking at your phone while at dinner. But the *bing* binged again.

'Please do take that if you need to,' Elise said.

I pulled the phone out of my pocket. I glanced at the messages. There was one from my daughter.

Just home from work … want to drop by now?

I texted back:

Give me an hour. All cool?

Klara's reply:

Life is never 'all cool'. But I'm okay. Just feel like having a beer with my dad. You 'cool' with that?

I found myself smiling; Elise asked:

'Good news?'

'My daughter wants to buy me a beer.'

I could see Elise turn away, trying to mask the sadness I saw in her eyes. She finally said:

'Lucky man.'

eleven

KLARA LIVED IN a crash-pad apartment in Echo Park. Not a bad street.

It was wide with a collection of indifferent modern houses. She was one of five people who paid $600 each per month for a three-bedroom place in a building that looked like a motel. Fifteen years back Echo Park was considered borderline no-go. Rundown. Gang warfare. Dangerous. Now it was all young professionals and arty kids who had to share a place to pay the excessive rent. Klara moved into this place just over a year ago after she'd finished her BA at UC Santa Cruz. I was proud of my girl coming out of one of the top UC schools with a *cum laude* degree and then choosing the social work path – working with migrants from south of the border. Privately I might have wished that she'd done the law school thing she kept telling me she would follow. But I knew that if I even hinted this to Klara it would get her back up. She'd say that I was pushing her into 'a secure career option' ... just as my father had done before with me. I could hear her tell me: 'I don't want to do safe, Poppa. Just as I know you'd really like to run away from that too.'

Maybe she had a point here. I said nothing. Because when my daughter felt cornered she refused to budge from a position taken on something. Two years previously she'd been seeing this real deadbeat guy, 'an artist biker', whose dream was to open his own tattoo parlor, and who struck me about as artistic as a garbage can. I also sensed that he had this resentful streak. Still, Klara was crazy about him. When Agnieska finally met him she went hysterical afterwards and gave our daughter a crazed earful about her bad choice in boyfriends. This naturally made Klara defend the guy even more ferociously. She was with him for another eight long months ... until she found out that he'd cheated on her with a fellow tattoo designer. I was quietly pleased that the clown had destroyed any feelings that my daughter had for him and that I had managed for once to put my foot down with Agnieska. I insisted that she did not go into her 'I told you so' routine which she liked to pull whenever something she disapproved of went wrong for somebody else. Especially as Klara showed real smarts and maturity in shoving the guy out the door. It was another important sign to me that, after a roller coaster of an adolescence, my daughter had become rational and focused – even though she got me a little worried when she told me a few months back that the shelter for battered women where she worked had suffered a security breach. Their armed guard had stepped away from the back exit for a two-minute bathroom break. It allowed the furious, crazy violent husband of a woman they'd been sheltering to burst in. He was brandishing a pistol and threatened to shoot the staff. Fortunately the other security guy on the front door was alerted and came running in, slamming his rifle butt into the guy's head.

'Security's been beefed up since then,' she said, trying to reassure me. But I was anything but reassured.

'We keep quiet about our work,' she said, 'but there are a lot of angry men out there who have abused women and now look upon us as the enemy for getting their partners away from their violence; a violence which, like most abusers, they refuse to acknowledge ever having committed.'

That statement of hers came back to me tonight as I pulled up in front of Klara's place. It underscored an unspoken rule that my daughter and I had: we were always there for each other. But we also respected the fact that we didn't have to speak about all going on in our separate lives. That was a hard rule for a father to adhere to. But when I considered whether I should tell her about all that I had driven into in Van Nuys last week I decided that, for the moment, I was going to stay silent about everything. Not because I didn't want to her to know. Rather because she might start applauding my own 'activism' – when it was nothing of the sort. And because I feared that the next time her mother called her – as I knew she did at least once a week – Klara might use this knowledge as a way of getting at her. Even if I told her that this was a secret between us, Klara so disagreed with everything to do with Agnieska's faith and politics that she went out of her way to provoke and anger her. I wanted what I had driven into not to become a point of family discussion.

Klara's place on North Beaudry Avenue was situated behind a high concrete wall. Pulling up outside and getting out of my car I sent her a text:

I'm here.

Her reply:

Be right there.

About a minute later the door opened. I could hear loud music from her place. She had a bottle of beer in each hand. She looked like she'd lost about five more pounds since I'd seen her two weeks ago. She also seemed very stoned.

'Hey, Poppa!' she said, all smiles, giving me a hug. 'Want an IPA?'

'Where we going to drink it?'

'On my porch – if you don't mind heavy metal and the whiff of weed.'

'It's legal now in California,' I said, following her in. 'And you are three years over the legal age for all that – so as long as you don't drive when high, what you do is not my business.'

'Even though you still clearly worry that I may drive when high.'

We reached the porch. A battered table spray-painted with graffiti. A couple of dented metal chairs. An ashtray piled high with butts. A couple of empty beer bottles. Head-banging music blasting away inside – where it sounded as if quite a crowd was hanging out in the living room; a place which, the last time I saw it, had little in the way of furniture and a lot of mattresses on the floor. I accepted a bottle of beer. Klara accepted a cigarette from me.

'If Momma could see you offering me a cancer stick and me giving you a beer when you're driving.'

'It's just going to be one beer,' I said, calculating that almost ninety minutes had passed since I'd finished that very good glass of Italian red in Westwood. I was not running any risks ... as long as I didn't touch anything more than one bottle of the fancy craft lager she'd put in my hand.

'Yeah but Momma is always looking for original sin moments to bring me down on.'

'Cigarettes and alcohol and weed aren't exactly original sin.'

'Momma still wants to think that everyone's in a fallen state of grace.'

'That's also called: her very own form of unhappiness.'

'Which you put up with.'

'Let's not go there.'

'Papa, you know she raises all sorts of objections with me, and has done so for as long as I can remember. Because I always remind her of the blessed first child who died. The son she worshipped. Unlike me. The girl she didn't want.'

'Don't say that.'

'Why? It's kind of true. And kind of sad. But it's what she sees me as: the consolation child whom she's never warmed toward.'

'It's a little more complex than that. And when you become a parent –'

'I'm never becoming a parent.'

'As you've told me many times. But, okay, if somehow, somewhere down the line you do become a parent –'

'As I just said, Papa: that won't ever happen.'

'Fine, fine, got it, not trying to convince you otherwise. But just understand this: to be a parent is to worry all the time.'

'To be a *proper* parent. Unlike Momma.'

'She does love you … in her own way.'

'Bullshit.'

'How's the job?'

'We're dealing with state budget cuts all the time. I didn't want to worry you – because I know you worry all the time – but last month my boss Helen told me that, as I was the last person they'd hired, I'd probably be the first to be let go.'

'Damn,' I said, trying not to overplay my distress at this news. Especially as good work was so hard to come by everywhere right now. And I knew that Klara loved her job – as difficult as it often was.

'Yeah – damn,' Klara said. 'But just a few days ago Helen told me that she had some interesting news. You know all about Patrick Kelleher … the great patron of "Uncle" Todor?'

'Of course,' I said. 'Who in LA doesn't know Patrick Kelleher?'

Because he was not only one of the richest men in a city full of very rich men – but also a serious Catholic who threw his considerable financial and political weight behind socially conservative causes. Like Angels Assist. Patrick Kelleher was a Wall Streeter who decided twenty years ago, while still in his late thirties, to move his entire mutual funds operation out to Southern California. I googled a great deal about Patrick Kelleher when I discovered he was the chief underwriter of Angels Assist. How, in his two decades in LA, his net worth had risen from a mere $50 million to close to $650 million. How he was, in his younger days, very much the hotshot financier around town, dating actresses and models, known for his extravagance and for having grown up in a bog Irish American background not dissimilar from me . . . only in South Boston where his dad had been a fireman. He too was raised a serious Catholic. But a very lapsed one. And famously unmarried. Until he got together with Cheryl Chandler – who, back in 2010, was one of the hottest young actresses in Hollywood with an immense fan base and a huge career in romantic comedies where she always played the beautiful, sought-after woman. She was twenty-five when she married the fifty-year old Kelleher. She was pregnant a year later – but had a much-publicized abortion when she filed for divorce, accusing Kelleher of physical and emotional abuse, not to mention being a control freak nightmare. Kelleher, in turn, went after her career – letting it be known that he had discovered (courtesy of a team of private detectives) that she'd been having an affair with her co-star on two of her more successful films, Jason Meese, an actor whom Klara once described as 'Mr Hunk who doubles in the role of Prince Not So Bright'. Kelleher also alleged that the reason his wife had a secret abortion was to eliminate the possibility of a paternity test . . . as it wasn't known if Kelleher or Meese was the father. Cheryl Chandler denied this version of events. So too did Jason Meese. But after word got out about her affair with her co-star her career went into something of a tailspin. Then, two years after her very publicized divorce (where she came out with $10 million – which, given Kelleher's net worth, was the equivalent of a speeding ticket) – she and Meese were killed in a car accident en route to Vegas. She was heading there to start work on a small independent film – her first acting gig since her private life became the stuff of supermarket tabloids and reality news shows. Her Porsche blew a tire while she was speeding along the interstate at 92 mph (according to the police records – which also went public everywhere). The Porsche somersaulted three times on this empty stretch of desert highway before exploding into flames. In the wake of her death Kelleher expressed what seemed to many to be genuine grief, saying that he had deeply loved his wife, had been heartbroken when she left him, and that all the bad publicity that circled her afterwards was the media's own doing; that he'd never orchestrated any of it. Cheryl's friends and fans thought otherwise – some even wondering out loud if Kelleher had been behind their deaths. The police investigation into the accident ruled it just that: an accident. But many in Cheryl's camp screamed that he had paid for a cover-up. Just as many of Kelleher's friends in the press (especially at Fox News and the also-Murdoch-owned *Wall Street Journal*) came out swinging in his defense, detailing Meese's extensive drug use (he was a cokehead) and Cheryl's many fines for reckless driving. They also published more lurid photographs of the couple in bed … which Kelleher maintained were masterminded by grubby paparazzi. In the wake of her death, Kelleher became (in Klara's words) 'a tsunami of bullshit compassion'. Not only did he set up five big acting scholarships every year in Cheryl's name at CalArts (her alma mater) – and indicated they should be given in favor of minority and LGBT students – but he also donated $20 million to a statewide 'anti-drug and responsible driving' educational program (which, according to my daughter, could all be boiled down to 'if you can afford to drive a Porsche don't break speed limits when coked up'). Most tellingly, Kelleher admitted in several carefully orchestrated interviews that his wife's tragic death had rekindled his Catholic faith. He was giving a great deal to Catholic food programs, Catholic Third World education programs. But his biggest project, without question, was Angels Assist. Todor had shrewdly become his priestly mouthpiece – who, in keeping with Kelleher's public image, was compassionate and apparently reasonable ... yet simultaneously relentless when it came to insisting that abortion was outright murder.

And now ...

'Around two weeks ago,' Klara said, 'we were told that we were having an important visitor come to the shelter that afternoon. We weren't told who ... just that, according to Helen, he was "a possible big-deal benefactor". Six hours later in walked Kelleher with an assistant and a bodyguard. He was also with Rachel Rancini – the woman who was one of the founders of our shelter and had been on record many times saying that Patrick Kelleher was one of the biggest enemies of women's rights in America. But there she was, showing the guy around, answering his questions, explaining very calmly how we were doing important work here. The weird thing was: Kelleher was taking it all in, showing real interest. I expected this total crazed Catholic monster who was probably terrified of women which is why he was doing his best to limit their reproductive rights. But he turned out to be smart and good with words. He was also super fit and was wearing the most immaculate gray suit I'd ever seen. Which made me even more suspicious of him. Especially as, when Rachel asked Helen to introduce all the staff there to him, he seemed to take an immediate interest in me ...'

Oh great … I thought, wondering what was coming next. Klara read me instantly.

'Fear not, Poppa. I haven't become one of his concubines. Given his taste in much younger women I'm over the hill at twenty-four, but it was clear that he'd decided to single out one of the staff to talk with – and he chose me.'

No doubt because she is beautiful and smart.

'What did he want to know?'

'He asked a lot of very well-informed questions about domestic abuse and were we dealing with women who walked in after being abused? If they called us did we send the cops to their homes? And how did I handle a woman who, say, had been beaten by her husband but still went back to him? I answered all his questions – and he turned to his assistant and said that he would like to invite me to lunch and learn more … "as I think you are exactly the sort of young articulate spokeswoman for the shelter that we need". I actually handed him my card – we all have them at the shelter to give to the women we take in – and said that I'd be happy to have lunch if he'd also invite my boss Helen along. I nodded in her direction. Helen's about fifty and rather severe. Kelleher put my card in his pocket and said: "We'll be in touch." Which struck me as also his way of saying: "If you won't eat lunch with me alone … goodbye."

That was that. Never heard from him again – which was a relief. Because had he asked me to lunch I would have probably felt obliged to go through with it for the good of the shelter.

'Anyway, five days ago Rachel came in and called a staff meeting and announced that the board of our shelter met yesterday with Kelleher's people ... and Kelleher wants to make an initial $2 million annual donation ... with the hope of trying to open another three or four of our shelters in LA within two years and starting to think about maybe opening an entire chain across the state.'

'So your job is now safe!' I said, raising my beer bottle to Klara.

'It looks that way,' she said, lighting up a fresh cigarette.

'Your enthusiasm isn't exactly overwhelming.'

'Patrick Kelleher was accused of assault by his wife; a wife whose career he ruined after she left him.'

'I think her career got ruined by the nude pictures of her with her lover boy when she was still married to Kelleher. And then having an abortion ...'

'That was her legal right to do so.'

'I'm not disagreeing with you on that one – but the fact that she didn't consult her husband ...'

'Why did she have to do that?'

'She never said it wasn't his child.'

'Maybe it wasn't. What does that matter? She was carrying it in her body. Which gave her the final say on whether to keep it or not. You've seen what Kelleher has done with that creepy Catholic home for scared young women – where he has my mother and her psycho friend Teresa convincing them to be battery hens. After the baby is born they sell the kid on to rich Catholic families who've had to make a donation of at least twenty grand to the Angels to get on their adoption list. Do you know what then happens to the mothers of those babies? A few days after they've given birth ... out they go onto the street.'

'How do you know all this?' I said.

'I've been doing some research into Kelleher ever since we've learned that he wants to take us over.'

'It's a charitable donation, Klara – and one that is going to allow you to keep your job.'

'Why do you think he wants to be our benefactor, Poppa? For the same reason why – as a right-winger who distrusts anyone who isn't white and Christian – he set up those acting scholarships in the name of the woman he initially dated when she was eighteen. No power imbalance there whatsoever. And yeah, I know that being eighteen makes you legal in this country. But he was still sleeping with a kid – and got away with it at the time.

Now those scholarships are being given to minorities by a man who has been on the record in the past as saying that homosexuality is against God's will. Just as he was once overheard at a fundraising dinner saying he still can't get his head around interracial relationships. Of course he denied it all afterwards.'

'Maybe he had a change of heart,' I said. 'Maybe he realized that he was wrong to think such things.'

'Oh please, Poppa. What's he's doing ... it's called "running interference" in football. Coming across like a good guy by supporting that which you privately hate, while meanwhile undermining the serious people who want to really change things. The guy was an alleged wife beater, so why does he want to throw money at a shelter for battered women? To show the world he is really into women's rights while simultaneously trying to impose his own program on us.'

'Which will be what exactly?' I asked. 'Is Kelleher going to professionally force you to forgive men who beat women?'

'Very funny, Poppa. But I am sure that, after a few months, he will have a "management structure" in place run by his own people. It's going to be what's known as a hostile takeover done under the guise of a big generous charity donation – and one which his media friends can spin as "*Patrick Kelleher: Protector of Women!*" Just as those scholarships he set up in the name of his late wife, whom he assaulted and whose career he ruined –'

'Allegations, nothing more,' I said.

'Why are you defending this guy, Poppa? Especially since he has *your* wife doing his dirty work for him.'

'Because his money saved your job. I might not like his extreme views, any more than I like the way Todor also does his dirty work for him –'

'That toad of a priest will do anything for Kelleher because he knows he's his meal ticket to a promotion in the Church ... or a big well-paid job in his organization should "Uncle" Todor decide he wants out.'

'Kelleher is still doing a good thing for your group. Especially with the State of California cutting your budget.'

'That's the other problem in the US today. If you want charity go beg a rich guy, not the state. Because we don't believe that our tax dollars should pay for anything but defense, law enforcement and tax breaks for the super-rich.'

A pause. I asked:

'Can I have another beer?'

'Is that your way of telling me: *enough!*' she asked, amused.

'Maybe I just want another beer,' I said, smiling back. She reached for the six-pack under the table and handed me a bottle. I twisted off the cap.

'Now if I drink this,' I said, 'you're going to have to put up with me for another hour … because that's how long it will take for the alcohol to wear off and I can drive again.'

'I think I can put up with you for another hour,' she said, opening a new bottle herself and clinking it against mine. 'If, that is, you can put up with me.'

'Only if I can have another cigarette,' I said.

'That's allowed, but only if I can have another one too … and if you don't ask me about my current boyfriend situation as Mom keeps doing.'

'You're talking to your mother?' I said, sounding far too hopeful.

'She called last week … saying she wanted to know if she could give away to charity the clothes I'd left behind in my room.'

'Why the hell did she do that? And no, you don't have to give away those clothes.'

'But I want to give away those clothes because they are old clothes. Mom did that as a way of reaching out to me … which was nice. Until she said that she was worried I was going to turn into an old maid. And that she was working with a really nice young guy named Chuck at Angels Assist who would be perfect for me …'

'Because, like you, he's a daily communicant?'

Klara let out a laugh and gave me a light punch in the arm.

'And I thought I was subversive.'

'Is his name really "Chuck"?'

'Yeah, there's something that makes me uneasy about a "Chucky" who's also a right-to-lifer. Mom lives in her own parallel fantasy universe – where I am her perfect little girl who is going to come to the church and meet the right guy and give her grandchildren. Even though she knows that all of those fantasies will come to nothing.'

'I think the truth is a little more complex and sad,' I said. 'She doesn't know how to talk to you. She really disagrees with everything you stand for. That scares her. Because she misses you . . .'

'Yet she also keeps me at a distance because she doesn't want to even consider my point of view. And, as I said before, she always looks at me and thinks about your dead son. Had he lived would I even be here?'

'Don't think bad stuff like that. You are everything to me.'

She touched my shoulder.

'I know that,' she said. 'And it means so much. But Mom . . . her faith, her belief . . . it's her way of seeing things or *not* seeing things. I feel lost with her.'

I lit up a fresh cigarette, telling myself it was the last of the evening … and knowing that to be a lie.

'Feeling lost …' I finally said. 'That's how most of us stagger through the day.'

twelve

I DRANK THAT one last beer with Klara – but didn't leave for another two hours. We kept talking and talking into the wee hours. Knowing that my daughter started work at nine, I finally called it a night when it was almost one in the morning.

'Sorry I kept you up so late,' I said when I stood up to leave.

'I'm a vampire,' she said. 'I need little sleep. And I am happy to have a dad I can hang with well after midnight.'

I was back at my house forty minutes later. As I parked out front I was surprised to see a light on in our kitchen. Agnieska was at the table, her hands around a steaming mug of tea.

'Couldn't sleep,' she said as I entered. 'Decided to make myself a cup of something to knock me out. Good day?'

'Same old, same old. But I did just spend several hours with our daughter.'

She suddenly looked very scared.

'Why were you with her? Did something happen?'

'She just wanted to talk.'

'About what? She's gotten into something bad, right?'

I touched the top of her hand lightly.

'And I thought I was the one in this household who always thinks the worst. All is just fine with Klara. No dramas, no emergencies. She just wanted to hang out.'

Agnieska's face tightened.

'That's something she never does with me.'

'Maybe if you asked her to hang out with you –'

'She hates me.'

'No, she doesn't ... but if you were to try to avoid bringing up the way the two of you have very different ways of looking at the world ...'

'Klara is my only child ... my *adored* only child. But she is beyond stubborn and refuses to see other people's side to things.'

I could have said much here – especially about how Agnieska herself was even more rigid when it came to her corner of the issue that had become her daily bread. But it was late, I was tired. I knew the argument that would follow between us and how it would go nowhere and how I didn't want the night to end grimly after all those excellent hours with my daughter. Instead I asked:

'Want another cup of tea?'

She shook her head but thanked me for the offer. Then she said:

'Had some nice news today.'

'Tell me.'

'Father Todor informed me that they're opening a new branch of Angels Assist in South Central LA and he wants me to be the manager. Which means running all the administration and trying to increase our influence in the community. And it's a paid job.'

'That's fantastic news,' I said, thinking: Klara is going to love this. Especially that 'increase our influence in the community' line – which sounded like some corporate spin from the management team that Kelleher had running this charity ... perhaps the same group about to take over Klara's shelter ...

'The pay isn't much – around four hundred a week. But it will cover some bills, right? And this is work I love. Work which is all about goodness. To get paid for that ...'

'Proud of you,' I said, kissing her on the head. Even if I had my doubts about the 'goodness' of that work ... to love what you do is such a rare thing.

I went to bed, I slept five short hours. I took a needed day off. That afternoon I got a text from Elise, asking if I was free to drive her 'and someone I am assisting' tomorrow? *Would picking me up at 2.30 work? I'll need you for about six hours. Can you do that?*

I texted back:

I can do that.

I was outside her apartment in Westwood ten minutes before the agreed time. Elise was already waiting for me on the street. She got into the car. She seemed distracted and tense. After saying hello and getting the address to where we were heading I asked:

'Something not good?'

'*Someone*'s not good. The woman we're picking up … spoke with her this morning. She's in a bad place. So if you hear things in your car when she is with us …'

'Hear what? I'll hear nothing.'

'You'll hear everything.'

'But like a priest I will discuss nothing.'

I asked Elise if she wanted to listen to some music on the way to the pickup. 'Yes please, Brendan,' she said so I hit the radio. Moody strings filled the car.

'Gray music for a gray day,' she said. 'Not that I mind the gray. When I lived in Paris the winter there was gray day after gray day. It went on for weeks, months. When I followed my husband out here to the land of endless blue in the sky, I was initially happy. After around a few months of nothing but sunshine I actually found myself thinking how nice it would be to see a little gloom from time to time.'

'I've never known anything but here.'

'Never lived anywhere else?'

I told her about my months way up an electricity pole in Sequoia. How it was the first time I experienced snow on a daily basis. And how free I felt.

'You being up among the tall trees was your version of Paris?'

'I wasn't getting a fancy degree like you were,' I said.

'But you were looking out on something amazing every day. And you were far away from all the ties that bind.'

'The terrible thing was – I came back when ordered.'

'And I gave in to Wilbur's marriage proposal ...'

'But he wasn't ordering you.'

'True. But still ...'

Silence. Then:

'Wilbur came to visit me for three weeks in Paris. We had this very passionate time. There was a night when, having drunk too much wine – something that is very easy to do in Paris – I forgot to put my diaphragm in. Around a month after he left ... I was late with my period. Three weeks later I went to a local clinic in the area I was living in. They extracted blood. A few days after that I came back and got the result: I was going to have a baby. I was just twenty-six. The last thing I wanted was a child. I did the difficult thing. I placed a long-distance call to California. I told Wilbur what had happened and that it was too early for me to become a mother. He told me he would respect my choice, my wishes. He never once tried to talk me out of it. He offered to fly back to be with me during the "procedure". He had just been given his first big trial in his law firm. One of the initial busing cases. This was 1975 when stuff like this was still going on … as it does in different guises today. I insisted he stay.'

'You had the abortion alone?'

She nodded.

'Was it okay?'

'Let me tell you something I know from personal experience and from the work I do now: there is never an okay abortion. By which I mean: the procedure can go flawlessly. There can be little or no pain whatsoever. But the emotions it engenders, the way you as a woman have to live with it thereafter … even if it is wanted, even if you are having it for all the right reasons, even if it is the result of sexual assault … the fact is: it is an immense roller coaster to ride.'

'And you felt … ?'

'Lost. Sad. Guilty. Self-Righteous. Tough. Proud. Crazed. Lonely. Full of regret. Determined. Feminist. Frightened. Wondering: did I act too precipitously? Knowing: it was the right decision for me. Knowing: I would always carry it with me.'

'It still haunts you?'

'On days when I regret the estrangement I have with Alison … when I think of the miscarriages I had some years after the abortion and that, after her birth, I couldn't get pregnant again … yes, it can provoke a modicum of melancholy. Especially when I still find myself wondering in lonely moments: who would he or she be now? But another part of me does understand that I really wasn't ready back then to make the vast commitment that being a parent involves. Who knows if the marriage would have been as happy as it largely was had we not had those first years for ourselves and ourselves alone?'

'Is that why you now do the work that you do at the clinics? Because of what you'd lived through?'

'What I lived through was me taking control of my body, my destiny. All significant choices in life are shaded by many complexities and ambiguities. But yes, after I retired and I learned from some friends about this charity that was helping women deal with the termination of a pregnancy, I thought I could perhaps help a little. Largely I am there for women who don't have a partner or a friend or family member to support them. They are often having the procedure without anyone's knowledge. I am with the woman beforehand. I listen to whatever they want to tell me. I attempt to talk them through any doubts or fears they have – never trying to convince them to have the abortion if they are beginning to have second thoughts. In several cases, the woman has changed her mind before the procedure. I try to get them to do breathing exercises if they are tense, scared. The abortion itself takes usually around five minutes. The woman is given normal over-the-counter painkillers afterwards. Advil or something like that. There are herbal teas and cookies in our recovery area. Most of all I sit with her after the procedure for as long as she needs me. Sometimes the woman breaks down. Sometimes the woman just wants to get dressed and get out the door. Sometimes there is anger. Sometimes regret. Sometimes hysteria. Sometimes absolute calm and a resoluteness about it all. Every abortion is different. Every woman has a completely distinct reaction to the whole business – and its ramifications … or lack thereof. I am simply there to support them in any way possible. Each time I am dealing with an atypical situation. Most of all I am there to let them know: they are not alone. If requested I give them my cell number and am there on the phone or to meet them later on if they need to talk. I function a bit like a therapist – but more than anything as a completely non-judgmental friend.'

Silence. I was trying to figure out what I should say next. All I could think was:

'I'm amazed you told me all that about your own abortion.'

'Why?' she asked.

'Because it's so private, so personal.'

'And something I've only shared with a very close friend – now sadly dead – besides you.'

'I'm kind of … honored, I guess.'

'But I trust you, Brendan.'

We went east – to Los Feliz. A little street off Franklin. A nice house. Very much renovated, with two very good cars – an Audi Q5 and a Mini Cooper – in the driveway. Before she got out of the car Elise said:

'I'll be about ten minutes,' she said. 'Her name is Jackie. Just to warn you she's a bit of a motormouth. But given what she's going through right now …'

Ten minutes. I could grab a smoke. I stepped out of the car and lit up an American Spirit. I took a couple of deep drags, with all that Elise had just told me still rattling around my head. I found myself thinking: *there's no easy way of looking at this. Even though we are being endlessly told that, yes, there is a right and a wrong when it comes to this issue.* But now I was coming to the conclusion: *personal choice is the one and only truth here. And all women had the right to that choice.*

The front door opened. Elise emerged with Jackie. Long black hair, denims, black sweatshirt, sneakers, sunglasses – all designer, all telling me: this woman was Hollywood. Someone high up in the business. Just as I could immediately sense her incredible distress. Twice walking toward my car she stopped and lowered her head and seemed to be on the verge of losing it. Elise had her arm around her, talking quietly to her as she moved her forward.

I hurriedly got back into the car and turned on KUSC. I waited. I stared straight ahead, worried: if that woman sensed me watching her in the middle of this very personal drama it could make things worse for her. The car door finally opened, the two women getting into the back seat.

'You sure he can be trusted?' she asked Elise.

'I chose him because he can be absolutely trusted.'

'Tell him to turn the music up.'

I was about to reach for the dial – but thought better of it. Because that would indicate that I was listening to her. So I waited for Elise to ask me:

'Would you mind turning up the music please?'

I reached for the dial. I cranked it right up.

'Jesus fucking Christ,' the woman said. 'Is he stupid?'

'We will have none of that, Jackie.'

'Sorry, sorry,' she whispered. I turned the music down. Elise asked the woman:

'Now that that is settled ... shall we head off and get this behind you?'

She nodded.

'Off we go then,' Elise said, letting me know I could put the car in gear and get us moving. I already had the destination. An address not far from the USC campus. Jackie started talking.

'That fucker known as my husband called me last night from Buenos Aires. No doubt he's got some woman stuck away there. Never marry an Argentinian.'

'How long is he gone for?'

'He had to go see his crazy mother in some rest home down there. And then he has this horrible sister who makes a killing as a plastic surgeon. More face jobs happen in Buenos Aires than –'

Elise cut her off.

'So your husband won't be back until … ?'

'At least Monday.'

'That's good. Six days. You should have recovered by then.'

'You mean, my twat should have recovered so that pig can shove his stubby little thing into me and –'

I heard myself take a sharp intake of breath. So did Jackie.

'You don't like my descriptive language, mister?' she asked me. I felt myself tense. Elise jumped in.

'He said nothing, Jackie. And regarding your husband … you don't have to let him have sex with you if you don't want to.'

'You don't fucking understand. He's sure I've been seeing someone else here in LA. But the guy I love lives in New York.'

'Are you sure your husband doesn't know about him?'

'No, I'm not sure. But he's been so obsessed with having me watched in LA …'

'Does the New York guy know he is the father?'

'I haven't told him. I'm not going to tell him until after the fact. I'm not risking losing my son.'

'What's your son's name?' Elise asked.

'Anton. He just turned twelve last week.'

'Do you really feel you have to terminate the pregnancy to protect your relationship with Anton?'

'I have no choice.'

'There is always choice. Couldn't you now file for divorce and move out and bring Anton with you and have your lawyer arrange a strict co-parenting agreement, insisting that Anton resides principally with you, and –'

'You sound as if this is all going to play out rationally. Trust me it won't. I got fired off the last show I was on and my professional stock is low right now. I'm also running out of money.'

'And your friend in New York … ?'

'It's possible he might just insist that I keep it,' Jackie said. 'Which would create even more complications. Especially if he also declared that he wanted me to move to New York.'

'You mean he hasn't definitively ruled out having a child with you?' Elise asked, her voice calm.

'He just intimated ...'

'Intimated isn't the same as him conclusively saying –'

'Thank you for the fucking lesson in semantics, Professor.'

'How did you know that?'

'What? That you are a retired UCLA prof? I think it's called Google. Let me ask you something: why are you doing such dismal work? Your idea of do-good charity? Some way-past-menopause notions of feminism?'

In the rearview I could see Elise studying her with almost clinical detachment. Then:

'I hope you feel better for having said all that.'

'Cunt.'

'I hope you feel even better for having said that too.'

There was a tense silence. I peeked again in the mirror. Jackie looked as if she was about to lash out again. I was ready to pull over. Then she put her face in her hands and started to weep uncontrollably. Elise sat by her, her arm around her shoulders, saying nothing. Now she glanced into the mirror and caught my eye. Her look told me: *it's okay, drive on*. Jackie took several minutes to calm down. By which time we were a block away from the clinic. And ... oh God, not this ... there was a crowd up ahead. As I edged closer I saw cops trying to clear away a bunch of men and women who had formed a human chain in the street just yards away from its entrance. In the back seat Jackie was going crazy, yelling at Elise.

'You didn't fucking know they were going to be here?'

'I checked with the clinic this morning. They said nothing about a demonstration, I guess it must have just sprung up now.'

Then Elise told me:

'Lock the doors, please.'

I hit the necessary button. All the doors closed with a loud click. Elise told Jackie:

'We don't have to do this today.'

'We're going in,' Jackie said.

'Fine by me,' Elise said, then asked me: 'You okay with that?'

'As long as this cop lets me through . . .'

The cop – white, young, tense – tapped on my window. I rolled it down, hearing nearby chanting: 'There is another way . . . there is another way.'

'Your business here?' he asked.

'Bringing these two women to the clinic over there.'

'Who's the patient?'

'Me,' snapped Jackie.

'And what are you doing with her?' he asked Elise.

'Giving her support.'

'You're going to need it. They're refusing to budge.'

I asked the cop:

'How close can I get?'

'Right up to the human chain. Once you let these two out we have officers there who will escort them right up to the door. But I'm warning you: it could get a little ugly.'

Jackie's face had turned into reinforced concrete.

'Let them try to stop me,' she said.

'Drive super slowly,' the cop told me. 'We don't want someone to decide to play the martyr and throw themselves under your wheels.'

I drove at about three miles an hour. The police were keeping the protesters in line. About ten of them, all with red roses, all forming a wall in front of the clinic entrance, all continuing to chant: '*There is another way ... there is another way.*' I looked over and saw two uniformed policewomen and one plainclothes cop right by the front door.

'Now here's what is going to happen,' Elise said. 'I'm sending a text now to two of my colleagues at the clinic. When they come out they will escort us both inside, with the police essentially keeping the protesters away. They are going to try to shove the flowers on you, taunt you with that horrible slogan of theirs and –'

'Say one of them takes a picture of me?' Jackie asked.

'The police will be there –'

'But they can't stop some lunatic right-to-lifer from posting my picture on some site. And if that went viral –'

Out of nowhere one of the women protesters shouted something to the others in the human chain. They all came rushing toward us.

'Turn the fucking car around,' Jackie shouted.

'Too dangerous,' I shouted back.

By now we were surrounded by this block of protesters, banging their hands on the roof and doors of the car. I heard Jackie dive to the floor. A smart move – because at least two of the people surrounding us had phones out and were taking photos of me and of Elise. The chants were now louder, nastier.

'*Baby killers! ... Murderers!*'

The cops were pulling the protesters away from us. I started revving the engine, my foot firmly on the brake, but ready to release it and get the fuck out of there as soon as the cops screamed that I could drive off. Elise, hearing the engine revving, yelled:

'Don't move until –'

'You think I'm nuts?'

But I don't think she heard me – because the banging on the car was now deafening. And terrifying. Especially as there was suddenly a woman on the hood of the car, pounding on the windshield, shaking her other fist at me, calling me a murderer.

No, it was not my wife. When I first saw the line of protesters I scanned them, thinking: what if Agnieska was here today?

She wasn't there.

But the woman roaring at me through the windshield was well known to me.

It was my wife's best friend, Teresa. Even when a cop managed to pull her off the hood she flung herself at my door, screaming my name. And telling me:

'You will die for this.'

thirteen

LATER THAT DAY I received the text message I was dreading: a message from Todor:

Brendan – you need to contact me ASAP.

The voice of authority.

I received the text just after darkness hit Los Angeles. I was elsewhere in the city, still with Elise and that woman, Jackie. She remained hysterical for a long time after the protesters surrounded us. She was smart to have thrown herself to the floor of my car. Not only were several of the protesters wielding smartphones, but some local news cameraman also filmed a segment of my car under siege. And like the demonstrators he also got pictures of myself and Elise.

The cops were ruthless once the demonstration got out of hand. A bunch of them rushed in and started arresting everyone who was attacking the car. Teresa managed to pound the windshield so hard that it actually heaved and suffered a slight crack on the passenger side. She was grabbed by a uniformed woman officer and handcuffed immediately.

'Get the fuck out of here,' the policeman yelled at me – and enough cops were on the scene to somehow allow me to move forward and make a getaway. As soon as we were a short distance from the protesters another officer stopped me and insisted on seeing my license and registration, then demanded to know why I had been stupid enough to wade into this chaos.

'He was driving us to the clinic,' Elise said from the back.

'He can't speak for himself?' the officer demanded. 'I want ID from all of you now.'

'You can have my ID,' Elise said, her voice hard. 'You can have this gentleman's ID. But you cannot and will not have the ID of the woman I'm supporting.'

'You're talking to the LAPD, lady. Who the hell are you to make the rules?'

'And who the hell are you to break the law, Officer? You have no right to ask this woman for her ID when she is exercising her legal right to go to a clinic and have her pregnancy terminated.'

'You telling me my fucking job?'

'Yes, Officer, I am doing exactly that: telling you your fucking job.'

'Out of the car now,' the cop yelled at Elise. 'You're under arrest for insulting an officer. And you too, fat guy.'

We both got out of the car.

'Hands up, both of you.'

Mine shot straight up in the air. But Elise was using her iPhone to scan the cop's badge.

'Hand that phone over right now,' he ordered.

'You'll have to take it from me,' she said, clicking on video mode and holding it now above her head and training it on him. His hand went to the holstered taser on his hip.

'I'm counting to three and –'

'What?' she yelled. 'You're going to pull a Rodney King on an old lady?'

At that moment an unmarked car with a siren and a flashing light pulled up by us. A man and woman – both in suits – jumped out.

'What the hell are you doing?' the woman roared at the cop.

'They were resisting arrest.'

'And I've got it all on video,' Elise said.

'Put your hands down,' the male detective said to us.

I saw Elise do some fast clicking on the phone and then she held up the screen for the two detectives to see.

'If I can explain –' the officer said.

'You can explain all you want to Internal Affairs,' the woman said, then pointed to a concrete barrier across the street. 'See that wall over there? You're to stand down and wait until we come for you.'

'You need to let me –'

'An order is an order,' the male detective said. 'And she has seniority here. Get over there, asshole.'

The kid walked slowly toward the wall, no doubt fearing that his career in the police was all but over.

'I'm sorry for all that,' the male detective said.

'If we could look again at the video,' the woman detective said, holding out her hand.

Elise did some even faster clicking on her iPhone.

'If you want this phone,' she said, 'you'll need to serve me with a court order. Just for the record: I've emailed all the video files and the photo of that disgraceful young officer and his badge number to my late husband's associates at the ACLU. But I would like you to take down our names and numbers, as I would like yours – so we can make a complaint against this officer and also seek compensation for police harassment while complimenting you to your superiors for being so professional and upright.'

I could hear the veiled threat going on behind all that. The way Elise was letting them know: *you don't think I know that you're going to try to grab the evidence and vanish?* She kept her nerve throughout this … and I could see the two detectives glancing in each other's direction, wondering what their next move should be. The woman detective pulled out her notebook.

'Point taken. Your names and addresses and phone numbers and emails … please. And who's the woman in the car?'

'She wants her identity kept secret … for obvious reasons,' Elise said. 'And under the law –'

'I know the law, ma'am,' the woman officer said. 'Before you ask, here is my card. If you do want to contact me or know who and where to make an official complaint, you can phone me directly. And if you can send me the video …'

Elise accepted her card. We supplied her with our contact details. The exchange ended with the male detective telling me I needed to get that windshield of mine repaired immediately.

'It was broken by the demonstrators, sir.'

'You can apply for compensation through the LAPD, as we were supposed to be protecting you when we let you drive up to the clinic,' he said, handing me his card. 'Though I've got to warn you: it might take a lot of paperwork and some months before you see anything back.'

I thanked him. I wondered what the hell I was going to do in the short term about my car – as I could see it was dented in about five places and the crack in the windshield was going to get me stopped by every cop driving by. And if they reported me to Uber …

As if reading my thoughts Elise said:

'Don't worry, Brendan. I'll make a call to the Women's Choice Group. I'm pretty sure they have an emergency fund for things like this …'

I was overcome by a sudden wave of exhaustion, a pain shooting up my arm; a pain I'd felt before during another bad moment when I thought I was about to drown in the craziness of others. I leaned against the now dented roof of my car.

'Are you all right?' she asked.

'I'll be with you in a minute,' I said. 'Please, get in the car.'

I didn't want her to witness this. When it happened the last time – six weeks after I'd been made redundant and it looked like there was nothing in the future – the doctor on duty at St Vincent's had me rushed into cardiology and slapped onto an ECG machine. No heart attack but he did warn me that I'd suffered from an overdose of stress and that I needed to keep a close eye on the way my body – especially my heart – reacted to moments when 'your entire system overloads'. He also suggested that I learn some breathing exercises to combat the stress, then gave me a severe talking-to about my cigarette habit. I told him I was planning to quit … something that I knew was never going to happen. But I did download some free app about 'calmness' or some such stuff and learned one simple exercise I could do standing up or sitting down to try to restore some quiet to my body when I felt it going into freefall and limit the pain going up and down my left arm.

So while Jackie continued shouting at Elise I shut my eyes and imagined that there was a straw going from my nostril into my lungs and that I was drawing air down through this straw and holding in my tobacco-charred lungs for a ten count, then slowly releasing all that trapped air through my mouth and nose … and repeating this around twelve times.

'I'm not fucking going home!'

Jackie was still screaming as I returned to the car, not feeling in any way calm after all that deep breathing … but with the chest pain under control. Back in the driver's seat, I stared out through the cracked windshield.

'I think we should get out of here – in case they break through the police line and come looking for us again,' I said, glancing at Elise through the rearview mirror. She nodded. Jackie yelled at Elise:

'Are you going to get this arranged or not?'

'It's not something that I can just do on such little notice.'

'You brought me here today knowing full well that there could be a demonstration –'

'I told you the other day there was a danger of a rolling demonstration at any of the clinics in LA,' Elise said.

'But they were clearly here before we arrived. Why didn't you –'

'Because I had heard nothing from anyone in this clinic. I can only assume that they were overwhelmed today when that human chain arrived –'

'Overwhelmed? Overwhelmed! What happened to *me* – what you allowed *me* to be put through –'

'She didn't allow this,' I heard myself saying. 'It just happened.'

'Who the fuck are you to butt in, Uber Man?'

'We're having none of that,' Elise said. 'You have no right –'

'I have every fucking right –'

'Drive,' Elise said to me.

I did just that, getting us out of there. Taking us to a shopping mall on the USC campus. Pulling up just in front of a Trader Joe's where all these well-heeled kids driving Minis and Audis and Beamers were cruising into the underground parking lot. Where everyone seemed blonde or Chinese. As soon as I parked Elise was out of the car with her phone, walking a few paces away, talking rapidly, the stress of the last hour everywhere on her face and in the way she seemed to be stabbing the air with her index finger. I so wanted to fire up a cigarette, but I still had memories of that smoking incident at UCLA. So I just continued to breathe deeply, trying not to think, for the moment anyway, about how I was going to pay for the car repairs and how long it might be off the road and how it would mess up what little cash flow I had left. Elise came back.

'We need to go to a clinic way out of town in Santa Clarita,' she said.

Santa Clarita. Todor's old parish. Jesus …

'I can get another Uber if you want to get the hell away from us,' Elise said. 'I won't blame you if you choose to do that.'

'No need to get another Uber,' I said.

'Are you sure?'

I nodded. Elise said:

'That woman on the car … she knew you.'

'She's my wife's best friend.'

'Oh my.'

'And my wife is a member of the same anti-abortion group as her friend … who happens to be the ringleader.'

'I feel terrible,' Elise said.

'Why? I chose to drive you. Not just today. But those other days. I chose to take you to those clinics. Just as I am choosing to take you to the one in Santa Clarita now.'

'Bless you,' she said.

My phone binged. I looked down at the screen. I then held it up, letting Elise read the message.

Brendan – you need to contact me ASAP.

'Bad news?' she asked.

'From my oldest friend – who happens to be a priest. The same priest who runs the anti-abortion group where my wife works. Word travels fast.'

'I'm so sorry. If you want to get home and talk this through …'

I had one, and only one, thought right now: *fuck them*.

I said:

'Let's hit the road.'

fourteen

On the drive up Jackie ranted non-stop. Threatening legal action against the protesters who stopped her from entering the USC clinic, against the charity that Elise worked for – on the grounds of 'endangering my sanity' – and against me.

'This man has done nothing except try to help you,' Elise said. 'You make a complaint against him, you start a lawsuit against the protesters, you attack the charity from whom you sought out help . . . you will be informing the world: *all this happened when I was trying to have an abortion to avoid vindictive blowback from my husband because I got pregnant by another man.* And you'll be handing your very unpleasant husband all the cards.'

I stopped myself from letting out an appreciative whistle of admiration for the way Elise had delivered that absolute takedown. I got us onto the highway heading north. To fill the silence that followed I put on the classical station that Elise liked, hoping it would also take the edge off the terrible tension inside the car.

Nothing further was said until we were on the 5 going in the direction of Sacramento. Traffic was building up, but we were an hour or so ahead of the big rush-hour mess. We made Santa Clarita in forty minutes. Around five minutes away from the clinic Elise pulled out her phone and made a fast call, talking in a hushed voice.

'All's clear over there, Jackie,' she then said. 'They're expecting you. Do you feel you can handle this?'

'I want it behind me. I want it done now.'

'Then it will be done now.'

'Before we get to the clinic,' Jackie said, 'can you find me an ATM?'

'They take credit cards.'

'Credit cards leave a paper trail. I'm doing this in cash.'

I found her a bank two blocks from the clinic. She got out of the car. Elise and I watched her use three different credit cards to pull out a significant amount of cash. Back in the car she dropped a wad of bills on the empty seat next to me.

'Guilt money for me being such a shit,' she said.

I looked down at the cash.

'Thank you,' I said.

I wanted to wish her well for what she was about to go through. But after all that had gone down saying nothing struck me as the right call. I put the car back into gear. I drove into the clinic parking lot. A woman in a white medical coat was standing outside, talking with the two security guards. I pulled up right in front of the entrance. The woman got out, followed by Elise.

'We should be in there for around two hours,' she said. 'Would you mind keeping your phone on, in case we need you before then?'

'No problem,' I said.

I watched them walk inside, Elise's arm linked in Jackie's, steadying her as the door closed behind them. I pulled into a nearby parking spot. I turned off the Uber app, indicating that I wasn't working right now. I scooped up the money and counted it. Five hundred dollars – all in twenties. What I sometimes made in a week. I knew that the damage to the car would cost four times that. Just as I also knew that the idea of asking Elise's charity for money to fix my car … no chance of me doing that.

I was hungry. I found a nearby food court and ordered sweet and sour pork and two egg rolls.

There was a couple next to me saying prayers over their General Tao Chicken. The slogan on the woman's T-shirt said: *Need Answers? Call Jesus*. That was a call I wasn't going to make, though another text from Todor landed on my screen:

Brendan – I know you're out there. You can't dodge this.

That last statement was indeed true. But I could dodge it for as long as it took to eat all this extra-greased bad Chinese food, enjoying the momentary MSG rush. There are times when stuffing your face with junk is the only way to combat the mess that has been swirling around you.

I took my time working my way through this fat-face meal. I walked to the edge of the parking lot and lit up a cigarette. My phone began to ring. Todor's name popped up on the screen. I sucked down a lungful of smoke. I took the call.

'So you finally deign to speak to me,' he said.

'I've had a busy day.'

'Don't I know it. The whole parish knows. And most of all your wife knows.'

'I'm sure she does, thanks to that fanatic. Did you hear how Teresa broke my windshield and battered my car?'

'Never mind that. She's now under arrest for breaching the terms of her last suspended sentence.'

'Good.'

'Lose the uncharitable tone, Brendan. You shouldn't have been driving those women to that place of fetal execution.'

'It was a job, *Father*. Don't act like I was making some political statement.'

'Weren't you at the abortion clinic in Van Nuys that was bombed?'

That stopped me short.

'I don't know what you're talking about,' I said.

'Yes you do – and don't ask me how and why I know it. I also know you've been driving around a woman who props up the local abortion industry.'

'You've no right to say that.'

'Why? Because you agree with her work? Are you pro-baby murder?'

'I'm ending this call.'

'Brendan, I want you to drop whatever you are doing right now and get over to my parish office.'

'I need to be working. I have a car to repair.'

'You come to me now I promise you I'll get someone to fix up your car and replace the windshield. Angels Assist will take care of it. And I can give you some work around here for a few days until the car is fixed to cover the money you're losing. Eighty a day until the car is ready to go back on the road.'

'What do I have to do in return for all this kindness?'

'Agree that you will not drive that woman again. Then just sit down with me and a few interested parties and tell us all you know about what you saw and heard driving this woman to those clinics.'

I was suddenly angry. Very angry.

'How the fuck do you know all this?' I heard myself shouting.

'Calm down, Brendan. I'll expect you in my office in one hour.'

'Otherwise what? You're going to keep me after school? Slap me around the head like Father Mulligan used to do forty-five years ago after putting his hand on my crotch?'

Click. The line went dead. I found myself reeling from all that had just jumped out of my mouth. And wondering: did it take the trauma of all that went down today to get it out?

Or maybe, just maybe, for the first time in my life, I was not listening to the man in the power position whom I'd allowed to play guilt games with my conscience. Especially some guy in a clerical collar who was doing polite gangster talk with me – and threatening to break me if I didn't play it his way.

Maybe, for the first time in my life, I'd just told the voice of authority to fuck off.

Back in the car, I allowed myself a moment to shut my eyes and black out the world. Then there was a *bing* on the phone, snapping me back into the air-conditioned here and now. From Elise:

We're done. Can you please come by in about fifteen minutes?

I was in front of the clinic on time. One of the security guys came out, his hand touching his holstered Taser. I rolled down the window.

'You got business here?' he asked.

'Picking up a patient.'

'Got two women inside, waiting for an Uber guy. You the Uber guy?'

'I'm the Uber guy.'

'Keep your hands on the wheel where I can see them while I signal them to come out. Want no trouble, got that?'

'I want no trouble either.'

'We'll see about that.'

He all but walked backwards to the clinic entrance, his eyes on me nonstop. He signaled to someone inside. Elise came out. He pointed to me. Elise gave him a confirming nod. She went back inside and returned moments later with Jackie. Elise was guiding her slowly down the stairs. She was subdued, lethargic. I got out and opened the door and helped Elise position her in the back seat.

'Where to?' I asked.

'A fucking disco,' Jackie said. 'I feel like dancing.'

She laughed a bleak laugh. She shut her eyes. She started to sob. Elise put her arm around her.

'I don't want your comfort,' Jackie said.

'Okay,' Elise said, taking away her arm, then telling me: 'Get her back to her house. Do you still have the address?'

'It's on the GPS,' I said.

We headed out of the parking lot in the direction of the highway.

'Want some music?' I asked.

'Because you think it will calm me down?' Jackie asked.

'I could put on the classical station,' I said.

'Because I am falling apart?'

'Are you?' Elise asked her.

'Did I fall apart when they spread my legs and gave me the local anesthetic and shoved a vacuum up my twat?'

'It wasn't a vacuum,' Elise said.

'Details, details. Want to know something, Uber Man? Want to hear my philosophic overview of this shit of a day? "*The things we do for love.*" Let me say that again in a nice shouty voice: "THE THINGS WE DO FOR LOVE."'

In the rearview mirror I could see Elise tense as the woman roared that last line. But she decided to pull back and say nothing.

Jackie went on:

'I'm glad it's behind me. As you promised, it only took five minutes. Outside of the local anesthetic they gave me which hurt like hell – that nurse should take lessons in administering a needle – it was painless. Five minutes to end any chance of having a second child; a child with the man I love.'

'You must stop this,' Elise said, her voice quiet, but absolutely firm.

'Listen to Madame Do Gooder telling me to calm down.'

'I am not telling you to be calm. I am telling you: you explored all the options. You did what you had to do.

You still have Anton. You still have the opportunity to fall pregnant again.'

'No,' she said. 'That's it.'

Silence. I'd come to hate this woman up until this moment. Now I felt terrible for her.

We were back in Los Feliz forty minutes later. Little in the way of words passed between us. Jackie shut her eyes and kept them shut all the way back. When we reached her house Jackie got out without saying a word.

'Do you want me to help you inside?' Elise asked.

Jackie shook her head, then turned and showed us her back. As we watched her walk up to her front door my phone binged again. A message from Agnieska:

Don't even think about coming home. All locks have been changed.

fifteen

ELISE READ THE text on my phone. Because I showed it to her. I also told her about the call I'd received earlier from Todor.

'How did he know about you driving me?'

'No damn idea. He must have his spies.'

'Or, worse yet, he knows the people who bombed us.'

'That's a big accusation.'

'I am just making an assumption. Why else would he be aware of all this?'

I had no answer to that question. But I did want to see right now if Agnieska had made good on her threat and changed the locks.

'I'm going to drop you off and head back home and see how big the mess is,' I said, 'and what I am facing into.'

'Let me come with you,' she said.

'Why?'

'Because I think it's often best, in a terrible situation, to have someone there to be behind you.'

'You're going to throw a punch at the priest?'

She smiled.

'I'd like to,' she said. 'Even if he doesn't have contacts among the terrorists who firebombed us, he still deserves to be slapped around for the way he threatened you.'

I wanted to laugh. Laughter just wasn't there right now.

'If my wife sees you ...'

'It won't be the first time I have come up against "the other side". Not that I like to think of them that way. So ... can I please accompany you on the drive back to your house?'

Truth be told: I didn't want to confront all that alone. But I knew that if I called Klara and told her what had gone down she would have come roaring over to the house ready for a major battle with her mother ... and then she might just take on Todor ...

'Okay,' I said to Elise, 'you can come along. But if it turns crazy –'

'I'll be able to handle myself.'

Of that I had no doubt.

'Let me sit with you in the front seat,' she said.

I nodded. She got out the back and came in through the front passenger door.

I turned the key and the engine fired into life.

'If the police stop me and see the Uber sticker and the cracked screen ...'

'I will tell them: I am your aunt and you are taking me home while off-duty. I want to also tell you: while in the clinic I made a call to the head of our group and explained all that went down and how heroic you were.'

'I was hardly heroic.'

'You didn't turn us out. You didn't drive away. You stayed with me and Jackie during that entire ordeal. You kept your nerve. Our group wants to make good on the damages to your car.'

I said nothing. I kept driving. When we got to my corner of the LA sprawl I weaved into some back streets until we reached my little house. It was boarded up for the night. The aluminum shutters that my brother-in-law Witold installed for us as a tenth anniversary wedding gift (after we were broken into for the fourth time) were all rolled down and closed up with padlocks that looked very new to me. I parked the car. I got out, Elise right behind me. On the front door was a large envelope addressed to me.

'That looks official,' Elise said.

'It can stay there,' I said.

Elise reached for it, putting it under her arm.

'Is there another door?' she asked.

'In the back,' I said. 'But I can promise you that the locks have been changed there too.'

We walked around to the back door. The locks had indeed been changed there too.

'It looks like she's making a point here,' I said. Elise held out the envelope to me.

'Open the letter, Brendan.'

'I don't need to. I know it's a barring order.'

I motioned that we should get back to the car, as I was worried that Agnieska and Teresa might come roaring up with Todor in tow. A confrontation would then follow, with Todor wielding all sorts of weapons of guilt – especially after me standing up to him earlier. An action that both surprised and terrified me.

Once in the vehicle I drove us around half a mile down the road, pulling into a gas station. Elise again tried to hand the letter to me. I told her to read it while I filled the tank.

'You're right,' she said as I got back into the car. 'It is a barring order. According to this your wife states that you were verbally abusive, that you broke a pot filled with scalding coffee at her feet, that you attacked her friend Teresa on account of her religious views, and that she feels threatened in your presence. I hate to tell you, but your priest friend vouched for her.'

'That son of a bitch. He knows I never did any of that.'

'But he certainly knows how to play dirty. I can turn this over to someone I know in my husband's firm and see if they can get it reversed. It's absurd, them telling you that you have to stay at least a half-mile away from your house. By the way, though, this is just a copy of the order. They need to have it legally served to you. Put directly in your hand by a process server. But if they don't know where you are right now ...'

'My wife will think I'm going to stay with my daughter.'

'Will you?'

'Klara lives in this crazy apartment with about six other people. I think she can find me a mattress on the floor.'

'I have a guest room.'

'No thanks.'

'Why not?'

'Doesn't feel right. I'd be imposing ...'

'On whom? I live alone. The room is empty.'

'I appreciate it. But I can look after myself.'

'Lose the pride, Brendan. We all get into places where we need the assistance of others. There's nothing wrong with that. I might also be able to help you with a car. My husband's Volvo is sitting unused in the garage.'

'Todor informed me he'd get my car fixed if I told him about you and your outfit.'

'*Outfit*? As in some kind of flying abortion hit squad, targeting innocent women who really want to have a baby after getting raped? Or someone who knows she'll be on the street with a child because she can't afford a roof over their heads. Or who has simply decided that this is the wrong moment for them to take on the huge responsibility of bringing a baby into this dark and dangerous world of ours. But the fanatics who spout Christian principles are the ones who show no compassion or decency, and who also think that sex should have a punitive side to it. And now I am having one of my diatribes. I hate when I get this way because I sound crabby. But look how your life is being turned upside down by these people.'

'One of whom happens to be my wife.'

'But she's very much caught up in the idea: this is all life or death. And why do you think she feels that way?'

'Because nothing about this life pleases her.'

'Not even her daughter?'

'Especially not Klara.'

'That's terrible.'

'I know that Klara has always wanted a connection with her momma. But she has just never been able to provide it. Kind of the reverse of you and your daughter.'

'I know I'm probably at fault as well.'

'Why?'

'For being so damn doctrinaire about so much.'

'But as a woman surely she approves of your …'

'What? My "militant feminism", as she calls it – along with her father's espoused socialism – clearly drove her to that usual form of post-adolescent rebellion that we've all been through. My God, you should see the fellow she's probably marrying. Mr Hedge Fund – who is about twenty-five years her senior and who told me that the secret of his success was deciding that, at the age of thirty-three, only having a personal worth of $50 million was just not good enough. Now he's worth about $300 million – as Alison told me recently.'

'There are guys like that out there.'

'And women like my daughter who have also bought into the whole program – to the point where she actually thinks that if you can't be a financial lion in this harsh world of ours you're cooked.'

'Then she'd really think me a total loser.'

'Perhaps. But she'd be so wrong about that.'

'But how else am I supposed to look at myself?'

She lightly touched my arm. And said:

'As a good man.'

I really didn't want to go back to her place. I knew it was going to make me feel shabby, down-at-heel and, yeah, a loser. But outside of floor space at Klara's I had few other options. Going to my daughter's also meant dragging her into the middle of all this. But sleeping in my car …

I glanced at my iPhone. It was now almost 9 p.m. The day – and all that had been in it – was suddenly hitting me hard. Elise could see this.

'Let's get you upstairs.'

She had two parking spaces in the garage below the building – and only used one. I pulled in, parked the car. She showed me the Volvo that she no longer drove. Dark gray. A saloon model. I walked around it. Perfect condition. Not a scratch or a dent. Nice leather seats inside. Automatic transmission. That was a relief as I hate driving stick shift. Tinted windows. I bet there was a two-liter engine under the hood. Thirty-five grand of automobile. So out of my league. Too nice for me to drive.

'I know what you're thinking,' she said. 'You don't deserve this car.'

'Are you a mind reader?' I asked, almost smiling. 'We'll talk about this tomorrow.'

'Yes, we will.'

We took the elevator up to the third floor. Her place was at the end of a corridor with six doors. Once inside what first struck me was: books. They were everywhere. There was a long hallway from the front door to the living room, with crammed shelves from the floor to the ceiling. Three of the four walls of the main room were also nonstop books. The furniture was all light wood and simple cushions in browns and reds. A whole shelf of family photographs. Her husband looked like a tall string bean with a taste for old-style tan suits and bow ties. Her daughter was equally tall and – even when young – had this look of superiority masking a lot of big-deal personal doubt. And Elise herself ... a total knockout back in her twenties and thirties. Just as she remained beautiful today.

There was a big kitchen with the sort of gas range that you expect to see on a cooking show. There was a cool marble table with four equally cool 1950s black chairs.

'That's some stove,' I told her. 'You must be quite the cook.'

'My idea of cooking is the microwave. Wilbur was the fanatical chef. He loved putting meals together. His way of dealing with stress – of which he had much.'

'It must be hard …'

'Being alone here? It's a bit quiet now. Forty-five years with my husband. Since he left the scene, the silence, especially in the evening … it gets to me a bit. I deal with it. I tell myself: you had all those years with that remarkable, sometimes difficult man. I know that he loved me. Seriously loved me … despite my own difficult side. Which might have lost me my daughter.'

'You haven't lost her.'

'I'm afraid I think I have. Regarding myself and Wilbur … I guess I have to be grateful for all those years together. I miss talking with the man who always considered me his equal, as I did him. That's pretty damn rare in my experience. Whenever the loneliness hurts I tell myself: you were lucky.'

'It sounds lucky to me.'

'You've never known … ?'

'What? That kind of closeness, of love? No way.'

'That is sad,' she said.

'Yeah it is. And if you ask me now: "why didn't you go, why did you hang in there all those years for something you knew was dead?" … if you ask me that I'm walking out the fucking door.'

I found myself surprised again at the anger pouring out. An anger I wasn't used to expressing. Elise raised her hand. A peace gesture.

'I won't say a word, Brendan. But I would like to propose that I open a bottle of wine.'

'That would work,' I said, thinking: I really want to fall asleep right now. I couldn't because I was here … imposing on this nice, classy woman who was being far too kind and understanding, and to whom I'd just acted like a creaky clown.

She went over to a wine rack, coming back with a bottle of something red and two glasses. She said:

'One of the few things I like about the modern world is that good wine is now often sold with a twist-off cap.'

She opened the wine in one easy motion, then half filled our two glasses.

'Drink, Brendan. Because it has been one mindfuck of a day.'

She raised her glass.

'To us – and to not giving up.'

I clinked her glass. And said:

'Speak for yourself. I gave up a long time ago.'

'No, you haven't.'

'How the hell do you know that?'

'Because look at what you allowed yourself to be put through today. That's hardly giving up.'

I threw back my glass of wine. I said:

'If you're sure you don't mind putting up with me for a night, could I please crash?'

'Of course you can. But on one condition.'

'What's that?'

'You drink one more glass of wine – to ensure you'll sleep. And if you want to smoke there's a little balcony with a table and two chairs.'

'Will you join me?'

'I can't smoke at night. It ruins what little sleep I get. These days I can only drink one glass of wine before bedtime.'

But as I sipped my wine I was hit by another wave of tiredness. I shut my eyes. When I opened them again I didn't know where I was. Until I saw Elise.

'You've only been out for around five minutes. Come on, I'll show you to your room.'

I stood up, my head full of cotton wool.

'Haven't really slept in about two days,' I said.

'Then you can sleep now.'

'Got to get my car repaired.'

'I told you: you're taking mine. But we'll discuss all that tomorrow.'

I followed her down the corridor to a nice-sized room. Wood floors. An old Indian carpet. White walls. A wood bed with white sheets. A whole wall of photos featuring her daughter at varying stages of her life. A small bathroom en suite with a shower.

'There's a new toothbrush and toothpaste in the bathroom. And when you nodded off I laid out a pair of Wilbur's pajamas on the bed.'

'I'm probably too fat for them.'

'You're not fat. And Wilbur was very tall – so they should just about fit. If you leave all your clothes outside the door I'll have them washed by morning.'

'You don't have to do that.'

'True – but I am going to do it. Anything else you need?'

I shook my head. I thanked her.

'You should sleep until you wake up,' she said. 'You need it.'

'So do you.'

She wished me a good night and shut the door.

I stripped off everything. I cracked open the door and dropped all my sweaty, grubby clothes on the floor. I went back inside. I took a long hot shower. I dried off and brushed my teeth and found that I just about fit into the bottoms of her late husband's pajamas. But my big gut did not work with the top. I climbed into bed without it. I turned off the light. Sleep usually takes a long time to arrive – all the bad stuff bouncing around the inside of my skull like a pinball out of control. Tonight the bed was so comfortable, the sheets so white and crisp, my fatigue so overwhelming, that I was lost to the world within seconds.

Then it was morning. On opening my eyes I didn't know where I was. For a moment or two anyway. I reached for my phone. 11.47 a.m. Fuck. The whole morning gone. Twelve–thirteen hours asleep. How did that happen? What allowed me to turn off for so long? The world rushed in. The need to get the car fixed. The need to get back to work. The need for a lawyer. The need for money. The need to find somewhere to live while this legal bullshit with Agnieska got sorted out. The realization: I didn't have the money to go anywhere.

I put on the pajama top, still unable to close it across my belly but knowing I couldn't walk in on Elise bare-chested.

'How did you sleep?' Elise asked as I staggered into the kitchen where she was sitting.

'I slept far too well,' I said.

'That's a good complaint. Got your clothes all laundered and pressed.'

'You really didn't need to do that.'

'But I did – and you now have clean clothes to wear today. Would you like a coffee?'

'I can make it.'

'But not the way I make it.'

'Would you mind if I lit up?' I asked, pulling my packet of American Spirit out of my pajama bottom pocket.

'Go right ahead,' she said, pointing to the balcony off her living room.

But once outside and halfway through my cigarette I heard screams and shouts. The same screams and shouts that we heard yesterday outside the clinic:

'*Baby killers ... murderers!*'

I found myself hunching up my shoulders, as if expecting the blows to hammer down again on my car roof. I took another steadying drag on my cigarette. I realized that the voices unnerving me were coming from within Elise's apartment. I stubbed out my smoke. I came inside – and found her standing in front of the television set on a shelf in the living room. On the screen I could see my car under attack. Elise turned to me and said:

'One of my colleagues just texted me to say that we were on the midday local news again. They're also saying that another clinic in Studio City is under siege by demonstrators. It's a clinic I know rather well.'

'Don't tell me we're heading there today.'

Elise laughed a bleak laugh.

'Fear not – I'm not on doula duty today. You have anything planned?'

'I was thinking that, after yesterday, a day off might be a good idea.'

'That sounds smart. I want you to make yourself at home here. And if you feel like venturing into the outside world you can take the Volvo for a spin, see how you like driving it.'

'I still feel bad about –'

'*What?*' Elise said, 'Me giving you a car I never use? And why am I giving you my car? Because yours was trashed. And why was it trashed? All due to me getting you to drive me and that distressed woman into the middle of anti-abortion madness. So why shouldn't you take my car? … and my God, I am sounding professorial this morning.'

'Okay,' I said, 'I'll take your car.'

'Thank you. That pleases me. Will you also have breakfast?'

'I can make it myself.'

'But it's my home, my kitchen. And you are my guest. So …'

She motioned for me to sit down at the kitchen table. The television played on for a few minutes as the journalist covering the current demonstration asked one of the doctors at the clinic in Studio City if she thought she was putting her life on the line by coming into work. The doctor's face tightened as she said:

'We are putting women's lives on the line by not coming in to perform what is still a legal procedure in our state, our country. But my two teenage children are now scared for my safety … and I am beginning to become so too.'

Elise reached for the remote control and clicked off the television, then leaned against the kitchen counter, her eyes shut.

'Are you okay?' I asked.

'No,' she said in a near whisper, 'I am definitely not okay.'

Then, after a short pause, she asked:

'Scrambled or sunny side up?'

I went for scrambled. Elise cracked and beat eggs. She made me two slices of toast. She poured out orange juice. She placed all this in front of me, nodding curtly when I thanked her. Then, telling me she 'needed some time to sort out a few things', she headed down the corridor toward her bedroom.

I ate the breakfast. I went back to the room where I'd slept. I showered and shaved and got into the clothes that Elise had washed and ironed for me. I started thinking about my next move. I texted Klara saying that we needed to talk. I got no reply from her. That bothered me. My daughter almost always shot back an immediate response to my texts. I felt the need for another cigarette. When I came back into the kitchen Elise was there. She had changed into a dark suit, a briefcase in hand.

'Something's come up,' she said. 'A business meeting in Mid-Wilshire.'

'What's in Mid-Wilshire?'

'My late husband's law firm. I have family business to discuss with them. I might be a good hour and a half. But as you deserve a day out after yesterday let me call an Uber.'

'No way,' I said.

We took her Volvo. It was smooth and sleek. It had kick-ass pickup. With all the windows closed and the air con cranked up the roar of Los Angeles seemed far away.

We made it to the address she wanted in Mid-Wilshire in about twenty minutes. From what she told me her late husband's law firm was anything but corporate or big money or flashy. I wasn't surprised when the GPS led me to a classic 1950s LA bungalow with a simple wooden sign out front: Flouton, Greenbaum, McIntyre and Milkavic. There was a banner over the door saying: Black Lives Matter. There was that multicolored LGBT flag which I was seeing everywhere and which baffled me (I thought it was a minor league sports team) until Klara set me straight about it, telling me I should 'get with the moment' ... whatever the hell that meant. As we pulled up Elise informed me:

'That nameplate out front – a WASP, a Jew, an Irish Catholic, a Pole – it was a point of pride to Wilbur when he and those three other iconoclastic guys founded the firm in 1978. Stan Greenbaum is the only living member of the quarter of original partners. He retired up the coast in Carmel, but still can be called in to rabble-rouse when the cause is right.'

I parked the car.

'You said ninety minutes?'

'Could be shorter,' she said. 'I'll text.'

As she walked up the drive I noticed that the windows on the bungalow had steel bars across them; that there was a CCTV camera by the front door – which was made of heavy reinforced steel. Damn. This firm had clearly been dealing with some threatening folk. Which given the sort of left-wing law they practiced – 'rattling the establishment, big money cage' as Elise had put it – wasn't surprising. I waited until she was buzzed inside. Then I drove off.

A minute later there was a *bing* on my phone. I pulled over. I braked. I glanced at my screen, hoping the text was from Klara. It wasn't. Instead I found myself reading:

I apologize for being so extreme. The heat of the moment. There is a solution to all this; a way back. I ask for the opportunity to meet you and offer my apology face-to-face and discuss solutions and a way for all of us to put this behind us. Please call me now. Todor.

I was suspicious. Very suspicious. Todor had always been my friend. And one of the few people I thought I could trust. Until he turned threatening on me. Maybe he now knew that he'd seriously overstepped. Maybe he could now be a reasonable intermediary when I announced to my wife that I no longer wanted our marriage; that I would give her half of everything and then get the hell out of Dodge.

I sat in the car. I shut my eyes. I tried not to think about Klara and why she hadn't texted me back. I failed. I tried not to think about the legal shitstorm that I was going to have to engage with when it came to the house and Agnieska. I failed. The only thing of comfort at the moment was the realization that, whatever came down, I would never be going back to her again.

Fatigue hit me. I nodded off. Then ... *bing.* Elise let me know she was ready. I checked my watch. It was 3.18 p.m. Rush hour in all its insanity was about to hit. I put the car into drive. After checking that no cops were in the vicinity I made an illegal U-turn. As I pulled up in front of the law firm Elise was already awaiting me.

'Home now?' I asked as she got in.

'When you say it that way you sound like my chauffeur.'

'I haven't started calling you "ma'am" yet,' I said.

Elise laughed. A bleak laugh. Then she shut her eyes and shook her head.

'You okay?' I asked.

'Not really.'

'A difficult meeting?'

'A sobering meeting.'

Silence. I checked the GPS. It was now going to take us over an hour to get back to Westwood.

'Shall we go?' I asked.

Elise nodded. But just before I pulled out into the street there was another *bing* on my cell phone. A new number, unknown to me. Which contained a text from Klara:

Poppa – heard you're in trouble. Some stuff has blown into my life and I had to make some choices, take some action. The result is: I'm now in hiding. Don't want to text you exactly where I am. I've ditched my old cell. This is my new number. It can't be traced. Call me now.

sixteen

I WAS NOW frightened. Beyond frightened. Elise read me immediately.

'That text,' she said. 'Troubling news?'

A moment of decision. In that instant the thought struck me: Elise is one of the few people whom I think I can trust. I held up Klara's text message for her to read, then asked if I could step out for a cigarette.

'Don't you want to call Klara first?'

'Not until I've had that cigarette.'

'Understood.'

I turned off the engine. I stepped out of the car. Elise joined me, standing by me on the sidewalk as I fished my packet of American Spirit out of my shirt pocket.

'I don't mean to interfere, but if your daughter is in a bad place …'

'Truth be told I am scared about finding out what that trouble might be … even though I'll have to know.'

I pulled a cigarette out of the pack with my teeth and lit it up.

'Might I take one?' Elise asked.

I pushed up a cigarette for her to nab. I lit it with my lighter. She took several deep drags, then said:

'I smoke when I'm anxious – and you've got me anxious. Please make that call now. And if you want my help –'

'That'll be up to her.'

'Understood. But if it wouldn't bother you maybe can you put the conversation on speakerphone … so I can get a sense of what is going on?'

'I'll have to clear that with her first.'

She nodded. We finished our cigarettes. We got back into the car. I took a deep steadying breath. I called the new number she'd sent me. She answered after just one ring.

'Poppa?'

She sounded very much on edge. No surprise there – but it still unsettled me.

'Sweetheart … where are you?'

'We'll talk about that in a moment. I saw all the news online about the violent protest at the abortion clinic and you driving into the middle of it all.'

'Is it a good idea you being online?' I asked, remembering some TV show I once saw about Homeland Security and how they were able to trace the whereabouts of anybody if they were on their computer or iPhone.

'Don't worry, I read all about your car getting the shit kicked out of it before I had to ditch my old phone.'

'Please tell me what trouble you're in.'

'We'll get to that. But don't worry. Besides having a new number I am not checking my email – so they can't figure out where I am. But where are you? Not at home, I hope.'

'Been locked out,' I said, then explained all that happened with her mother and Todor.

'That fucker,' she said. 'Who are you staying with?'

I told her all about Elise and her doula work; how I'd been driving her to and from clinics; how she'd been with me yesterday when we drove into chaos – and how I got the woman she was looking after to another clinic and then discovered that I was legally barred from going home.

'So she took you in?'

'It was the best option.'

'And you're planning to stay there for a while?'

'I've got no choice – and she's cool.'

'You can trust her?'

'Absolutely.'

'She's on our side?'

'Of course,' I said, simultaneously wanting to ask her: *have you decided that we are on the same side?* But that was opening up a discussion that was not appropriate right now – as there were more important things to know. Like how deeply in trouble Klara found herself.

'Can you tell me where you are?' I asked.

'Out in the east of California. A place near Twentynine Palms.'

'What made you run there?'

'We'll also get to that, Poppa. But I've got to ask you a question: that woman you're with … what does she do vis-a-vis abortion clinics?'

'Why do you need to know that?'

'Don't worry, Poppa. I'm not knocked up. But the "situation" I'm dealing with … I need someone with that sort of expertise. Can you get me in touch with … what's her name?'

'Elise … and she is sitting right near me.'

'She's heard all this? You've had us on speaker?'

'Of course not. But, as I said, I trust her. And she's helped a lot of women.'

'Would you put her on then?'

I handed over the phone to Elise, saying Klara wanted to speak to her.

Elise took it from me and was immediately professional and friendly with a hint of take-charge in her voice. As their conversation continued I decided that a fresh cigarette was needed. I got out of the car, closing the door quietly behind me. There was a bus stop nearby with a bench inside its shelter. No one was waiting there. So I took up a corner of the bench and lit up.

Fifteen minutes and three cigarettes later Elise got out of the car, waving me back. Once I was inside and behind the wheel she handed me my phone and said:

'Your daughter is a brave young woman. Maybe recklessly so – to the point where I fear that she could be in possible danger. But we have a small window of opportunity here. She got a call two days ago from a young woman named Amber. She told Klara that, for the past three years, she's been kept in seclusion ... by a man who essentially found her in a home for homeless adolescents. And this very rich and powerful man happens to be a certain Patrick Kelleher.'

'Jesus Christ ...'

'Jesus is certainly part of his twisted theology – even though I sense Jesus would be against everything that Kelleher is doing in His name.'

'Why did this girl contact Klara?'

'It seems that Kelleher is going to subsidize the women's shelter where Klara works. Your daughter met him there and he got her phone number ...'

'Yeah, I heard all about that meeting. And how he asked her for her card and invited her to lunch.'

'Amber got hold of that card. It seems that she's been kept in a separate cottage on a corner of Kelleher's estate in Brentwood. He comes to see her a few times a week when he wants to have sex. It's not like she's being held in a tiny room. It's an actual little house. And she told Klara that, after the bleakness of that Catholic home for homeless girls, she initially felt spoiled at Kelleher's. Like he was a surrogate father. Until, that is, he started insisting that they have sex whenever he wanted it. That started very quickly after she arrived there three years ago. When she was just fourteen years old.'

I felt myself take a short intake of breath.

'It gets worse,' Elise said. 'She's only allowed out once a week – a shopping spree with one of his bodyguards. She has internet at her home, but no email access. No cell phone. But she can watch all the television and Netflix she wants. She can drop a thousand dollars a week on clothes and stuff. She can work out in the compound's gym and swim in its pool. But otherwise … no freedom. And now she's five months pregnant … having turned seventeen two weeks ago.'

I shut my eyes. This was Todor's great benefactor. This was the man paying my wife a salary to do his anti-abortion bidding … and also now covering my daughter's salary.

'How did she get Klara's number?'

'According to Amber when Kelleher came back that day from his visit to the shelter he had sex with her immediately – and fell asleep on her bed afterwards. She went through his pockets, found Klara's card and hid it away in her bedroom. Kelleher never noticed its absence … or, at least, he never said anything to her. Just two days ago, when she was out having her weekly shopping spree at the Beverly Center mall, having already tried on a skirt and having worked out that there was a staff exit off the changing rooms, she came out and found a T-shirt and told the bodyguard that she was going back to try it on. With the bodyguard waiting by the entrance to the changing rooms, Amber went back in with the T-shirt, tossed it aside and made a dash for the staff exit. She ran down a corridor and right into a security guard. A sympathetic young woman – and, as Klara later found out, a graduate student in social work doing this mall job to earn a bit of extra money. That was her first bit of luck. She begged her to hide her – but wouldn't explain why. The guard offered to call the police. Amber feared that as soon as the police found out she was Kelleher's 'ward' he would use all his influence to get the whole thing hushed up – and she'd be sent back to him and never allowed out again. Taking a chance, she gave Klara's card to the guard who decided to call Klara. After explaining the situation she put Klara on to Amber … and that's when your daughter decided to take matters into her own hands.'

'What do you mean by that? Surely she told her boss …'

'She was worried that, given Kelleher's backing of the shelter, were she to bring Amber in there her bosses would have insisted on calling in the law – or even Kelleher himself. The security guard told Klara to meet them at an obscure side entrance to the Beverly Center. Klara drove over and picked up Amber. She thought it best to get the young woman out of town, since Kelleher and his people would be looking everywhere for her. One of Klara's roommates inherited a trailer from an eccentric old hippie uncle out in the desert near Twentynine Palms. She'd been there once, knew that the key was kept under a stone near the front door … and her roommate was out of town for a week in Seattle. She decided to make a run for it now and explain all to the roommate later. But before they went out to this safe house Klara managed to get Amber to a doctor – who confirmed that the pregnancy is about five months along. Meanwhile Kelleher is determined to get her back. Especially after his first wife had that very publicized abortion while they were still married.'

I found myself reeling. I said:

'Klara has to bring that girl to the cops *now*. I don't care how powerful and connected Kelleher is. He's committed at least two big crimes: statutory rape and kidnapping. The police will have no choice but to arrest him.'

'The snag here is: Amber is insistent that she's aborting the child. And because she's beyond the legal time limit for terminating the pregnancy, the state will probably insist that she go through with it. She is still just seventeen years old. Meanwhile, according to local news reports which Klara has heard, the security guard at the mall who called her after Amber ran into her arms … that young woman has disappeared. Her parents have gone public, asking if anyone knows her whereabouts, which is why it's been on the radio and in social media. This has Klara thinking that Kelleher's people might have something to do with her disappearance; that after Amber vanished at the mall they threw some money around the mall's management and found out what happened … and the name of the guard Amber ran into. Then they picked up that brave woman after work. And …'

'Finish that sentence,' I said.

'I don't need to. I'm just telling you Klara's hypothesis about what happened to that security guard. What isn't a theory is the fact that before she ditched her old phone Klara got an anonymous text, saying in so many words: *We know whom you're hiding. We have your name. We will find you both. Drop the girl back in LA – we will tell you where – and there will be no consequences for either of you.*'

'They haven't worked out where she is?'

'Not yet,' Elise said.

'But they will. She has to call the police now.'

'I agree,' Elise said, 'and Klara agrees – but only after Amber has had her abortion. Which she is currently trying to arrange.'

I hung my head. This was beyond bad. This was a nightmare.

Elise reached over and put her hand atop of mine. And said:

'I have a possible plan … a way out of all this. But I didn't put it to Klara just now on the phone – because I could tell that she was absolutely resolute about her own game plan.'

'That's my daughter's greatest strength and most dangerous tendency: when she becomes resolved about something she refuses to budge from her position.'

'Let's see what I can do to change that position. She gave me the address of the safe house out in Twentynine Palms. We have to get out to the desert today.'

seventeen

It was now crowding 4 p.m. The crazed height of the Los Angeles rush hour. I plugged the address Klara had given Elise into my phone. Google Maps indicated that we would make it to Twentynine Palms in four hours and twelve minutes. Elise scrunched up her face as she looked at my screen and saw the journey ahead of us. She was clearly thinking something through. Just as I was about to hit the ignition button she said:

'Not just yet.'

'Something wrong?'

'I need to make one last call before we head off.'

'Time's not on our side.'

'I'll be five minutes, no more.'

She was immediately out the door and on her phone. As I watched her head to the sidewalk and turn away from me there was a *bing* on my own phone. A new text from Todor:

We still need to talk, Brendan. I know you probably don't trust me after my outburst yesterday. But if you remember Paul's conversion on the Road to Damascus … well, I'm not saying that I have had an about-face on the abortion issue. But having watched video footage of what went down when you were at that clinic near us yesterday, I am now making it clear to everyone that this sort of intimidation protest has to stop. I just gave an interview to the local NPR station for the national 'All Things Considered' show tonight. I really hope you'll call me.

What the fuck? Why did I smell even deeper bullshit? And yet there was that other part of me – the blue-collar Irish boy brought up to respect the parish priest and consider him the local moral barometer – who wanted to believe that Todor might just have come to the conclusion: *this is all so out of hand.* Maybe I was wrong to think that Todor knew all about the terrible crime that his benefactor had committed. Maybe Kelleher had kept his priest friend unaware of this dark secret. I knew that Todor remained deeply ambitious and always on the lookout for advancement. I also knew that, given his serious moral discomfort about all things to do with sex and the unborn child, the story of what had happened to Amber would horrify him – especially if he found out that she wanted an abortion while five months pregnant. Just as I also knew: my oldest friend was increasingly unknowable. A stranger to me.

Elise came back to the car. Shutting the door behind her she said:

'Now what I am going to say you probably won't like – but I felt I needed to get some legal counsel on all this. So I called Stanley Greenbaum.'

'Klara doesn't want anyone to know any of this.'

'I'm aware of that. But Stan is my lawyer – and an absolute Jesuit when it comes to keeping secrets … even if Greenbaum is hardly a priest's name. He is the best of the best when it comes to something like this. As such I thought he should know what's going on.'

'Did you tell your lawyer guy about Kelleher?'

'Yes – but with the understanding that nothing could be put into action until I met the girl and found out the whole story. He told me that, as Klara got that threatening text, they might put a trace on her father's phone as well.'

I found myself trying not to slam my fist against the dashboard.

'I can't use my phone?' I said, the anger rising.

'No way. We'll use mine for the GPS. And I am also going to call Klara on my cell and tell her that she should not try you again; that it's just my phone she should call.'

'Fuck fuck fuck.'

'We'll get through this. "The coolest head in a gunfight" and all that …'

It took us over an hour to inch our way onto the 10 East. Elise decided to simply text Klara that we were on our way. Her reply:

Can you bring food please? Can't leave her alone.

'That doesn't sound good,' I said.

'No it doesn't,' she said. 'We need to find a supermarket somewhere and get supplies for dinner.'

'I can google –'

'No you can't.'

I looked at the digital clock on the dashboard. I asked Elise if she knew the frequency of the local NPR station. She told me to hit preset 2 on the radio.

'The news should be on any moment now,' she said.

I explained about Todor being interviewed by NPR, his about-face on violent anti-abortion protests and that I was now wondering just how much he knew about Kelleher and Amber.

Elise thought this through, her lips tightening. Then said:

'I'd prefer imagining that a man of God would not cover up for a monster like Kelleher. But that's also wishful thinking.'

I hit preset 2. An educated voice came on the air, telling us that we were listening to *All Things Considered* from NPR. I was too preoccupied to take in the top stories, but suddenly gave the broadcast my full attention when they began a report on recent aggressive demonstrations outside abortion facilities in the Los Angeles area. The head of the clinic where we tried to bring that angry, frightened woman yesterday was interviewed. She talked about how 'these alleged pro-life extremists are showing themselves to be unethical and ruthless when it comes to ignoring the central legal rights of other women to terminate a pregnancy. They are flying in the face of established laws. They are flying in the face of separation of church and state. Most of all they are flying in the face of basic human decency and a woman's absolute reproductive choices.'

Then Teresa came on, introducing herself as 'the most militant of our militant group. We will stop at nothing when it comes to defending the rights of the unborn child and eventually seeing the end of Roe v Wade and the closure of every abortion death factory in the country. How dare the abortionists act as if they have the moral upper hand by protecting women who, having become pregnant, must accept responsibility for the fact that they are carrying a human life in their uterus, and by "terminating" that life – to use their sanitized term – they are committing an act of homicide. Anyone who doesn't believe this is complicit in the murder of the unborn. As to their comment that we are violating their human rights – we are not attacking them physically. We are not threatening them with physical violence –'

The journalist cut her off, stating that yesterday her group did attack the car of an Uber driver bringing a woman to the clinic and – according to a cameraman on the scene – causing this woman to fall to the floor of the back of the vehicle, completely traumatized by this assault. Teresa remained cool and as hard as concrete.

'Is banging on the roof of a car such a terrible thing when a human life is at stake?'

Next to me Elise let out a sigh.

'I've heard it all before,' she said. 'The truth is: you can never convince their side to show decency and empathy to those women who are making that very difficult decision – and who are doing anything but murdering –'

She cut herself off when the journalist said that a voice in between these two very different positions was Father Todor Kieuchikov, the parish priest for St Ignatius Loyola in Beverly Hills, who had been an important figure in the local pro-life movement for many years and whose charity, Angels Assist, was funded by 'the well-known financier, Patrick Kelleher'.

'Your one-time priest friend has just gotten himself a national profile,' Elise said.

I said nothing. I just wanted to hear what Todor's new point of view might be.

His voice now filled the car's speakers.

'Let me say from the outset that I am morally and ethically against abortion. And I have convinced many of my parishioners who have been wavering between abortion and bringing the pregnancy to full term to choose life for their child. If the mother is unable or unwilling to raise the child herself we have always been able to place the baby with couples who are desperate for a child or are delighted to add this baby to their family. From my pastoral experience women who agree to abortions often suffer immense regret afterwards – because they know deep down that they have stopped a child from being born. They have denied that child a life. But I know that those who carry the child to full term and give it up for adoption can indeed reach out to that child at a later juncture and even have a relationship with that child. Just as the child might indeed in time want to know his or her biological mother – and will have a possible wonderful reconciliation with that woman.'

Elise was shaking her head.

'These guys always spin out fairy tales,' she said. '"Possible wonderful reconciliation" . . . after years, decades of agony.'

All I could think was: what agony is worse? Ending the pregnancy or handing the child to someone else to raise? Father Todor continued:

'Having said all that, I still condemn without reservation the intimidation of women who are having to make what is essentially a life or death decision about the child growing within them. Screaming at these women. Banging on car roofs. Even approaching them with flowers and saying there is another way . . . I can see why those who believe in the sanctity of life can get so enraged at those who are going to put themselves in the hands of the abortion industry. But that still does not give them the right to intimidate and frighten these very vulnerable and emotionally distressed women. Nor can they make these women feel like criminals. That is not humane. That is not Christian. That is not right.'

The journalist asked Todor what he felt was the right approach for pro-life activists to take … and what was his benefactor's take on these aggressive protests.

'Now I would never dare to speak for Mr Kelleher, but I can say with authority, from the conversations we've had on the subject, that Mr Kelleher is not only against the intimidation of women, but also that – as shown by his magnificent donation of $2 million to the women's shelter in downtown LA – he is also helping the fight against all violence toward women.'

Elise came in here.

'My word, Kelleher truly knows how to play the PR game brilliantly and cover his socially conservative tracks with money.'

On the radio Todor continued.

'So to answer your question … what is the right approach for pro-life activists to take? To begin with: back off frightening women needing abortions, while using all the legal means possible to curb these clinics from performing abortions. Use education as a way of showing women that there are reasonable other choices. But coercion and terrorism as part of the anti-abortion campaign ... that must stop now.'

My immediate reaction was: good on Todor for speaking out against Agnieska and Teresa and all their other fellow radicals. Elise thought otherwise.

'That man speaks horseshit. Very dangerous horseshit.'

'It didn't strike me as dangerous,' I said. 'The guy is clearly anti-abortion. But he's still insisting that the crazy behavior stop'.

'What he's really saying is: we cannot stop until abortion in this country is driven underground again. He's doing what Wilbur used to call "the *bearded nice priest* routine": coming across all understanding and humanist, but actually articulating a deeply intransigent position – and one which shows he knows nothing about women and the fact that everyone who opts for an abortion has a different reaction to the process; that there is not one set emotional response to it – as that fool seems to be implying.'

I'd not heard this anger in Elise before. It threw me. But it didn't surprise me. She'd survived a clinic bombing, after all – and one of her colleagues didn't.

'Look,' I said, 'you have every reason to hate the right-to-lifers given what you've been through. And yeah, Todor tries to play the cool padre dude. But the guy has always taken the hard Vatican line when it comes to abortion. I know that he's been in cahoots with that woman Teresa and her crew – which includes my wife – for years. For him to now come out and advocate no violence against clinics and no protest … sorry, that's a big thing.'

I could see Elise scrunch up her face. Then she just shrugged and said:

'His public pronouncements make me dubious. Still, maybe you've got a point. Maybe I'm just too flattened out by the endless fight that all this is. And the realization that we're never going to find a common ground, no agreement to meet in the middle. When it comes to this issue the battle lines are completely drawn. It's our new Civil War. Not exactly North versus South, although that's now part of it. Rather, hardline Christian versus those of us who still believe that we're supposed to be a secular country. But who is right here? Me and my point of view? That priest fellow? I'm just trying to protect women and help get them through a difficult passage – with the knowledge that there is going to be a degree of psychological pain. Why turn such a personal choice into a frontier? A way of dividing us even further?'

Bing. A text on Elise's phone. From Klara.

'*Hurry*,' Elise read. '*Things going to shit here.*'

She clicked back to the GPS. We still had almost two hours of driving ahead of us.

'There's no alternative route?' she asked.

I shook my head.

'Surely after all your years here,' I said, 'you know that one of the great rules of Southern Californian life is: the traffic will always be at its worst when you absolutely need to be somewhere fast.'

She texted back:

Nightmare on the 10. Cars backed up for miles. Getting there as fast as we can. How bad?

Seconds or so after Elise sent it … *bing.*

Bad. She has a gun. She's pointing it at me.

eighteen

THE NEXT TWO hours were among the longest of my life. The traffic started to clear as we got through the town of Whitewater. I was able to speed up once we reached Cal 62 – but was conscious of highway cops on the lookout for anyone who did ten miles over the speed limit. A patrolman lecturing me on going too fast – then handing me one of those nasty big tickets ... always some weird sum like $334 – was further bullshit I didn't need right now.

'You okay?' Elise asked me. Then seeing my expression she said: 'I am sure that this young woman isn't going to use the gun. Something made her panic and –'

'If she's crazy enough to point it at the woman who risked her life to get her to fucking safety she's crazy enough to pull the trigger. Text Klara back.'

'You know I sent one thirty minutes ago. Just telling her where we were, how much longer we would be. I have no idea what would happen if Amber saw Klara texting back and forth all the time. She's come out of sexual abuse and captivity. Even though part of her realizes that Klara is her savior another part of her has no idea where she is, what will happen next. I'm just surmising here. Trying to figure out why this is happening … and also: where the hell did she get the gun?'

We were supposed to stop and get food. I told Elise: 'To hell with that. We're getting there as fast as we can.' But Elise insisted, when we were just fifteen minutes away and passing through a series of strip malls, that we find a supermarket and arrive with a bag of groceries.

'She'll see it as a sign of normality,' she said.

'There's nothing fucking normal about this. And my daughter is –'

'Trust me here. Amber needs to see that we are not coming in hostile. I'll get the shopping done in ten minutes, maybe less.'

We stopped at a Ralphs.

I stayed outside and smoked and tried to not think dark thoughts. Klara. My only child. The only person for whom I have felt unconditional love and whom I sometimes think is the only reason I haven't slammed my Toyota into a brick wall and given in to the idea of permanent darkness. Were anything to happen to her …

No, no, don't go there again. Don't invent a nightmare before the nightmare has actually arrived. Listen to Elise. She's smart when it comes to other people's worlds. She knows what to do.

Elise emerged eight minutes later with two big bags of groceries.

'I got a very rich chocolate cake along with a six-pack of Corona.'

'You think we're going to drink that much? I'm driving … and the girl is pregnant. She's also seventeen.'

'She's not going to be drinking for all those reasons – even if she tries to argue that, as she's not keeping the baby, she can have a beer.'

I said nothing. The whole idea of having an abortion at five months … it struck me as all wrong. But I didn't feel right speaking up about it. Not with everything else that was going down.

The GPS brought me down the highway for another three miles, then off onto a two-lane blacktop that snaked up into sandy hills. We were in the desert – and even though it was early evening the temperature was still in the high nineties. The air here was bone dry. Not a hint of moisture. High desert plains. Low hills. A cluster of houses. Then a back road. Narrow. Winding up a slight incline. Reaching a small trailer. The car tires crunching across sand. I told Elise to text Klara when we were minutes away. The trailer had lights on inside and out. It was a battered old thing with a tin roof and corrugated cream metal siding. There was an air-conditioning unit rusting in one of its few windows, its fan creaking away. The door opened. Klara was there. I waved hello. She nodded tightly. Behind her was a cheerleader-tall young woman with a bump defining her belly. Her hair was blonde and cascaded to her waist.

'Hi, Poppa,' Klara said in a hushed voice.

Amber gripped Klara by her left arm. In her other hand was a pistol, nuzzled into the jaw of my daughter.

'You bring food?' Amber asked.

'Yes, we brought food,' Elise said.

'Who's the old lady?'

'The old lady,' Elise said, 'is here to help you.'

'You a doctor?'

'I work with the doctors you need. My name is Elise. And if you let us in I will cook you dinner.'

Amber waved us in with her free hand, the gun still up against Klara's head. She motioned for my daughter to sit in a broken-down armchair. The trailer decor was hippie crash pad from somewhere back in the 1970s. I moved over to my daughter and tried to reach for her hand.

'Who said you could do that?' Amber shouted, brandishing the gun in my face.

'Is there any need for that?' Elise asked, her tone light, almost strangely breezy.

'You shut up,' Amber snapped back.

'No problem,' Elise said, unpacking the groceries. 'Hungry?'

'I told you to shut up,' Amber said, cocking back the hammer of the gun and putting it up against Klara's temple, making it impossible for me to make a grab for it.

'Are you going to shoot her if I don't?' Elise asked, scouring the kitchen drawers for a knife.

'I'll shoot you all.'

'Why?' Elise asked, finding a small black chopping knife and going to work on an onion.

'Because how do I know you won't fuck with me?'

'When did you last sleep?' Elise asked.

'You shut up.'

'When did you last sleep?'

'Two days ago.'

'No wonder you're acting crazy.'

'You say that again I'll kill her.'

Elise said nothing for a moment. When she spoke again her voice was still moderate, easy – as if this was some sort of normal conversation.

'Why would you do such a thing? Especially to a woman who has risked her life to save you. Especially in front of her father. What? You kill her and then us? Then where do you go? Jail forever. But maybe this is what you have become. Maybe this is how you feel you need to be now – as evil and sick as the man who –'

Suddenly Amber swung the pistol at Elise. As she did, Klara slugged her in the face. Amber reeled backward, pulling the trigger at the same time. The explosion was vast, deafening. She fell toward the sofa, waving the gun again. I jumped at her, grabbing her arm, pinning it against the sofa. She tried to pull the trigger again, but Klara was now over her, slapping her repeatedly across the face. Screaming:

'You fucking, fucking idiot! You want me to throw you back to LA, back to the wolves?'

Amber began to howl. Klara slapped her again.

'Drop the fucking gun.'

More howls. Another slap. Even louder howls. I tightened my grip on her wrist, ready to snap it if she tried to again pull the trigger. Elise had thrown herself behind the counter when the gun had gone off. Now coming back to her feet, she walked over to the sofa and grabbed Klara's hand just as she was about to administer another slap.

'No more of that,' she said to her, then turned to Amber.

'I know you are crazy angry, crazy furious at the world. You have every right to be. But Klara is correct: this is madness. This is turning against everyone who wants to help you. Adopting the same tactics as the man who has been a monster to you. But again, you must understand: we are here for you. You have to stop now. And trust us. We are your only hope.'

Amber closed her eyes. She dropped the gun. I scooped it up. After letting go of her wrist with my other hand she collapsed into Elise's arms, wailing, out of control.

Klara fell back against the sofa, beyond stressed. I picked her up, raised her to her feet, put my arms around her and held her for a very long time. Then I whispered in her ear:

'You are gonna take ten years off my life.'

She buried her head in my shoulder and started to sob. Klara was someone who never sobbed.

'Let's go outside,' she finally said.

Klara turned to Elise, her arms still around Amber, asking:

'You can handle this?'

Elise nodded.

We stepped outside. I fished out my pack of cigarettes and handed it to Klara.

'Give me the Glock,' she said.

'How do you know its make?' I said.

'Because it's my damn gun.'

'Since when the fuck did you get a gun?'

'Since doing this work. There are a lot of angry men out there who resent having time called on their violence toward women.'

After a moment's hesitation I handed it over, thinking: there is something not at all good about turning a gun over to my daughter. She expertly clicked on the safety, then unloaded the magazine, checking it thoroughly. I lit up two cigarettes, handing her one.

'You take lessons with that thing?'

'You don't pack a Glock without taking lessons.'

'The gun is legal?'

'Of course it's fucking legal.'

'How did that sad crazy kid get hold of it?'

'Had to go to the bathroom real bad. So tired after forty-eight hours without sleep. Stupidly left my bag in the kitchen. When I walked out I found her pointing the Glock at me. Tried to explain over and over again that I was on her side. Six fucking hours she had that gun on me. Screaming lunatic shit about shooting me, shooting the baby, then going back to Brentwood with the corpse of Kelleher's dead child – it's the boy he's always wanted – and shooting the man who enslaved her in his balls, then pouring gasoline over him and tossing the match and watching him become a human torch.'

'Mother of God ...'

'Yeah, it's a real Disney movie. The truth is: that kid inside the trailer has been so abused and degraded and cut off from the world, I'm not surprised she's beyond loco. It still doesn't give her an excuse to turn a gun on me or fire the fucking thing. Slapping her around ... I'm kind of ashamed of that. But after six hours having my life threatened by her –'

'Is she really going to abort the baby?'

'She is absolutely insistent on it.'

'But she's more than five months pregnant.'

'Stay out of it, Poppa.'

'I can voice an opinion, Klara.'

'And I am telling you: I don't care how late the pregnancy is. It's her choice, her call. The baby was born out of rape. The father is a man she loathes – which is using a nice word to describe what she really feels about that monster. If she wants to terminate it –'

'That's not a fetus in her. That's a fully formed child.'

'This is not your business.'

'You've made it my business, Klara.'

Silence. She gave me that petulant look I remembered when she was fifteen years old and I told her to clean up her room. I checked my watch. It was now 9.08 p.m. I wanted nothing more than a place to lay my head.

'What's the plan now?' I asked.

'That depends on Elise. We've only got the one bed and a sofa.'

'I'll talk to Elise,' I said.

'Let me check if things have calmed down.'

Klara went up to the trailer front door and peered in.

'Yeah, we're good,' she said.

Inside Amber was tucked into the bed, Elise having somehow arranged the sheets and the blanket to make it appear almost hospitable. She was curled up tight like a ball. She had her thumb in her mouth. Seeing her looking like this … it sideswiped me. Klara went over to the bed and took her free hand and spoke with her quietly for a few minutes. At one point, Amber pulled her closer, sat up and allowed herself to be rocked back and forth.

'Amber, I didn't want to hit you,' Klara told her. 'It was the last thing I wanted to do. But you could have killed one of us. Let us get you through this, find a way for you to start a new life …'

'But he will come find me …' Amber said.

'You're safe now. We will work out a way for you to have a new identity. We'll make sure he cannot find you. Rest now. We'll have dinner soon.'

She lowered Amber back onto the pillow. Immediately her right thumb returned to her mouth, her eyes wide in fear and exhaustion and confusion. Meanwhile in the kitchen Elise was frying up onions and garlic and a bunch of now-chopped vegetables, adding to the frying pan chili powder and a can of beans and one of the tomatoes.

'The beer's in the refrigerator,' she said. 'Help yourself … and if someone could open one for me …'

I went over and pulled out three bottles of Corona, twisting off the caps. I handed one to Elise and one to Klara. We didn't bother raising them and toasting ourselves. We just drank. The beer was cold and very needed. Klara fell into the caved-in armchair, pulled on her beer, then put her head in her hands and exhaled loudly. I came over, sitting on the arm of the chair, expecting it to collapse thanks to my big gut. It somehow held together. I put a hand on my daughter's shoulder. I squeezed it and said:

'That is behind us.'

To which Elise, stirring the chili, replied:

'She's calm now. She'll be a lot better after a night's sleep. But things are not going to go the way I thought they would.'

'What do you mean?' Klara asked.

Elise said:

'She's keeping the baby.'

nineteen

I SLEPT THAT night in a motel around fifteen miles from the trailer. Elise googled it. She also insisted on paying the $60.50 for the room. It was beyond basic. But the double bed didn't sag. The air conditioner just about worked. And there was a television with all the channels. Elise gave me two more bottles of Corona to bring with me. She said that she was going to sleep on the sofa and, in turn, ensure that the plan she wanted to put into effect would take place the next morning. I think she was also concerned that, given Klara's initial ferocious reaction to her news, she might try to do something radical in the middle of the night.

I was happy to get the hell out of that trailer. After the gunshot, the crying and wailing, then came the knock-down, drag-out exchange between Klara and Elise. It started with the pre-dinner announcement that Amber had decided to keep the baby. Or, at least, not to abort it before its birth. Klara was outraged – but needed to eat. As Amber came out of bed to join us we all tried to keep the conversation calm. Klara held back from saying anything else. Until after dinner – when Amber ate two pieces of the chocolate cake and accepted a mug of the herbal tea that Elise had also bought. Then she thanked us, hugging Klara and Elise, telling them both that she felt safe now. 'I apologize for going totally crazy on you.' When she finished the tea she crawled into bed and was asleep in moments.

That's when Klara motioned to Elise that they should step outside. I said I was coming too – because I sensed they might need a referee and I was worried that Klara might go hothead on us … which is exactly what happened.

'You some secret operative from the pro-life assholes?' she hissed at Elise as the trailer door closed behind me.

'If I can explain …' Elise said.

'Explain what? All the way here from LA Amber must have mentioned around ten times that, as soon as we got to the safe house, she wanted me to find a doctor who could end her pregnancy. Immediately. Then you spend ten minutes with her and suddenly she's keeping the baby. It all smells bad to me.'

Klara's tone was borderline angry and taunting. Elise did something remarkable. She came right up to her, face-to-face, and glared at her in a way that put me in mind of a headmistress who did not take kindly to being talked down to.

'I have been doing my abortion doula work for over five years. On average I have sat with three women a week going through a pregnancy termination. Well over 130 women in varying mental and emotional states. Never, *never*, have I tried to force anyone to adopt a moral position. Never have I ever told any of those women they should not go through with the procedure. But there are two crucial matters at play here. Amber is seventeen, as you well know. She could not – according to California State Law – have an abortion now without parental approval. More to the point, she is not five months pregnant as you first told me, but six months and ten days.'

'See, see,' I said to Klara. 'I told you –'

'Stay out of this, Poppa,' she said.

'Why should he do that?' Elise asked. 'You pulled him into this. You got him to bring me into it. We drove hours to help you and this terrified young woman.'

'She told me she will not carry the baby of the man who raped her. You force her to do that –'

'I will not participate in an abortion of a fetus at twenty-five weeks and three days,' Elise said. 'Nor, young lady, will any legitimate doctor.'

'Don't you fucking "young lady" me. If you can't deal with this, I'll get someone who can,' Klara said.

'Then you will be dealing *not* with a legitimate doctor, but a dangerous, backroom quack.'

'I can find someone. Anyway, California law is vague on this: between twenty-three and twenty-eight weeks. She's now just into the twenty-fifth week.'

'But she is still a minor. She needs an adult to sanction the abortion. At her age twenty-three weeks will be judged the frontier beyond which this pregnancy should not be terminated. Personally speaking I too believe that twenty-three weeks is the right limit. After that the fetus is too formed. Terminating the pregnancy now will mean turning to the sort of illegal, grubby abortionists whom women had to turn to before Roe versus Wade. And you will be actually committing a heinous offense.'

'But she wants to terminate –'

'Yes, that is what the hysterical, battered, raped and – as she told me – repeatedly sodomized seventeen-year-old said that she wanted. The state will probably rule that, as she is underage –'

'Fuck the state.'

'What are you saying? That we don't abide by the rule of law? In doing so we are giving the other side all the ammunition they need. The law is right on this matter. Just as it is also right to insist that an underaged young woman cannot be allowed to make this sort of decision without parental approval.'

'Her parents are dead. She was taken in by that rich anti-abortion monster who will do everything to get his baby.'

'Not when we go to the sexual crimes squad of the LAPD with Amber and get her to tell them her story ... as you should have done the moment you picked her up at the mall.'

'But the first thing she told me – after letting me know that she'd been Kelleher's sex slave since she was fourteen – is that she was not giving birth to this baby made in captivity. If I'd gone to the cops –'

'I know why you decided to do what you did – which was, first and foremost, to get this young woman to a safe place. The fact still remains: she is a minor. And –'

'Stop fucking repeating yourself.'

'I respect the work you are doing,' Elise said. 'I am more than impressed by your willingness to live dangerously for Amber ... though you've certainly terrified your father with all this daredevil stuff.'

'It's not daredevil work,' she said, 'it's crucial work.'

'It can still get you killed,' I said.

'I'm like an alley cat,' Klara said. 'Nine lives.'

'You know that's nonsense,' Elise said. 'If anything were to happen to you it would destroy your father's life.'

'I think my poppa can talk for himself.'

'Then listen to me' I said. 'You now have one of the most powerful men in Los Angeles pissed off at you.

Which is serious shit. Look at what happened to that poor security guard who called you when Amber ran into her. Has she been seen since?'

Klara shook her head, looking more than anxious. Then:

'As soon as she's had the abortion I'll go to the cops and have Kelleher put away forever.'

'Oh please,' Elise said. 'You go to the police having arranged an illegal abortion for an underage girl – especially when you could have gone to them before – you yourself will end up arrested. And you will hand Kelleher a great trump card to play against you in the court of public opinion: instead of saving the baby this reckless pro-abortion liberal harpy insisted on forcing this underage girl to have a backstreet abortion. Even if Amber insists it was her call, her choice ... even if Kelleher is arrested and exposed as the hypocritical brute he is ... the media will jump all over you as the worst sort of feminazi baby killer. You know damn well this is exactly how they work. This child Amber is carrying is now ten or so weeks from birth. He deserves life. We have to honor that, Klara. I explained this to Amber tonight. I asked her directly if she could live with herself if the child was aborted at this very late juncture. I explained that her best revenge against the man who brutalized and raped her was to bring his son into the world and, as she doesn't want to keep it, give him up to parents who would ensure that he has all the opportunities in life. My group can find solutions when it comes to getting her to a safe, comfortable home in which to see out the rest of her pregnancy, to find proper excellent medical care for her to have the baby delivered, to arrange its discreet adoption, and to then tell her story to the LAPD and the world.'

I came in here, telling Elise:

'I still think what you said earlier makes the most sense. We should go to the cops now.'

'But Amber's right,' Klara said. 'If we go to the police Kelleher and his people will step in … and who the fuck knows what will happen next. Especially when Kelleher has the Church and the city establishment behind him. For all your nice reasoned talk, Elise, about moral gray zones and civic acceptability, the fact is: we're in a war here. Against the endangered white male who will do everything possible to make certain he is still running the show. And those assholes never play by the rules. They fuck over women's rights. Fuck over minorities. Fuck over emigrants. Fuck over anyone LGBT. They are essentially turning us into a banana republic with a superrich elite who now control all our lives.'

'You think I disagree with you?' Elise said. 'You think I don't see all this? You think that, like any thinking American, I'm not fearful of the dark road we're now going down? But you and I can argue all night, Klara. The big "macro" stuff. But we've got a huge "micro" problem to deal with right now. Getting Amber to safety. Out of sight, out of danger … and then somehow getting you out of danger too. But tell me if you have a better idea than the one I've given you? Tell me.'

Klara was pacing back and forth. I could see her fear. But when I reached out for her, wanting to put my arms around her, she shrugged me off, hissing:

'I don't need your fucking steadying hand, Poppa. I've gotten myself into this mess. I'll get myself out.'

'But only if you let Elise help you. And help Amber.'

Silence. Klara turned away for a while, then came over to me and pulled the cigarette packet out of my shirt pocket, fishing one out and motioning to Elise if she too would like one. She nodded. Klara put two cigarettes into her mouth, accepted my lighter, lit them both up, then handed one to the only woman I've ever seen able to get my daughter to go silent and actually consider a different point of view.

'I want to have a talk with Amber when she wakes up tomorrow,' Klara said, taking a deep drag on her cigarette. 'I won't pressure her. I promise that. I also won't tell her what choice to make. But I need to hear from her directly that she is cool with the idea of keeping the baby. If she says yes, that's the plan she's following, I'll put it all in your hands. Then I'm going to have to figure out a way of disappearing for a while.'

'Our group can help you with that too. The women who run it ... they will happily take you in and keep you out of harm's way.'

'You mean: hiding me for the rest of my life?'

'If Kelleher is locked up it should end there,' I said.

'There's the possibility that he'll want his people to settle the score with me,' Klara said.

I swallowed hard. Klara had spoken the truth.

'Let's see how things play out first,' Elise said. 'But you can – *you must* – have a talk with Amber when she gets up tomorrow. And if it's okay with you I am going to drive off now with your father and get him into a motel and use my phone away from the trailer. Just in case someone has put a trace on it. That priest of yours, Brendan, says he knows you've been driving me.'

'But he's not put a trace on your phone.'

'Nothing would surprise me with that asshole,' Klara said. 'Especially as he's in Kelleher's pocket.'

'I need to sleep,' I said.

Two minutes later, after giving Klara a long hug, Elise and I got into the Volvo and drove down the long winding path to the village below. Once there we hit the highway and continued on down to a town called Yucca Valley where there were the usual strip malls and budget motels.

We pulled into the first one we found. Elise insisted on using her card to pay for it. Then we found a 7-Eleven. She went inside and made a call and bought a few things. I remained inside the car, hoping the air conditioning would keep me awake. When she returned she looked at me and asked:

'You sure you can get me back to the trailer?'

'I'll somehow keep going for a little while longer.'

As we drove off she took a notebook out of her purse and scribbled a name and number.

'My colleague's name is Judy Rainer. She's been briefed. She's now going to start making arrangements. Tomorrow we can drive back over here and I can call her and see what the next steps will be. But here's the thing: once we get Amber to my group's safe house we will, with her permission, begin to see how we can get this quickly handed over to the criminal justice system before Kelleher turns the tables on us. Our group has many lawyers working with us – and even a few retired judges. We can quietly but effectively get a case built against Kelleher very fast – and also ensure that the state entrusts Amber to our care until her baby is born. I'm sure of this. I also know that Klara will raise all sorts of hell and insist on doing things her way. I want this to be in the hands of the District Attorney within forty-eight hours. Because Kelleher is a formidable opponent – and if he finds us before then …'

'Klara's always going to be a target now, isn't she?'

'That is a possibility, Brendan. But we will deal with that, the law will deal with that ...'

'I can't lose her. If she had to go into permanent hiding –'

'Brendan ... let's not go to Catastrophe Corner just yet. Let's wait and see how it all plays out.'

I sensed myself getting shaky. Fatigue, fear. I gripped the wheel. I choked back a sob. I again found myself thinking: there is no life for me without my daughter. I have nothing but her. Elise reached over and touched my arm.

'You are not alone. Please know that.'

But I still felt very much alone.

I drove on. We passed a modern church off the highway – Victory Calvary – with a big message board outside reading: *We can help you see the light!*

'Everyone's looking for the light, aren't they?' Elise said. 'As if, once they've been illuminated in its radiance, they are finally going to have the answers.'

'I don't know much,' I said. 'But I do know this: there are no real answers.'

'Not to you or me. But for those who think they've found the light there's ... the glow of certitude. Which makes so many of us so wary of the glow they possess.'

'Because their answers are not our own?'

'Maybe because answers are usually not very flexible thoughts. If history teaches us anything it's this: people who say they have seen the light are often leading the rest of us into darkness.'

We said nothing more until we were back in front of the trailer. I was going to come inside, see how Klara and Amber were doing. But the lights were already out.

'You sleep until you wake up tomorrow,' Elise told me.

'How are you going to sleep?'

'Badly. But at least by being in the trailer I will feel that I am somehow watching over the two girls.'

'I should be with you.'

'Get out of here now,' she said.

Once back in the motel room I stripped off my clothes. I took a very long, hot shower. I drank the two beers. I watched some late-night talk show. I got into bed. Sleep arrived in seconds.

Then it was morning. Late morning. 11.08 a.m. by the bedside digital clock. I sat up immediately, wanting to know how the night had passed at the trailer. I reached for my phone, thinking: if something urgent had come up Klara would probably have risked sending me a text. Even if there was a trace on my phone I was so far away from the trailer as to not let 'them' know our whereabouts. And I hadn't checked messages in a day. And ...

I turned the phone on. *Bing. Bing. Bing. Bing. Bing.* Five messages from someone I never hear from: Grazyna Pawlikowski. My wife's youngest sister. All containing one word: *urgent*. The last one reading:

Where are you, Brendan? It is essential that you contact me now. Anytime day or night.

Immediately I hit the redial number. Grazyna answered after one ring.

'Brendan,' she said, sounding beyond troubled, 'where have you been? I have been texting, calling nonstop.'

I ignored the question. I asked:

'What's happened?'

'I have some terrible news. Agnieska had an embolism last night. It caused cardiac arrest. I'm afraid the doctors think she might not make it through the day.'

twenty

Guilt. It eats the soul. It makes you believe that you are irredeemable; that – as the Church kept telling us when we were young and ready to believe their stuff – life is an endless hardship. With the big payoff coming when you die – but only if you've played by their rules while you were walking around.

Guilt. All the way back to the trailer I told myself: this is not your fault. The way Grazyna explained it over the phone to me Agnieska had been under a lot of stress during the past couple of days. Yesterday around 9.30 p.m. she'd called her up, saying she had this 'crazy bad pain' in her chest. Grazyna rushed over. She found her semiconscious on the kitchen floor. She called an ambulance. She told me that, before she drifted into what seemed to be a coma brought on by the embolism cutting off oxygen to the brain, she whispered to her:

'Tell Brendan I know I was a terrible wife to him. Ask him to forgive me; to pray for me.'

'I should have been there,' I said.

'I'm saying nothing, Brendan. Except that she also told me she forgave you. Personally I fear Agnieska got far too emotionally involved with this fight Then, when you disappeared I'm afraid that was too much for her. Where have you *been* for the last twenty-four hours?'

'Didn't your sister tell you that she locked me out of the house?'

A silence. Then:

'Yes she did tell me that … and why.'

'After that happened I checked into a motel. Turned off my phone. Something I now regret doing.'

'Get here now. You need to get Klara here as well. She has to say goodbye to her mother. Where is she now exactly?'

'Working,' I said. 'But I know how to find her.'

'When can you be here?'

'A few hours. Will she hang on?'

'I can't say. When the ambulance men brought her to Dignity last night the ER team informed me that there was little they could do for her; that she was essentially in the throes of death. As the costs of keeping her in hospital were frightening, and as I couldn't reach you and am sure Agnieska would prefer to leave this life in her own bed, I had to make a decision on your behalf this morning. I had my sister brought back to your home.'

'Thank you, Grazyna. Is she suffering, in pain?'

'She's beyond that now.'

'Does she have other people with her?'

'Our brother is on his way to her from Fresno. I'm so sorry about all this, Brendan. Please get here as soon as possible – and please know that I am not just praying for Agnieska, but for you as well.'

I felt that tightness coming across my chest again. I was certain that the big one was coming; that this was the final retribution for all that I'd caused. I turned off my phone. I lay back on the bed. I shut my eyes. I actually said a decade of the rosary and three Hail Marys. The pain stopped at the top of my left arm, no longer traveling down to my fingers. I won't say that prayer worked. I will say: some force within me, blocking an artery, waiting for the right moment to snuff out my life, decided I should at least get through today to face my dying wife at the home she had me barred from.

When the pain subsided, I forced myself into the shower. Then I hit the road. I was back in front of the trailer by twelve-thirty, dreading how Klara was going to react.

But it was Elise out the door first. She looked at me with care.

'You've just had bad news, right?'

I told her. She went white and flinched as if someone had just hit her.

'That's terrible. How long do the doctors think she has?'

'Maybe until the end of the day.'

'You have to get back there now.'

'I know. And I have to tell Klara …'

She came over and put her hand on my shoulder.

'I am desperately sorry.'

I went into the trailer, Elise following right behind me. Amber was in a corner, the television on, some cartoon flickering across the screen. Klara was chopping vegetables in the kitchen, her gun on the counter in front of her. She looked up as I came in.

'What's happened?' she asked.

I told her. She tossed the chopping knife aside. She lowered her head. She gripped the countertop. She shut her eyes. She uttered one word:

'Mama.'

I went over to her. I put my arms around her. She buried her head in my shoulder. She cried. But only for a brief minute. She asked:

'How long do we have before … ?'

'I don't know. Your aunt said … hours maybe.'

'I can't leave Amber,' she said.

'Yes, you can,' Elise said. 'I'll stay with her. Amber will be fine with me. I can take the car you came in and drive with her to a safe place and make contact with my people at the Women's Choice Group and see what arrangements they've made for her. I can then message you on your safe cell phone, Klara. All going well, Amber will be with them tomorrow – out of danger.'

'Amber is my responsibility ...'

'She's everyone's responsibility now,' Elise said. 'She will be in the right hands for the next stage of this business. Your mother is dying. You must go see her.'

Elise reached over and picked up Klara's gun.

'You give that back,' Klara said.

'I will when I see you next.'

'Don't fuck with me.'

'You talk tough, you act tough – but you are also still an adolescent when it comes to letting your emotions run you; of not being able to count to ten.'

Long silence. Amber stood up from the television and – sensing something was up – came over and asked us what was going on. She was especially wide-eyed to see the gun in Elise's hand. Elise explained all. Amber immediately put her arms around Klara – who stiffened at her embrace. She began to speak with her, offering condolences, telling her:

'You must get to your mother now.'

Klara started to pace back and forth, as I had often seen her doing when indecisive, overstressed. Then:

'I'll only go if you give me back my gun.'

'It stays here,' Elise said.

'Says who?'

'I'm insisting on this – because you don't need it where you're going. And you shouldn't be visiting your dying mother carrying a concealed weapon. Would you agree with me, Brendan?'

I nodded.

'Then I'm not going,' Klara said.

Amber suddenly turned on Klara, saying that Elise was right; that she had to go now and see her; that Elise was a woman 'we could all trust' and 'we will be safe here until tomorrow'.

'I lost my mama when I was thirteen. As bad as she was I don't think I'd have ended up in this terrible place had she lived. Your mama might be an angry woman, and against all you're about, but I know that she still probably loved you more than anything.'

This battered, violated child was so forceful, so outraged in her tone, that even my daughter was taken aback. When she finished she put her hand on Klara's shoulder. This time Klara lowered her head, her eyes filling up.

'She never liked me,' she said.

'Amber's right,' I said. 'She loved you. But she couldn't handle anyone or anything outside her limited way of looking at the world. And she was also easily influenced by people more persuasive than she was.'

I was already using the past tense to speak about Agnieska. An hour later – as we headed west on the interstate – Klara turned to me and said:

'I never told you this – but when I was six, I came home from first grade and spilt a glass of milk at the kitchen table. Momma got furious, started slapping me around, telling me how it was my brother Karol who should have lived, not me. Saying that, though she loved me, she never liked me. And she doubted she ever would.'

'She was still crazy with grief then.'

'You trying to excuse what she said, Poppa?'

'I'm just saying … she was in a hellhole … .'

'And the thing is: all these years later Momma still hasn't come out of it. Until she found her calling at Angels Assist she couldn't work. But now she can go out and harass women wanting abortions.'

'Is this any way to talk now? In a couple of hours she'll be gone from us forever. Maybe even before we get home. Surely you can forgive her now.'

'That's the difference between you and me, Poppa. You put up with other people's shit. Including my own.'

I smiled. The only smile of this terrible day so far.

'I was finally planning to leave your mother after all this calmed down.'

'I'm not surprised. I've suspected that Momma's not been there for you in years.'

I thought about that comment for a moment or so, thinking: Klara is too damn observant. Then I said:

'One thing I do know which you definitely *don't* know yet. When it comes to someone else's marriage – especially your parents' – never attempt to try to figure out what goes on inside it. It's often a mystery to the two people who happen to be in it.'

Klara's response was to look out the window for a very long time.

'It's hard knowing that a parent doesn't really care for you,' she finally said.

'That's a tough truth. I wish it was a different one. But yeah, you're right. I never talk much about your grandfather. But he was a hard guy. I was never good enough for him. Which still leaves me thinking: I'm never really good enough for anyone.'

'That's not what I think. And that's not what Elise thinks.'

'You're in a lot of trouble, Klara,' I said, ignoring that last comment. 'Kelleher has all the power that a billion dollars can buy.'

'Let's get Amber to her safe house. Elise says I can stay there as well for a while. After that ... Elise's group has money and connections. I might have to disappear for a while. But you won't lose me. There is a way out of this which doesn't involve a coffin.'

'That's not funny.'

'I know it isn't.'

The traffic was light until we got near the Los Angeles city limits. I turned my phone back on. I let the GPS find our location. It informed us that there were bottlenecks everywhere. Night was falling. We would arrive at 7.13 p.m.

'I better text your aunt,' I said, 'give her our arrival time.'

'I'll do it,' Klara said.

I gripped the wheel tighter. Trying to keep all my mixed-up emotions in check. Grief, anger, the realization that I was about to say goodbye to the mother of the wonderful daughter sitting next to me; a woman whom I talked myself into thinking that I loved when we first met, even though I knew it not to be the case. Someone I should have said goodbye to years ago. Which now left me with the sense of a sad long-term compromise; of staying put instead of walking out the door; of wasted time. All my timid, scared choices. All done in the name of . . . what? Keeping up appearances? Proving to my priest and the community that I was a responsible guy? Always having to do what was expected of me?

And now . . . ?

Bing.

A text from Grazyna. Klara read it out to me:

Please hurry. Time is running out.

There was an accident on the highway. I ducked off the 10 and went surface all the way to North Hollywood.

This cost us another twenty minutes. When we turned into our street it was almost 8 p.m.

'If she's gone now . . .' I started to say.

As we pulled up in front of the house Klara asked:

'What the hell is with the steel shutters being down?'

'That's another conversation,' I said.

Out front I saw the white Subaru that Grazyna had been driving for the past few years. Klara and I looked at each other.

'We'll get ourselves through this,' I said.

'One way or another.'

We parked. We got out. Walked up to the front door. I rang the bell, knowing that – as the locks had been changed – I couldn't get inside my own house. After a minute I rang again. No answer. Myself and Klara exchanged a worried glance. I turned the door handle and was surprised to find that it was unlocked. Knowing we were en route Grazyna must have decided to leave the door open. I pushed it forward. We walked inside. The front hallway was dark, lit up only by the fluorescent tubes in the kitchen down the hall.

'Grazyna?' I said.

'Where is she?' Klara asked.

Behind us came a voice. A woman's voice. A voice I knew.

'She's out taking a walk until this is over,' Teresa said.

The front door slammed shut and we were both grabbed from behind. I was spun around, my arm shoved up against my back, as the man who'd grabbed me forced his gun barrel into my mouth. Teresa had Klara also in a chokehold, a pistol against her head. Then, in a voice thick with doom, the guy asked:

'So who's going to die first?'

twenty-one

'I TOLD YOU, Ricky, no guns, no violence.'

The voice of Todor coming out of the kitchen. Todor. Fuck. Behind me the guy holding a gun to my head hissed at him:

'The CEO told me I should do what I had to do.'

This Ricky guy stepped around to face me, the gun barrel still in my mouth. A big guy in a black suit, a white shirt, a tie. Klara was struggling against the grip of Teresa. When my daughter tried to turn toward me, Teresa suddenly jabbed the barrel against the right temple of my daughter. She did it with such force that Klara cried out in pain.

'What the fuck,' I yelled.

Now it was my turn to get jabbed in the head by a gun barrel. It hurt. Badly. I felt as if I had been knocked sideways.

'No talking,' the guy said. 'You're bringing us to them now.'

'Bringing you to who?' I asked.

Teresa hissed at me:

'You want a bullet in your daughter's head you keeping acting stupid.'

'I want to see Agnieska,' I told Todor.

'She's not here,' he said, approaching us.

'She's already passed?' I asked, my voice hushed.

Todor looked directly at me.

'She is elsewhere tonight,' he said.

'What do you mean by that?' I said.

'I got her to go somewhere else so she wasn't involved in all this.'

'She's not dying?' I said, my voice raised.

'She's just fine. But I had to find a way of getting you back here. So I got her sister to call you and spin that little story.'

'You fucking creep,' Klara yelled and was rewarded with another hard poke in the temple by Teresa and her gun. When she cried out in pain Todor waded in, whispering something to Teresa.

'You fucking stay out of this,' Ricky shouted at Todor. The priest turned on him.

'You might have the gun ... but you don't have the baby. And your "CEO" assured me that we are going to try to do this all as civilly as possible.'

'Talking nice ain't gonna make this come out the way the CEO wants,' Ricky said.

'And if you want your boss to end up with his baby,' Todor said, 'you will stop acting like the thug that you are and be reasonable.'

Then he turned to me and said:

'I'm going to need your cooperation here, Brendan. I apologize for playing this trick on you. However, what I can promise is that, in exchange for helping us, no harm will come to the mother … and you will be well remunerated for all this.'

'Let me guess,' I said. 'The guy with the gun to my head is one of Kelleher's bodyguards. And, like Crazy Teresa here, he's being paid serious money to get Amber back?'

'Very clever,' Todor said. 'I'm impressed by your powers of deduction. You may think me appalling for doing this. But the girl you mention is the ward of someone who was very upset to discover that she got pregnant by one of his bodyguards. All he wants is that the girl comes back home and has the child – which the gentleman is planning to raise as his own son.'

'The "gentleman" is Patrick Kelleher,' Klara shouted, 'and he repeatedly raped that underage girl who's now carrying his baby –'

Teresa hissed at Klara to shut up.

'And if I don't?' Klara screamed. 'You shoot me? Then what?'

'Enough!' Todor shouted. 'No more craziness.'

'You've created this craziness,' I said. 'You're doing the money grab.'

'You will have enough from this one evening to walk out of your life and start over again.'

'And you, you fucking Judas?' Klara screamed.

'Stay out of this,' Teresa said, again jabbing the muzzle against her skull. 'Amber will be kept safe. No harm will come to her. We know what we're doing. And you're both going to now hand over your phones to me.'

'You're going to have to fucking well take it off me,' Klara said.

Teresa pulled back the hammer on her gun.

'I've never liked you,' she said. 'Always saw the trash way you disrespected your mother, with your nasty feminist bullshit. And you're a baby killer. So why shouldn't I blow you away?'

I felt myself go into something like freefall. Especially as Teresa's finger was trembling around the trigger of the gun.

'There's no need for all this, Teresa,' Todor said. 'I know Klara will hand over her phone to me right now.'

He held out his hand. Klara, looking absolutely terrified, reached into her right pocket and fished out her phone, dropping it into Todor's open fingers. Then he came over to me and held out his hand. I too handed my phone over. Todor now nodded at Teresa – who lowered the barrel of her pistol.

'See,' Todor said. 'No more melodrama. I sense we've got a long drive ahead of us.'

'Get them to give you the address,' Ricky said to Todor. 'Brendan will do that.'

Then he said to me:

'We're taking two cars.'

Klara, as it turned out, was driving the second car – with Teresa riding shotgun beside her. Teresa marched her to a white Camry, the gun pressed against her. Ricky pushed me forward, a black duffel bag swinging from his shoulder, with Todor keeping an eye out if anyone was on the street. Todor used his key remote to open his car door. Klara got in behind the wheel, Teresa training the gun on her. She told Klara that she should put her hands on the wheel and keep them there until she said otherwise. Todor handed the keys over to Teresa. She clicked open the passenger door and walked to the other side of the car, the gun always pointed in my daughter's direction. She got into the passenger seat. Then she used the remote to turn on the engine. It fired into life. Todor turned to me and said:

'I want Ricky to do the driving, so you are going to program the address into his phone. Then you and I are going to sit in the back seat and have a little talk. I told the CEO that, as he put me in charge of sorting out this problem, I would be running the recovery operation by my own rules. I don't want Teresa to have the address on her GPS. Just in case that hothead side of her comes out and she decides to get ahead of us and take matters into her own hands.'

'What the fuck is she doing here in the first place?' I said.

'All will be explained. Right now Klara and Teresa are going to follow us. If we get separated I'm going to tell Teresa to call me and we will pull over somewhere and wait for them to catch up. How far is it from here?'

'Maybe three hours.'

He checked his watch.

'Then we'll be there just after midnight. I'm going to talk to Teresa.'

He went over and knocked on the passenger-door window. Teresa lowered it. They had a fast exchange. She raised the window back up. Todor motioned to Ricky that we should head to the Volvo. Ricky nudged me with the gun. Before I turned away I raised my hand towards Klara. She had a look on her face I'd never seen before: pure terror.

'Get moving,' Ricky said to me.

We walked over to the Volvo.

'Keys,' Ricky said.

I pulled them out and handed them to him. He and Todor had a rapid-fire exchange, then Ricky opened the back door and ordered me in. With the gun trained on me I took my place. Then he gave me his cellphone.

'Put in the address now – and if you fuck around, put in something false ... *bang*.'

He shoved the gun against my head as he said this.

'No need for theatrics, Ricky,' Todor said, 'especially as Brendan is going to do everything we say. Isn't that right, Brendan?'

I nodded and tapped the address into the phone. Ricky studied it, hit a button and told Brendan:

'Two hours fifty-three minutes.'

'Good,' Todor said. 'Let's get on the road.'

He came around to the other side of the car and opened the door and slid into the back seat next to me. Ricky meanwhile opened the trunk and dumped his duffel bag inside. Slamming it shut, he walked to the front door and got into the driver's seat, adjusting the mirror, then hitting the ignition button and firing the engine into life. Before he put the car into drive Ricky turned around and again pressed the gun up against me.

'Any trouble and you are checking out of this life.'

Todor didn't like this.

'Did you hear what I said before? You get the gun out of my friend's neck now. We have a long drive ahead. He will get us there, we will get this business finished without violence, and we will part company reasonably. Now be smart and drive.'

I could see Ricky's face tighten. But he said nothing. Instead he glanced at the GPS on his cellphone and shifted down into drive. We pulled out into the road. We passed by the Camry, Ricky flashing his lights as we approached. Once out in front I turned around and saw that Klara was right behind us. I gave her the thumbs-up signal. She nodded back at me. Teresa still had the gun trained on her. We drove off. Ricky hit the radio on the dashboard. Classical music filled the car. He immediately touched his phone screen and some heavy metal music blared out.

'I wanna hear my music,' he said.

'Then hear your music,' Todor said.

I exchanged a glance with Todor. He put a finger to his lips. We said nothing for many minutes. Ricky was concentrating on the road up ahead, the crash and bang of his music making conversation impossible.

'Can you ask him to turn it down?' I said.

'I'd rather he not hear us,' Todor said, then raised his voice up a level and asked Ricky whether he could turn the music up even higher. When he didn't seem to catch the question or glance back in our direction Todor nodded to me, saying:

'It's safe to talk.'

'Then talk,' I said.

'I'm sure you hate me right now. But before you confirm that hear me out ...'

'I'm listening.'

'The price was right, Brendan. You are my oldest friend. I will lay all my cards on the table. When this young woman disappeared Mr Kelleher came to me, desperate. Saying that he'd taken her in from a very bleak refuge for homeless adolescents, given her a place on his estate, made certain she was very well materially looked after. But then, after a couple of years, she started a thing with one of his bodyguards ... and found herself pregnant at seventeen. She didn't want to keep the baby. And you know Mr Kelleher's viewpoint on abortion ...'

'Do you really believe this story, *Father*?'

Todor glanced again at Ricky who was somehow singing along to this crash and burn music. Having made certain he truly couldn't hear us he turned back to me and said:

'Truth is a flexible construct, Brendan.'

'Of course it is ... when you're doing someone else's dirty work. Maybe I should be asking: how much is he paying you?'

'That's my business. What I've negotiated for you ... I think two hundred thousand will make a difference in your life.'

'No thanks,' I said.

'Your call. Your loss.'

'And your gain. I'm sure you're getting paid five, ten, maybe fifteen times that amount.'

'Again that's my business.'

'Indeed it is, *Father*. But as you have gotten me and my daughter involved in your scheme –'

'Correction: it was Klara who got herself way over her head by stepping in to seemingly "rescue" this young woman and get her the illegal abortion she wants.'

'Man, you really know how to twist the story to make it morally acceptable to you. Your "CEO" – as you and that thug behind the wheel call him – essentially took in a fourteen-year-old girl and turned her into his sex slave. Are you telling me you seriously didn't know about *this*?'

'Hand on heart, I knew nothing whatsoever about it all. Because the few times I had been invited to meet Mr Kelleher at his compound it was in his office or one of the many living rooms he has there. When the young woman went missing and they found out that your daughter had collected her from the mall –'

I jumped in here:

'They found out it was Klara because they grabbed that young woman security guard whom Amber had run into when she was fleeing. Did you know that guard hasn't been seen since?'

Todor's eyes were wide now.

'First I've heard of it,' Todor said, then added: 'I am telling you that, hand on heart. The first I learned of any of this was when Mr Kelleher found out that Klara was involved, that Klara was Agnieska's daughter, that Agnieska now has a paid job with him, that Teresa is her best friend, and that you and I go back –'

'So instead of sending one or two of his goons in to shoot everyone up and get Amber back Kelleher thought: send her father's priest friend and her mother's best pal and the whole thing can be settled without bloodshed.'

'Don't you think that's a more reasoned approach?' Todor said. 'Yes, he insisted that one of his bodyguards comes along just in case Klara wouldn't turn the girl over to us ... or if she refused to leave. But though he might be Prince Not So Bright Ricky has still been told not to pull the trigger under any circumstances; that this all has to be carried out quickly and without violence.'

'When he gets Amber back,' I said, 'then what? Do you really think Klara and I are going to stay quiet about this? Especially given the crimes he's committed against that young woman. And I'm sure she was hardly the first.'

Todor's lips tightened. Again he glanced toward Ricky, making certain the heavy metal was still drowning out our conversation for him. Then:

'I am certain I can also negotiate a generous payoff for Klara in exchange for her silence. If you and your daughter chose *not* to be silent ... well, that could have unfortunate consequences.'

I glared at my friend, knocked sideways by what he just told me.

'You're giving us a choice: take the money offered and shut up ... or get a bullet in the back of the head. Or maybe Kelleher's people will make it look accidental like they did with his ex-wife and the guy who got her pregnant?'

'Those deaths were legally ruled just that: a terrible accident.'

'Money can whitewash so much in this wonderful country of ours. You know all the dark shit about this guy, don't you?'

Todor leaned back against the seat and said nothing for a very long time.

'I am also Mr Kelleher's confessor. My priestly vows forbid me from breaking his confidence. But I will tell you this, Brendan: I'm not threatening you or your daughter. On the contrary, I'm offering you both a lucrative way out of the "problem" we all find ourselves in. Is that also buying your silence? Absolutely. Will bad things happen if that silence is breached – or either of you refuse to abide by it? I'd rather not say ... because it won't be me behind what follows thereafter. But as your friend –'

'You are no longer my friend.'

'I hope that's not a permanent state of affairs. Be that as it may my advice to you and your daughter is: take the money and let Mr Kelleher handle things his own way. I can assure you that no harm whatsoever will come to the girl. Once she is delivered of the child and he formally adopts it Mr Kelleher will have her set up nicely somewhere, allowing her to start over again at a very young age. You have my word that she will be just fine.'

'Your word means shit to me now,' I said. 'And you know full fucking well that Amber will never be fine. But I really need to know something, *Father*. What are you going to do with the million or two or maybe even more he gives you? Clearly you have decided to finally push all your priestly vows out the window ... if you haven't done so already.'

Silence. Then:

'I have spent decades giving everything to my parishes, my church. Now I want to ... *diversify*. I'm starting to crowd sixty. I would like to think that, having sacrificed so much for a higher calling, a payback is allowed.'

'Even if it goes against all your high moral teaching.'

'Ah yes I forgot – you are actually one of the few ethically pure men I know. You have played by all the rules.'

'Because you've told me repeatedly that I *must* play by those rules. I should have left my marriage. I stayed. But, in a certain way, I left it a long time ago. I am guilty of neglecting Agnieska. Just as I also know she has made it impossible for me to stay. Who's right here? Neither of us. But you like to play the right/wrong card. Like when you threatened me a couple of days ago because I dared to drive an honorable woman –'

'Nice ride, by the way,' he said. 'Her Volvo?'

'You're a scumbag, Todor.'

'I am, in fact, your only friend in the world – and someone who is about to earn you two hundred thousand dollars . . . which I am going to get you to accept. From the CEO's standpoint you being paid off will guarantee your silence.'

I turned away, looking out into the black California night. Todor went on:

'Just think what you can do with all that money. You want to walk away from Agnieska tomorrow, you can do just that. Leave her the house, drive off somewhere. There are many places in this fine country of ours where you can buy a house for one hundred thousand and have enough left over to cushion you while making a new start. And you get to divorce the woman I know you now hate.'

'I don't hate Agnieska. I pity her. But it was you who for years, decades, insisted that I stay with her.'

'Guilty as charged. But now I am giving you a Get Out of Jail Free card. You can change your life tomorrow.'

'You act like all this is going to go so smoothly. You're dealing with the brute in the front seat – and someone who has a ruthless thug paying him. Who's to say he hasn't been ordered to kill us all once he has the girl?'

'Because I have already put an insurance policy in place. Mr Kelleher insisted that Ricky come along to provide muscle if your daughter won't let Amber go quietly ... but you and I will ensure she goes quietly. Mr Kelleher also knows that if I do not call my secretary by 7 a.m. tomorrow she is to alert the police. Why do you think I brought Teresa into the story? Because as agreed with Mr Kelleher she is going to take Amber to a safe location for the last weeks of her pregnancy, keep her very comfortable and healthy, get the baby delivered by doctors that Mr Kelleher will supply, and then give him the child – on the proviso that Amber is left alone.'

I could have said: that was our plan as well. Todor went on:

'Once this is all wrapped up you give me your bank details. I am certain Mr Kelleher's legal people will want you to sign certain non-disclosure forms. But trust me, he wants this wrapped up as quickly and quietly as possible. The money will be with you days after this is done.'

‘*If* I accept the money … which I won’t. But you will. That’s the big, serious difference between us: you’re a mercenary creep.’

‘Call me all the names you like, Brendan. I am solving a problem for a man who will solve many problems for both of us.’

‘When this night is over we are never having anything to do with each other again.’

‘Glad to see that being with that baby-killing older woman has so emboldened you. The new aggressive Brendan.’

To which I could only reply:

‘Fuck you, Father.’

We drove on in silence. Todor now asked Ricky to lower the music. He didn’t looked pleased about doing it – but he did it. At which point Todor nodded off. I kept looking back to make sure that Klara was behind us in the Camry. She never once lost us all that long way east. I kept telling myself that Todor had indeed sussed this all so well as to ensure that the handover went smoothly, though I knew that Amber would be horrified to see that one of Kelleher’s bodyguards was with us. I decided that I would insist on going in first to the trailer, bring Elise outside and outline the situation and how we had little choice but to follow Todor’s plan for Amber. Then Elise would have to go back inside and explain all to that terrified young woman. How would she react to this? Very badly indeed.

Ricky's eyes were absolutely fixed on the night road in front of him, glancing once or twice back at me with deep stupid menace, just to remind me (and, no doubt, himself) who had the power in the car. Todor stirred awake around an hour later. He rubbed the sleep from his eyes. I could see him trying to figure out where he was.

'How long was I out for?' he asked me.

'A while.'

'How far to go?'

'Maybe an hour.'

'The girls are still behind us?'

I glanced for about the fortieth time out through the rear window, waving toward my daughter – who probably couldn't see me in the darkness of the empty highway we were both traveling down.

'They're still there,' I said.

'I want to talk to Amber first when we get there,' Todor said.

'That's not a good idea. She doesn't know you. She might get hysterical. Let me go in first, try to explain things very slowly, very calmly.'

Todor considered this.

'I'll give you two minutes. I want this finished up fast.'

We drove on. I kept obsessively staring out the back window every few minutes. Klara was right there behind me. I kept thinking over and over how I was going to explain to Elise that my daughter and I had walked right into a setup, and how – given the guns trained on us – we were going to have no choice but to let them leave with Amber. I knew already how turning that desperately abused young woman over to her thug of a captor was going to make her frantic. How Todor's reassurances that no harm would come to her would send Elise's bullshit meter into that deep red zone where outright lies are registered. And how I so wished I had never let her speak to Klara and get involved in all this madness.

'You feeling tired?' Todor asked me.

'It's hard to feel sleepy when the guy driving has a gun on the seat next to him,' I said.

I could see Todor smiling a tight smile. Then he asked:

'When you were younger did you ever think about becoming a priest?'

'What a question.'

'You strike me as ideal material. All that principle and virtue.'

'But no belief.'

'Really?'

'I knew when I was around thirteen – as an altar boy being touched up by the local parish priest – that all the doctrine and dogma you all preach, along with that very comforting, dumb idea of eternal life, just didn't add up for me. Call it my engineer's brain. But I couldn't make the leap into faith. Unlike you.'

'Faith is something that has to overwhelm you. A bit, I guess, like falling in love.'

'You ever fall in love, Father?'

'Don't ask me that, Brendan.'

'Why not?'

'Once.'

'Did you ever act on it?'

'That's between me and my confessor.'

'So that vow of chastity ... ?'

'We're not going there, my friend.'

'To repeat what I told you earlier: I am no longer your friend.'

'That's a shame, Brendan. I still remain yours. Though you might hate me now for tricking you into all this you will thank me later ... when you will have the latitude and new life you've been craving for years.'

'But how can you have latitude, a new life, when it's bought by dirty money?'

Nothing further was spoken until we passed by the motel where I slept the night before.

'Fifteen minutes,' I said.

'I'll text Teresa,' Todor said.

'Tell her in no way to approach the door when she gets there. As agreed I'm going in first.'

'Okay,' he said, 'but we'll be right after you.'

He now told Ricky to kill his music, as they had business to discuss. The silence after all those hours of heavy metal was a relief. Todor explained to him 'the game plan' once we arrived at the address. Ricky didn't like it.

'Say they try to sneak out the back?' he asked.

'It's a trailer,' I said. 'There's no back door. And it's in the absolute middle of the desert. There's nowhere to run to.'

'I still don't like the idea of him going in first,' Ricky told Todor.

'I trust him.'

Bing. A text on Todor's phone. From Teresa.

'She's all cool with the plan,' he told me.

'She's holding a gun on my daughter. She's not cool.'

Silence for the last eight minutes of the journey. We crunched on the sandy gravel as we hit the dirt road leading to the trailer. As we came closer I could see the floodlight ablaze above its front door. We parked side by side. We all got out. But when Klara tried to move toward me Teresa grabbed her and shoved the gun into her back.

'Don't even think about making another move until I give you permission,' she hissed. Todor glared at her, putting his finger to his lips, indicating silence was necessary right now. I wanted to go over and throttle Teresa. But with her pistol pressed against my daughter I could do nothing. Klara stared straight ahead, rage across her face. Ricky was jumpy. Hair-trigger jumpy. Pacing back and forth, wanting to burst into the trailer. Todor put a steadying hand on his shoulder and told him to stand back. He then indicated that I should now go in through the front door.

But suddenly I heard shouting inside. Elise yelling:

'No, Amber, no!'

Then the door flew open. There was a gun in Amber's hand. It exploded. The shot hit the dirt at Teresa's feet. Immediately Teresa returned fire, hitting Amber in the belly. At which moment Elise dived out from the trailer, pushing Amber into the dirt below. Teresa now blasted away, hitting Elise in the chest and the neck. I screamed. I rushed forward, managing to break Elise's fall as she tipped over. I could hear Klara yelling. Ricky went insane. He ran over to Teresa, slammed his gun across her face, screaming murder. Then he turned his pistol on her, firing several times into her head.

Blood was pouring out of Elise. I held her close, one hand on her gaping wounds. She tried to touch my face. She couldn't. I looked into her eyes. They were swimming with trauma, disbelief. She whispered one word:

'Why?'

Then she went still in my arms.

I buried my face against her. Howling. For a moment I lost all sense of where I was – clutching Elise, my hands trying to stop the blood pumping out of her, telling myself over and over: *she can't be dead … she can't be dead …*

Then I heard Klara screaming at me to call 911. I looked up, seeing that she'd thrown herself across Amber's gaping wound. Ricky fell to his knees by us, reaching for his phone, crying while telling Amber that she would be all right, that the baby would live, that he'd get her to a hospital, that …

But then there was gunfire. Ricky's head suddenly came apart. I looked up. Todor had raised the pistol out of Teresa's hand and, keeping his fingers around her own, fired the last of three shots into the back of Ricky's head. Then he staggered over to the Volvo, falling against it like a man who knew that the entire bottom had dropped out of his world. Klara jumped up in shock as Ricky keeled over by her into the dirt. She now dashed into the trailer, racing back out with a blanket. Pressing it against Amber's wound she screamed at Todor:

'Get over here now, you fuck.'

I could see Todor, his head bowed, pounding the car with his fists, then stopping as if – in the midst of all that rage – he suddenly realized what had to happen next. Staggering back over to Teresa's body he pulled a handkerchief out of his trouser pocket and vigorously rubbed the gun everywhere. Then he turned to me and handed me the handkerchief, saying:

'You need to shoot me first.'

'What?' I screamed.

'Shoot me.'

'She'll *die* if we don't get her to a hospital now,' Klara said.

'Where's the nearest hospital?' Todor asked.

'How the fuck should we know?' Klara said.

'I passed a small one down on the main road,' I said. 'Maybe ten–fifteen miles from here, near Joshua Tree. I'm calling 911 now.'

Todor said:

'But before that you are going to lift Ricky's hand, aim the gun in it at my shoulder, pull the trigger, then get the hell out of here.'

'And let her die?' Klara said. 'No fucking way.'

'I will keep my hand on her wound, will try to stem the blood,' Todor said. 'If the hospital is that near they should be here fast. She'll make it.'

'We are not leaving,' Klara said.

Todor reached into his jacket pocket and handed me the cellphones that he took off us.

'You are definitely leaving,' he said. 'Because you don't want to be involved in all this. I'll tell the story. My version of it. Without you in it. Which is why I need to be found shot too. You go. You walk away. And you take the bag that Ricky brought with him. Now fucking shoot me.'

'I am not listening to this bullshit,' Klara said.

'I am,' I said. 'Call 911 now.'

'Poppa …'

But Todor had already dialed the number. He spoke in a frantic voice. Said there had been a multiple shooting at Caravan Fields 32 in Twentynine Palms. Three dead. Two wounded – one of them a pregnant woman.

'She'll die if you are not here in ten minutes … Right … Right … You've got to hurry.'

He ended the call.

'They will be here in nine minutes,' he shouted at us. 'Do it now.'

Walking over to Ricky's lifeless body I wrapped my hand in Todor's handkerchief, making sure my fingers were completely covered. Ricky's hand was still around his pistol. I raised it. Todor leaned forward, fear in his face. It was tricky putting my handkerchief-covered fingers around those of Ricky's, but I managed it somehow. I told him to come closer. He walked right up to me. I placed my finger against Ricky's lifeless finger to pull the trigger. I'd never fired a gun before. I didn't expect its backward kick that knocked me off balance. Todor howled as the bullet tore into his right shoulder. He fell to the side, but somehow managed to scramble back to Amber – who looked semiconscious and kept muttering incoherent words. He grabbed the blanket and pressed down against her bleeding wound. Shouting at us:

'You're out of here. Now.'

I ran to the car. Klara followed, but then had a second thought and turned around and ran back to Amber and whispered something to her. Then she took the gun out of her hand and dashed to the car. But halfway there Todor shouted:

'The bullet Amber fired. It must be near Teresa's body. If they find it they'll trace it to your gun … and you're fucked.'

Klara and I ran back to the area around which Teresa had fallen. All sand. Life sometimes deals you a lucky card. The moment I ran my hand through the immediate vicinity near her body I felt it touch a small metallic object. The bullet.

'Got it,' I said, putting it in my pants pocket along with the handkerchief.

Seconds later Klara and I were in the car.

I gunned the motor. We shot off into the night.

twenty-two

I DROVE FAST. Stupid fast. Barreling down the gravel road at forty miles an hour. I was covered in blood. So too my daughter, hysterical in the seat next to me and trying not to fall apart. I knew that I would never get out of my head the image of Elise falling dead into my arms. Elise. Who saved Amber's life by pushing her out of Teresa's final crazed volley of shots. Elise. My friend. Who showed me decency and kindness and respect: rare qualities in this strange, angry life we live now. Elise …

I felt myself about to explode into the most deranged sort of grief; that kind of heartache which threatens to drown you in the belief that life is just not worth the agony it so often is. I felt horrible leaving her on the ground back there. It was as if I had abandoned her. Left her for the cops, the ambulance guys, the coroner. Didn't hold her until they arrived. Didn't keep her close to me …

Oh fuck, my head was going to detonate. And Klara was crazy crying next to me. I wanted to pull over and fall apart too. But I knew that the cops and the ambulances would be here in moments and I had to get us off this fucking dirt track. Even if we were innocent … once Kelleher found out that we were witnesses to all that went down we might just have a price on our heads. And a cheap price at that.

It was a relief to leave the gravel and hit the two-lane blacktop. I turned right, heading toward the highway. As soon as I made that turn I heard the roar of sirens in the oncoming distance. Two cop cars, two ambulances, racing down the road. Zooming right past us. Immediately Klara popped open the glove compartment and shut away the gun in her hand.

'They should be there in a couple of minutes,' I said.

'If she dies ...'

'She won't die.'

'The baby is dead,' Klara said.

'And Teresa was the murderer.'

'We could have stopped it.'

'How? We had nothing to do with –'

'We could have fucking stopped it!'

I said nothing. Except:

'We are going to run out of gas in about thirty miles.'

I glanced at the clock on the dash. 1.12 a.m.

'We can find a station that's closed,' I said, 'where they have one of those cash-machine pumps. No one can see us with all this blood.'

'That fucking priest ... he's the one with blood on his hands. He's the one who killed Elise, who killed Amber's baby ... and maybe Amber herself.'

'She's going to live.'

'How the fuck do you know that?'

'She's going to live. And so are we.'

Ten miles down the road, right before the turn onto the highway, there was a small Sunoco station closed for the night. I fed a twenty into the slot that allowed you to buy gas after hours. As I filled the tank I asked Klara to pop the trunk and bring out the black duffel bag that Ricky had brought with him. When she opened it she let out a sharp 'Holy shit'. When I got back into the car Klara announced to me that the bag was filled with cash. A large amount of cash.

'That must have been Kelleher's advance to Todor,' I said, 'as he told me that Ricky brought it along for him. Or maybe it was going to Teresa as a payoff for helping out. Todor also told me I was going to get paid for being dragged into this – not that I'd take their fucking money.'

'That cash has blood all over it. And I now need to get out of the country for a while . . . but not with that money.'

I knew she was right. Just as I also knew that she had little savings . . . and I only had maybe fifteen thousand left in the retirement fund I was endlessly dipping into whenever the Uber money didn't go far enough to cover all our bills.

'I've got my passport with me,' Klara said. 'We need to go somewhere and sleep. We need to get rid of these clothes and buy new ones. Then if you can get me to LAX I can get a flight somewhere out of America.'

'Where will you go?'

'I'll decide that tomorrow. You should come with me.'

'No passport.'

'You might want to get one now. Fast.'

Though still in deep shock, Klara was now going into that rational mode of hers. She was trembling. She sobbed when she spoke. But I could see she had her mind set on an exit strategy – and I was determined to get her out of the States as soon as possible.

'I don't think I should turn on my phone,' I said.

'Nor mine. We should get off the interstate. You think she had navigation installed in the car?'

'She never said.'

It suddenly struck me that we were talking about Elise in the past tense.

Klara began to play with the touch screen in the center of the dashboard. She tapped away, telling me she was going to find a route that avoided all highways.

'If Kelleher or the cops or anyone else is looking for this car they are going to be setting up a dragnet on the main roads. On reflection maybe we shouldn't head back just yet to LA. Maybe I should fly out of San Francisco.'

'Okay then. Back roads to San Francisco. But I've been up for too many hours. And you didn't sleep much ...'

'Didn't sleep at all.'

'We need to pull over and crash,' I said.

'But if some backwoods cop sees our car parked on the side of the road – and the blood all over us ...'

'You have less on you than I do,' I said, seeing that it was just Klara's T-shirt that had the remnants of Amber's terrible wound. 'If we could find something to cover all that ... and a motel where you can drive right up to the rooms ...'

'Pull over for a moment.'

'Why?'

'There's a big junk car lot over on the right. I need to get rid of the gun.'

Indeed there was one of those graveyards for rusted and abandoned vehicles on the side of the road. I stopped in front of its entrance. It was chained. There was one of those playground fences around it. Though it was pitch-dark we were lucky that there was moonlight tonight. Klara made a quick tour of its perimeter.

'No camera surveillance. And no barbed wire. Then again who would want to steal junk cars?'

'You'd be surprised.'

'I'm going over.'

'Be fast.'

I watched Klara tackle the fence with rapid determination. Though it was about twelve feet high she scaled it in under a minute. I was anxious when she had to lift one leg over and carefully manage her way to the other side – as a twelve-foot fall can do some serious damage. But she handled crossing over to the other side with great skill. Once on the ground she walked over to where a line of cars seemed to be waiting for the giant metal compactor that took up a major part of the yard. She approached an ancient, rusted Oldsmobile. I saw her reach inside and slip the gun under its front seat. Then she returned to the fence and was back over to me in two minutes.

'Neatly done,' I said.

'Decided not to put it in the glove compartment or the trunk as someone might do one final check in there before the thing gets turned into a cube. Hid it in the springs under the passenger seat. And I removed the magazine and put it nearby so the gun doesn't go "boom" when crushed. Hopefully that's the end of my Glock. Now I want to check the trunk of our car.'

'What might be in the trunk?'

'A way out of this.'

I got out of the car. As soon as my feet touched the ground I was hit with a full-scale attack of the shakes. I had never known anything so severe as this before – my entire body overcome with a tremble that caught me by the throat, sent waves of pain up my left arm, and had me clutching the door handle of the car, holding on to it as if it was the only thing that was going to keep me upright. Klara didn't see any of this – as she was at the back of the car, digging into the trunk, suddenly holding up a green vinyl object.

'She kept a windbreaker in the trunk.'

An hour later, as the clock was closing in on 2.30 a.m. and I was truly beginning to fight exhaustion, we found ourselves on the outskirts of a small town. There was a Motel 6 up ahead.

'We've got to stop,' I said.

'Okay, let me handle it all,' Klara said. 'Pull over first.'

We were still around five hundred yards from the hotel. It was pitch-dark outside and hot. Eighty-five degrees according to the indicator on the dashboard. I braked for a moment. Klara stepped out and put on the windbreaker, cursing the heat outside. When she got back in moments later I asked her if the clerk at the front desk might wonder why she was wearing a jacket in the middle of a night when it was nearly ninety degrees outside.

'It's almost two in the morning and this is a Motel 6 in the ass end of nowhere. He or she isn't going to care. Give me your driver's license.'

I reached into my wallet and handed over my California license. We drove on. Moments later we pulled up into the parking lot of the motel.

'Wait here,' Klara said, zipping up the jacket. She went into the little reception area, emerging a few minutes later with two keys.

'We've got rooms next to each other. She told me there was a Walmart around fifteen minutes from here. What's your waist and shirt size?'

'Forty-two-inch waist, XX large shirt.'

'You've got to lose some weight, Poppa.'

'Not tonight, Klara.'

'Gotcha.'

'I've got about sixty bucks on me in cash.'

'I took out cash before I left LA. The clothes and the rooms are on me. We'll figure out the rest later.'

She handed me a key.

'I'm in Room 17,' she said. 'The woman at the front desk said you dial 7 then the room number to call. If you need me I'm next door. Checkout is noon. I'm getting up and going to Walmart at ten. I'll come back with clothes and coffee by eleven. Can I have the car keys please?'

As soon as I was inside the room I stripped off all my clothes. I threw them into a pile under the counter that served as a makeshift desk. Once under the shower I finally let go. Crying uncontrollably. Unable to stop. The sense of horror colliding with the sense of loss. Elise …

killed in rage by someone who screamed her 'pro-life' credentials all the time. Vanished forever.

I climbed into the polyester sheets. I hit the light. Sleep wouldn't arrive, I wanted to ring Klara's room, see if she too was having an insomnia jag, if she was coping. But if she had managed to pass out I didn't want to jolt her back to the middle of the night. There was a minibar in the room. I drank two beers and two miniatures of Jack Daniel's. That did the job. I blacked out.

Then the phone was ringing. I reached for it. Klara was on the line.

'It's 11.15. We've got to be gone in less than an hour. I'm going to knock on the door in a moment. There will be a bag outside with your new clothes and another with a coffee and a Danish. Then turn on CNN. The story is everywhere.'

I was awake immediately. I heard her knock. I waited another moment, then opened the door about three inches, brought in the two bags, turned on the television. Nothing on CNN – but I figured the story might be broadcast on the half-hour. I pulled out the clothes that Klara had bought for me – khakis, a T-shirt, a hoodie – along with underwear, socks, a toothbrush, toothpaste, a stick of deodorant. The coffee was still warm. The Danish was needed. I hit the shower. I kept the TV on loud. As soon as I heard the talking head mention 'a shocking multiple shooting in Eastern California' I was out of the shower, drying myself, watching a reporter standing in front of the trailer, police crime-scene tape everywhere, several dried brown stains in the sand, explaining how three people died and two were injured in a multiple shooting for which there was still no explanation. One of those shot was a Catholic priest. The other was a pregnant woman who was in a stable condition in a local hospital, though the child she was carrying had died. The priest was also in a stable condition. No further details were given.

I got dressed. I looked at myself in the mirror. A fat guy in black. With deep dark circles under the eyes.

Two minutes later there was a knock on the door.

'We should roll,' Klara said. 'And get those bloody clothes off the floor and into this bag.'

She held open a plastic Walmart bag with all the blood-splattered clothes she wore yesterday already inside.

'The last thing we want is to leave any trace of anything behind.'

I gathered up everything I'd worn yesterday. Dumping them in the bag I couldn't help but think: the blood on them was Elise's blood.

I added the bullet to the bag as an afterthought.

'You see the CNN report?' Klara asked as we walked to the car.

'Yep. Didn't say much.'

'No doubt the padre is spinning a yarn for the cops. Let's just hope he hasn't decided to blame it all on us.'

'Our fingerprints aren't on the guns.'

'That's why I went back and took mine out of Amber's hand. Because it's registered in my name ... and would be a direct forensic link to us.'

'Smart thinking.'

'You do what I've been doing you've got to think smart all the time.'

'And now that you've retired from all that,' I said.

'Don't think I'm walking away from the fight ...'

'Why don't we think about getting you to somewhere in Europe and then you can go quiet for a while? We're still not out of the shit yet. And you're right: we don't know what Todor's telling the cops.'

'I'd put money on him putting the blame squarely on us.'

'But the forensics will show otherwise,' I said. 'Who knows what he'll do. Todor is an opportunistic asshole. And he's got the CEO – as he calls him – to answer to. No doubt some cover-up is being hatched as we speak ... if it's not already in place.'

We drove six hours – with breaks for gas, the toilet and two meals at backroad diners. We found another cheap off-the-grid motel. It had a public computer in its lobby. Before we checked into our respective rooms Klara spent some time surfing travel sites on the internet. She found a direct flight from San Francisco to Amsterdam the following late afternoon. A last-minute deal. Actually reasonable.

'Why Amsterdam?' I asked.

'It's still supposed to be cool,' Klara said. 'And everyone speaks English.'

I insisted she wait until tomorrow before paying for the ticket, wondering if they were now putting tracers on her credit card. So maybe she should buy it hours before departure. During this exchange I had a stab of desperate sadness. My little girl would be leaving for the other side of the world tomorrow. I had no idea when I would see her again. We went to our rooms. I lay down on the bed, grief sideswiping me again. Then the phone rang. Klara.

'Turn on CNN now.'

I reached for the remote. I found CNN. And saw Todor – in a hospital gown, his left arm heavily bandaged, looking like he hadn't slept, his voice heavy with what I sensed immediately was manufactured anguish. He was telling the reporter:

'As I explained to the police Mrs Elise Flouton was a retired UCLA professor, a women's rights activist who'd become involved in helping abused women flee from violent spouses and partners. This young woman – whom I can't name for legal reasons – was pregnant after a relationship that started three years ago when she was fourteen with a certain Richard Grout – who had been employed as a bodyguard for Mr Patrick Kelleher. Last week, after an abusive episode at home, she made contact with the group for which Mrs Flouton works. Mrs Flouton took her in and, discovering that Richard Grout was hunting her, whisked her off to a safe house in the desert. Unfortunately he made contact with one of my parishioners, Teresa Hernandez, who has indeed worked for the charity I founded: Angels Assist. Being a fierce anti-abortion activist she was obsessed with the work of Elise Flouton – who was known in the LA area for helping many women in need to get abortions. Morally and ethically I follow Pope Francis's teaching against abortion. But like His Holiness I am also very much against violent activism – of which, sadly, Teresa Hernandez was an advocate. It seems that she was able to put a tracer on Mrs Flouton's phone and found out where she was sheltering the young woman. When she told me that Grout was desperate to find the mother of his soon-to-be-born child I felt it was my pastoral duty to intervene. I suggested the three of us drive east to where Mrs Flouton was harboring this much mistreated woman. Alas when we got there,

there was an angry exchange between Mrs Hernandez and Mrs Flouton. When Mrs Flouton called Mrs Hernandez a terrorist she became outraged and pulled out a gun and shot Mrs Flouton. She fired indiscriminately and also hit the young woman in the stomach, killing her unborn child. Grout then went crazy. I tried to stop him and was shot by him. Then he turned his gun on Mrs Hernandez – but not before, in a final response, Mrs Hernandez took several shots at him. But before he died he still managed to return fire, killing her. It was a horrifying business – especially as that poor woman lost the six-month-old boy she was carrying. And it just goes to show that we must rethink extremism on all sides when it comes to the debate about abortion. I am praying hard now for this young woman who has lost her precious child and will, no doubt, grieve over his death for the rest of her life.'

The journalist then came on, saying that the California State Police were continuing their investigations into this brutal multiple killing. And that a spokesperson for Patrick Kelleher would be making a statement shortly.

As soon as the segment ended Klara was pounding on my door. I opened it immediately.

'Quite the fucking performance,' she said in a low, angry voice. 'He should win an Oscar as Best Jiveass Immoral Priest.'

I ushered her inside.

'At least he kept us out of it. Thank Christ you grabbed your gun and he reminded us to find the bullet Amber fired. Todor gave us a Get Out of Jail Free card.'

'That asshole is now going to be celebrated and honored for getting shot and probably saving Amber's life. No doubt, as soon as we left the trailer, he called Kelleher and told him everything that happened – and Kelleher immediately had his lawyers on to it. Creating an alibi. Putting all the blame on that now-dead bodyguard. Everyone will think Ricky was the father of Amber's dead baby. Whereas I know from Amber herself that Kelleher and only Kelleher had sex with her. No doubt he's having someone visit Amber in the hospital to offer her a small fortune in exchange for her silence. No doubt the police have been paid off. Everyone's going to buy into the storyline they've put out there . . . because it means they can close the case quickly and without any of the truth coming out. Most of all Patrick Kelleher is going to come out of this with clean hands. Welcome to Modern America. The bad guy wins.'

I didn't know what to stay to that. Except:

'Maybe having wrapped it up like this Kelleher and his people won't be looking for you.'

'The police still haven't found that security guard who helped Amber then went missing. I'm taking no chances, Poppa.'

It was another insanely long day. As we finally came closer to the coast we stopped in a shopping center and Klara went into a branch of Staples and bought time on one of their computers there. Twenty minutes later she emerged holding a printout of her flight at 6.45 p.m. that night. When I asked her how much it cost she said:

'Don't worry about the money, Poppa. I just got paid last week and have around two thousand in my checking account. Enough to cover the ticket and live for a month or so over there.'

'I feel a failure.'

'For not having money?'

'For not being able to help you.'

'Stop talking shit. You are the best. Know that.'

'But I still have no money.'

'You have a bag of money in the trunk.'

'Which I won't touch.'

'And that's why you are the best.'

A few minutes later I made the suggestion that we could risk the highway north from Prunedale to the airport. Klara agreed. She also slept for an hour. I nudged her awake when we were around twenty minutes away from San Francisco International, just as the 2 p.m. NPR news was coming on the air. The third item was 'about a horrendous shooting in the desert region of Twentynine Palms near the Joshua Tree National Park'.

There was an interview with a former colleague of Elise's at UCLA who said that she was always noted for being someone 'with a strong ethical viewpoint and a horror of cruelty and injustice; a woman who believed that you had to truly act on your beliefs in a very corrupt modern world. But to discover that Elise lost her life helping a sexually brutalized, underage woman … it's the stuff of modern legend, isn't it?'

After this there was a spokesperson from the California State Police saying that 'Professor Flouton's murder at the hands of an anti-abortion activist – who also shot the young woman whom Dr Flouton had decided to shelter – points up the terrible price paid when such activism turns violent. The woman who shot Dr Flouton did so – according to the priest eyewitness on the scene – when Dr Flouton threw herself in front of the teenager who had been the victim of statutory rape for years … and was over five months pregnant at the time. The fact that the woman who killed Dr Flouton first shot the teenager in the stomach … well, I don't have to speak further of the tragic irony inherent in the fact that a "right to life" activist killed an unborn child while allegedly defending the rights of unborn children.'

There was one final item on this story. A woman named Patricia Babson – who was the 'director of communications' for Patrick Kelleher – made a statement:

'Given that the late Richard Grout worked for the organization in security for several years – and that Mr Kelleher has a long-standing commitment to both women's rights and the rights of the unborn child – he is beyond devastated by what has transpired. We want to assure the public that this young woman will be taken care of for the rest of her life … and that a chaired professorship is being funded by Mr Kelleher in Dr Flouton's name at UCLA.'

When the news item ended I told my daughter:

'What you said would happen has happened. Amber is being paid off big time to stay silent. In the meantime Todor and Kelleher have also ensured that Elise is going to become some sort of a folk hero. Maybe even a saint.'

'Yeah, she'll probably end up canonized by every progressive group in the country.'

'Your tone is strange. Don't tell me you wish you were the one being martyred now?'

'Martyrdom is cool.'

'Stop talking shit. Be happy you're alive.'

'I am …'

'But a part of you hates the fact that she's getting all the credit for your daredevil stuff.'

'Perhaps. But she also saved Amber's life.'

'And Todor saved yours. Now given how Kelleher is playing the great humanitarian you might not have to go to Amsterdam.'

'I am definitely going to Amsterdam,' Klara said. 'Because I still think I should lay low for a while. And because this country of ours ... it's just too hard a place right now.'

We made the airport exactly two hours before the KLM flight. I walked her directly to the entrance of the security area and she gave me a long hug.

'Thank you for getting us out alive. And for always being there for me.'

I bit down on my lip and felt tears.

'I don't want you to go,' I said.

'I'm freaked too. Landing in a foreign city I know virtually nothing about. But, Poppa ... I have to disappear until we are sure no one evil is looking for me.'

I couldn't argue with that. I still felt that jolt of inevitable separation that knocks a parent sideways when the realization hits: she's truly leaving home. What made this even harder was the thought: Klara is all I care about in the world. And if things break wrong she might not be able to safely return. We could be apart – not within crosstown reach – for a very long time.

'You could wait and see how things play out,' I said.

'I'm getting on that plane, Poppa.'

I felt myself starting to sob. Klara took my face in her hands.

'No teary-eyed goodbyes, Poppa. None of the sadness that I know I will feel for as long as I am apart from you.'

'Whatever's easiest.'

'None of this is easy. I'm still a little girl who needs her daddy. And who now has to get on a plane out of here. You can probably turn your phone on again in about three hours – as I will be safely up in the air.'

'Okay.'

'Will you get a passport and visit me soon?'

'Just send me word and I'm there.'

'I don't deserve you,' she said, giving me one last long hug.

'You come back as soon as you can.'

'You come see me as soon as you can.'

Then she was gone, vanishing into the security area. I felt myself getting shaky. I turned, tears now running down my face. I walked back to the parking lot. I popped the trunk of the Volvo. I looked down at the black duffel bag. I zipped it open. Bundles of $50 notes. I zipped the bag closed. I turned the car south, determined to make it to LA by the end of the evening. Three hours later I turned my phone back on. There was a text from Todor:

Still under 'medical observation' in Twentynine Palms. I should be discharged by early next week. We need to talk.

But I didn't want to talk to Todor.

There was another message. From Elise's lawyers.

We are trying to reach you on an urgent matter ...

Thirty miles further south on the Interstate I pulled into a rest stop. I used the men's room. I bought a bad coffee. I called the number that the law firm had texted me. I was put through to a guy named Dwight Simplon. He asked if I was in Los Angeles. I told him I was out of town.

'Have you been following the news? Have you heard that Mrs Flouton was killed several nights ago?'

'Yes, I did hear that. I was ... shocked.'

'We all are. Her husband was one of the founding partners of the firm – and even after his death Elise kept a keen interest in our goings-on here. We all considered her a class act. And we are appalled at the circumstances of her death. When might you be back in LA, sir?'

'Late tonight.'

'Might you be able to come in to see us as soon as your schedule permits?'

'I suppose so ... but why do you need to see me, Mr Simplon?'

'I'd rather we talk face-to-face.'

'It's that serious?'

'Well ... yes, I suppose.'

'Mr Simplon, I will be driving for the rest of the afternoon and most of the evening. Please don't leave me in suspense. Please tell me what is going on here.'

I could hear a long intake of breath on the phone. Then:

'All right. If you insist. Mrs Flouton left her apartment in Los Angeles to you.'

twenty-three

I WAS CONFUSED. Very confused.

'I don't understand, sir,' I told Dwight Simplon.

He said:

'Mrs Flouton owned an apartment on Malcolm Avenue near the UCLA campus. She owned it outright. No mortgage. And she left it to you – along with the sum of $24,000 to cover the apartment's $1,000 per month maintenance charge for the first two years.'

Because she knew that I could hardly afford $1,000 a month – and would default on those payments immediately. Elise: she seemed to think ahead. Especially when it came to the needs of others.

'I still don't understand: why didn't her daughter get the place?'

'I can't discuss how Mrs Flouton decided to distribute her estate. I am just telling you the legal facts of the matter. You are now the owner of Mrs Flouton's apartment. Can we see you at our offices at, say, twelve noon tomorrow?'

'That should work,' I said.

As I drove on after the call I couldn't help but remember Elise telling me, the morning after driving into that protest in front of the abortion clinic, that she needed to drop by her lawyers to do a little business. Did she sense darker danger to come? But why leave her home to me? I was distressed and feeling deeply guilty about Elise's daughter. I knew that she and her mother had had a breach. Elise did say that she made serious money and was building a life with a fellow financier. But I couldn't, in all good faith, accept this gift. It wasn't merited. I was determined to tell her lawyers that I was handing it all over to Elise's daughter; that I wanted nothing from her estate whatsoever.

I stayed away from NPR or any news channels on the radio. I didn't want to hear another damn thing about the horror that was still haunting my every moment. I kept telling myself to just keep my eyes on the road, keep clocking up the miles, keep making to-do lists in my head. But I couldn't blank out that image of Elise falling into my arms, her last whispered word, the strange shock on her face – as if, in that moment or so before her heart stopped, she realized: this was it. The end of her. A death so sudden, so violent, so out of nowhere. Though everyone would now say that she died doing a heroic, ethical deed I knew that Elise's decision to throw herself in the way of the gunfire was all split-second instinct. She just wanted to save the girl's life.

There was only one other text message during the trip. Right around 8 p.m. The one I was truly dreading. From Agnieska:

Father Todor suggested I go to my sister's house for a few nights. I heard about Teresa's death. I spoke with the Father who told me that you and Klara had been on a father–daughter trip – you showing her your old stomping ground of Sequoia – when all that happened. I was so relieved that you were both far away from all that – and from that woman you were driving. I feel terrible about what happened to her. I feel even more terrible about that poor teenage girl who she rescued. I know people will blame Teresa for what happened to her baby but had your friend gotten that woman the proper care she needed maybe this would never have happened. I fear that Teresa is now in purgatory for what she did – and may be there for eternity. I know you probably don't want to see me but there are things to discuss. And I hope Klara has, in the wake of this terrible business, seen that she must stop supporting the baby killers and –

I stopped reading after that sentence. I felt rage shoot through me like a faulty jolt of electricity. I had just come out of a Shell station on the 101 south of Santa Barbara. I broke off from her text, not wanting to deal with any more of her sanctimonious self-justifications. And deciding at that moment that I would get a divorce done as quickly as the courts would allow it.

I knew that Klara had to read her mother's text – especially as it did show that Todor had covered us on all fronts and kept us out of the story. It would also let Klara know that her mother had entered that denial territory where her own fellow believers could be absolved of murdering an innocent woman and an unborn baby because, of course, they were doing what they believed to be God's work.

But on reflection I decided not to send it on to my daughter until after I'd heard that she'd arrived in Amsterdam and found somewhere to temporarily call home. If she read it now, she would be so enraged, so furious, that she might not sleep. She needed sleep.

It was strange passing across the LA city limits, telling myself that I would not be staying here much longer; that I was moving on as soon as that was possible. I got off the 101. There was a jam on the freeway – even though it was almost 11.30 p.m. Los Angeles: the endless tangle. All the money. All the promise. All the longing. All the failure. All the despair. All the sense of not being one of the rare chosen few. How jammed we all were in this town, crawling along in our lives at inches per hour.

I finally made it to my little street. And parked in front of the house that had just been shuttered against me

– and to which, according to a new text from Todor (*You home yet? Meant to say: keys for the new locks are under the flowerpot to the left of the front door*), I was now welcomed back ... by no one.

I got out of the car. I popped the trunk. I pulled out the bag with the clothes that Klara had bought for me. I dug out the duffel with all the money in it. I walked up our little drive. I lifted up the flowerpot and found the keys. Once through the front door I slid the shutter back down and locked it from the inside. I didn't know if Kelleher's people would be looking for me. I was taking no chances.

I turned on a light, figuring that with all the steel shutters down it would not be visible to the world outside. I walked down the hallway, past the living room and into the sad simple bedroom in which I had spent the last fifteen lonely years. I hated this house. Hated everything it represented. I was determined not to spend another night beyond this one here.

The trauma of the last few days – and the insane drive since early this morning – forced me into the shower and off to bed. Another bad night. I was up at five. I dragged myself back into the shower. I made coffee. I smoked two cigarettes. At seven there was a text from Todor:

They are letting me out today. Can I come by around 7 tonight? Happy to take you out to dinner.

I thought about this for a moment. I decided: there was still one last piece of Todor business to deal with. I texted back:

See you at 7 p.m. No dinner.

Not because I was busy, but because I would never sit across a table from Todor again.

The text I most wanted to read was awaiting me on my phone. Klara had landed safely in Amsterdam. Someone at a tourist information desk at the airport had given her the name of a student hotel a little way from the center but only fifteen euros a night … *and there's a tram and a metro right nearby and I can be at the Centraal Station in about ten minutes – see, I'm spelling it the Dutch way! – which puts me really close to everything. Tomorrow I'm going to start looking for a room to rent in someone's apartment. I am tired and still in what I guess could be described as weird-ass shock after all that went down. And I am missing my poppa terribly.*

I sent a reply, saying how relieved I was to hear from her and how I was on the end of my phone 24/7 if she needed me. *Please send me a daily bulletin of what's going on with you. Meanwhile take a deep breath and read the text I've just forwarded to you from your mother. It will, I'm sure, enrage you. I just felt strangely sorry for her when I read it. But try to see it as just further evidence of her craziness. And know I am with you always.*

I got dressed into the one suit I owned – a brown-striped job that looked around twenty years out of date and which I could just about squeeze into (I really was going to have to lose some weight and cut down on the smokes). Before forcing myself into the jacket I put on a white shirt and black tie, then, reluctantly, I got into the Volvo and let the GPS lead me to Mid-Wilshire and the offices of Flouton, Greenbaum, McIntyre and Milkavic.

The receptionist was expecting me. He was pleasant and quiet and respectful, asking if I needed water or coffee, showing me into a conference room with many framed photos; one of which was of Bernie Sanders and another elderly man.

'Two old rebels without a true power base,' came a voice behind me.

I looked up and found myself staring at a diminutive guy in his eighties, wearing a simple tweed jacket and a blue button-down shirt and khaki pants. He had round wire-rim glasses and the air of a retired professor.

'You must be Brendan,' he said. 'I'm Stanley Greenbaum. I started the firm with Elise's husband, Wilbur. And I was still close to Elise after his death. We are all beyond shocked by what happened.'

'It's ... terrible,' I said, unable to meet his eyes.

'It is indeed,' he said, just as an African American in his early forties, dressed in a severe black suit, came toward us.

'Brendan, very good to meet you. I'm Dwight Simplon and this is my associate Jennifer Cooper.'

She was in her late twenties, also wearing a black suit and edgy black glasses.

'It's very good to meet you, sir,' she said.

I was pointed to a seat at the conference table. Coffee was offered. And water. There was a plate of cookies. I wanted to eat them all, I was so tense. Stanley Greenbaum saw this, saying:

'I know this all must be an immense strain for you.'

'And for you.'

'From what Dwight told me: you expressed immense shock at the discovery that Elise left her home to you.'

'I can't accept it,' I said.

'Why is that?' Mr Greenbaum asked.

'Because I don't deserve it. Because she has a daughter.'

'Her daughter has been informed that you are the sole beneficiary of the apartment and that the rest of the estate is going to the Women's Choice Group with which she was associated,' Mr Simplon said. 'Her daughter has raised no objections.'

'That makes no sense,' I said.

'Ms Flouton has indicated that she does not want to contest her mother's will. We have a scanned statement from her attorney in New York, signed by his client that she accepts her mother's wishes ... and she pushed us to get all probate matters settled straightaway. This is why we contacted you so quickly. Because we were instructed to.'

Before I could ask why, Stanley Greenbaum's lips tightened as he said:

'Alison Flouton is a law unto herself. As such the apartment is yours and yours alone.'

Jennifer Cooper opened a file.

'The apartment has an estimated market value of around $880,000. As I think Dwight mentioned to you on the phone Mrs Flouton also left you $24,000 to cover two years' maintenance on the apartment. If you choose not to live in the Westwood apartment, the balance of that $24,000 is yours to keep. And the Volvo is yours to keep as well.'

'I won't be living there,' I said.

'That is, of course, your call,' Dwight Simplon said. 'After state taxes, the realtor's commission, transfer taxes and the like – and estimating everything on a price of $800,000 – I would estimate that, once a buyer is found, you will be receiving a net of around $650,000.'

I stared down at the table.

'I don't deserve it.'

Stanley Greenbaum came in here:

'Elise thought otherwise. And just to go off the record for the moment: though clearly we are not contesting that priest's version of the events that led to her death and that of the unborn child and those other two players in the tragedy ... what's his name again?'

'Father Todor Kieuchikov,' I said.

'He is your priest as well?' Mr Greenbaum asked.

'My oldest friend. Not anymore. But he is my wife's confessor.'

'That is an interesting detail – because we do know that he had connections to the anti-abortion group that your wife and her late friend belonged to. Nonetheless he has decided to tell a version in public of events that makes Elise the mastermind who got that desperately abused and pregnant woman away from that thuggish security man who worked for the deeply suspect Patrick Kelleher. We know for a fact that Elise never engaged in such derring-do. According to our police contacts, ballistics show that the security guard shot the woman Teresa Hernandez after she shot Amber and Elise. We understand and appreciate why this Father Todor fashioned his story to make it out that a dead woman was responsible for getting Amber away from that brute. It will hopefully protect everyone who was actually involved in this very brave endeavor.'

He looked directly at me as he said this. Was this his way of letting me know 'we have a shared secret here'? His next question indicated just how much he knew.

'You have a daughter, don't you?'

'A wonderful daughter. Klara.'

'Yes, we've heard all about her.'

A pause. My response was to simply nod an acknowledgment to Mr Greenbaum and his associates at the table – and one which said: I appreciate your absolute discretion here.

'May I ask,' Mr Greenbaum said, 'where Klara might be right now?'

I explained that she flew off to Amsterdam yesterday – and was hoping to set up a life for herself there.

'I'm very pleased to hear that she has made it there,' Mr Greenbaum said. 'It's a far saner option than our own country right now – and a safer one as well. We work with a law firm over there who know all the buttons to push when it comes to helping someone get work and get settled. So with your permission –'

'That would be fantastic,' I said, knowing that Klara would be so pleased to have such help.

'Consider it done,' he said.

I kept staring down at the table. I had a question to ask that still ran against everything I was raised to believe, but I still needed to ask.

'I want to divorce my wife. Can you handle that sort of thing for me?'

'Of course we can,' Dwight said. 'Jennifer is one of our family law specialists.'

'I want this done quickly and fairly. I know what I want to offer her. I will do so on a "take it or leave it" basis.'

'Let's talk it all through after this meeting,' Jennifer said, 'and get things in motion.'

'Thank you.'

I then asked if they had heard anything about the whereabouts of Amber. Stanley Greenbaum said:

'According to our law enforcement contacts she's still under police guard – but she was transferred down to Palm Springs after it was clear that, given the damage caused by the shooting, she had to have an emergency hysterectomy.'

'Oh my God,' I said.

'As has been announced around the media the great Patrick Kelleher is taking care of everything to do with her future. Because, of course, his bodyguard got her pregnant. Did Amber talk to one of you about the father ... the *actual* father?'

A long silence – in which I knew he was waiting for me to say something. Now it was my turn to stare down at the conference table. I chose my next words with care:

'All I will say is this: if her silence isn't bought Amber has a story to tell.'

'And if it is bought?' Stanley Greenbaum asked.

'She still has a story to tell.'

*

Todor arrived at my house at exactly 7 p.m. His right arm was in a sling and there was a heavy shoulder bandage protruding from the loose Hawaiian shirt he was wearing. He looked pale and exhausted and very much on edge.

'Right on time,' I said.

'I didn't want to keep you waiting.'

'I wanted to see you for one and only one reason,' I said.

I reached behind me and lifted up the duffel bag that Ricky brought along with him. The bag filled with money. I tossed it at Todor's feet.

'It's all there. Not a dollar taken from it. You can give it back to your "CEO" with my compliments. Not that it will stop him having me gunned down if he wants to do that.'

'Where's Klara?'

'Hiding far away from here.'

'There's no need for her to hide.'

'Stop acting naive, *Father.*'

'No harm will come to either of you. In fact, given all that went down, the man in charge is very grateful for your ... *discretion*. As long as that discretion is maintained ...'

'What? He won't kill us?'

'There's no further danger, Brendan.'

'Does the CEO know that Klara and I were there?'

'The story spun is the story that has been accepted by everyone.'

'Bullshit.'

'Why are you trying to further complicate a *very* complicated situation?'

'Because you're still not answering my question.'

'Yes I am. And now ... the matter is closed.'

'How lucky for all of you. I presume you're still getting the huge payoff promised to you?'

Todor stared down at the floor and said:

'I'm carrying on my parish life as normal ... until the time is right for me to announce that I am taking early retirement.'

'The perfect cover. Because disappearing now would have people wondering –'

'Can I come in?' he asked.

'No.'

'Can't we sit down and try to –'

'No, we can't.'

'Why?'

'Because three people and a baby are dead thanks to you.'

'That's not fair.'

'Yes, it is. You did a deal with the Devil. You accepted his money. You set me and my daughter up by lying about my wife dying. You forced us to drive you and his bodyguard thug and that lunatic Teresa to the place where the girl was being hidden. It was all your handiwork, Mr Man of God. Now you're getting your big retirement payoff, your money. And now you are going to fuck off out of here. But before you do, you are going to pick up that bag and take it out of here.'

'The money is yours, Brendan ... with more to come. I did promise you two hundred thousand.'

As he said that he leaned in toward me. That's when I spat right in his face. He reeled in shock. He looked like he wanted to take a swing at me. But he stopped himself. Perhaps because he saw that I was ready to rearrange his face; to pound him to a pulp. Without even stopping to wipe my spittle off his cheeks he made a dash for the door, the money bag still at my feet. I hoisted it and followed him out onto the sidewalk, tossing it right out into the street. A UPS truck was barreling right toward the bag. Without thinking Todor dashed out and grabbed it, jumping back just before he was sideswiped by the van. The driver swerved and yelled out at him:

'Fucking idiot.'

Back on the curb Todor gripped the bag against him, like a parent who had just scooped his child out of the way of an oncoming vehicle – and realized that he'd been microseconds away from calamity. That bag was now one of a true box of horrors that he would tote behind him forever. I slammed the door, knowing I would never see Todor again. But before it closed in his face I did manage to hiss out one word as he vanished into the heat of the night:

'Murderer.'

Elise's funeral was held ten days later. She had been born and baptized in the Episcopalian Church and wanted her sendoff from the world to adhere to their rituals. The university chapel was the place chosen. All pews were packed. A bishop officiated along with two priests. A choir sang the Anglican Ritual – their version of the Mass. It was a sound so pure, almost divine, that I kept thinking: I'm hearing some version of the voice of God. Elise's coffin was a plain pine box, lightly varnished. I imagined she'd had written into her will the instruction that she was to be put into the ground in something basic, not at all fancy. Between the prayers and the scriptural readings, two people talked about Elise's life and work. Stanley Greenbaum was the first. He spoke about Elise's progressivism, her need for serious political engagement, and her long marriage to Wilbur.

'It was a great love story which, like all great love stories, weathered difficulties and somehow managed to find even greater strength and commitment in the wake of great doubts. As Wilbur once told me, one of the many things he admired about Elise was that she never believed there were actual answers to life's huge questions. Only more questions. And the idea that, "in a world ridden with cruelty and hate, we really do have to do best by each other". That was the great moral duty we owed not just society at large but most of all ourselves.'

The other speaker was her daughter Alison. I'd seen her earlier, greeting people as they arrived. She was, like her mother, a tall, slim woman. Perfectly made up. Perfectly in control. I saw the man sitting next to her. Older. Equally very tall and immaculate. Looking like he wanted to be anywhere but here. During the prayers and the readings and the eulogy he was busy messaging on his cell phone, using an open hymnal to mask the glow. The thing was: Elise's daughter never once leaned over and told him to show a little respect for the woman in the coffin – and acknowledge the terribleness of the occasion – by turning off his fucking phone. She stared straight ahead, rigid, holding it together. Only when it was her turn to speak did her guy finally put down the phone. She mounted the stairs to the pulpit. She had a single piece of paper in her hand. I could see her take in a sharp steadying breath. She stared out briefly at us, then started to read out loud:

'Even when we were politically on other planets – which we were almost all the time – even when we disagreed furiously about the state of our country and the world at large, I always knew that my mother's love for me never wavered. Even when my take on things – especially economic and social – drove her nuts. Even when I called her a "relentless do-gooder" and someone "who believes that she can fix everything and everyone ..."

'The hardest thing to get your head around when someone close to you dies – especially a parent – is the realization that the conversation is over; that I will never hear Mom's voice again. All those terrible ideological exchanges we had; the times we fell out for weeks – like a really angry exchange we had when I defended supply-side economics and Mom called me a Gilded Age capitalist ... all that seems to be the height of absurdity now. Mom ... she was a much better person than I am. She cared passionately about the fate of others. She was – I see this now – genuinely good. And tough as hell. And relentless in her belief that we can all better ourselves. Maybe she had a point. Maybe we do need to be kinder. Especially to each other. Maybe I never understood how fortunate I was to have a mother as remarkable and upstanding as my mom. When my dad died a couple of years back Mom read at his funeral the following poem by Edna St Vincent Millay. Trust Mom to choose something by a crazed 1920s Greenwich Village beatnik feminist on the terrible unfairness of death. I looked it up again the other night. These final words are worth quoting again now:

Down, down, down into the darkness of the grave
Gently they go, the beautiful, the tender, the kind;
Quietly they go, the intelligent, the witty, the brave.
I know. But I do not approve. And I am not resigned.

There was sobbing in the chapel as Alison finished speaking. As she returned to the front pew she stopped and put her hand on her mother's coffin. For a moment it looked as if she was going to break down. But all eyes were on her – and she knew that. Which, I sensed, kept her fiercely in control. She bowed her head and kept it bowed as she walked back to her place. Had she looked up she might have seen her guy with his own head bowed – as he'd started texting again on his phone.

An hour later, after Elise's coffin was lowered in the ground and we all turned back to our cars, I felt a hand on my arm. Alison was in front of me.

'I asked Stan Greenbaum to point you out to me.'

'I'm so sorry,' I said, extending my hand. 'She was … remarkable.'

I saw her eyes fill up, her bottom lip tremble.

'So … you got our home,' she managed to say.

'I didn't want it. I told Mr Greenbaum that I didn't want it. Say the word and I will sign it all over to you tomorrow.'

'But she wanted you to have it as much as she wanted me *not* to have it. Because she figured I have more than enough. Which, on a certain material level, I most certainly do. Whereas . . .'

She glanced around, looking for her fellow. He was standing not far from the hearse that would return empty to the funeral home. He was on his phone, deep in a conversation that seemed to be turning heated. Alison made eye contact with him. He waved her off, gesturing that this was an important call, then showing her his back. She bit her lip again. Out of nowhere I heard myself say:

'You can do better. You deserve better.'

Her eyes went wide. She regarded me with cold contempt.

'Who the fuck are you to tell me that?' she hissed.

'I'm not your servant, ma'am. Stop acting as if the house boy has said something out of line. I was your mother's friend. I cared about your mother deeply. And I know how much she loved you. Despite –'

Alison lowered her head and began to sob. When I tried to put a steadying hand on her shoulder she shrugged me off.

'I'll never get over it,' she whispered. Then, with a fast shake of her head, she tossed away that moment of pure truth, pure grief ... and slipped back on her mask of control.

'I gather you're selling the apartment,' she said. 'I hope you use the money well.'

'Believe me I will.'

Many days later, in the conference room of Flouton, Greenbaum, McIntyre and Milkavic, I found myself seated between Jennifer Cooper and Dwight Simplon. Opposite us was Jorge Suarez. He was a local attorney – and someone I knew from church and who very much had Father Todor in his ear. He'd arrived to represent Agnieska. I'd been asking her for a face-to-face meeting for days. After all these years together, there was no way that I was going to inform her of my intention to leave the marriage by email or text. I wanted to speak directly to my wife.

But she chose not to meet. When I sent several text and voice messages asking if we could perhaps have a coffee or lunch somewhere 'to talk things over' her response was silence. After a week of trying to get in touch with her, I called Jennifer Cooper and asked if she could intervene.

'Of course. Give me her sister's address and we'll send a courier over with a letter informing her that you are filing for divorce and asking her and her legal representative to meet us here at a mutually convenient time blah blah blah.'

'I wish she'd just agree to meet. I hate doing this by letter.'

'The reason she refuses to talk with you,' Jennifer said, 'is because she knows you want to leave her; that it is now definitively over between you. You told me how she reacted to all that happened in Twentynine Palms – and how she denied that her pro-life friend was in any way responsible. She is now also refusing to face the fact that your marriage is over. A couriered letter, I'm afraid, is the only way forward. With your permission, I will point out that if she or a legal representative doesn't respond to our request for a meeting, we will simply begin divorce proceedings in the Superior Court of Los Angeles. Are you okay with that?'

I said nothing. I just nodded agreement.

The letter had the desired effect – and now Jorge Suarez was opposite us in the conference room, apologizing for his client's absence, explaining that she was 'feeling a bit under the weather'. Jennifer then explained that I was putting the following offer on the table – but that this was a non-negotiable offer: the house to be signed over to Agnieska and a one-off payment of $200,000 in lieu of alimony or any other sort of 'spousal support'.

Suarez smiled a smarmy smile and said that, as it was clear I had come into considerable money, the offer was not acceptable – and he was going to demand a full disclosure of the sum I had inherited and would be seeking a fifty/fifty split. Jennifer was fiddling with a pencil as Suarez came out with this threatening statement, laced with considerable arrogance. Jennifer suddenly snapped the pencil in two and slammed it down on the table. That took Suarez aback. Then in a low voice – filled with indignant menace – she informed him:

'How dare you? In fact, since we are not in court here and nothing is being recorded, let me rephrase that: how *fucking* dare you? Your client was part of a violent militant anti-abortion group whose leader was responsible for several deaths, including that of an unborn child. We have reason to believe that your client is borderline mentally unwell. I advised my client not to offer her much. My client is a generous and decent man. More than generous. Your client will have a mortgage-free house and a significant sum of money. If you dare – I will repeat that, *dare* – to go greedy and mercenary on us, I promise you that (a) the offer will be withdrawn by 6 p.m. tomorrow evening, and (b) I will become merciless on my client's behalf. We will offer next to nothing and we will argue that this woman deserves nothing. And if you think I am angry now – angry that you dare try to gain more for a woman with terrorist connections – because her political mentor and best friend, Teresa Hernandez, was just that, a terrorist – wait until we are in a court of law. Do you get that, Counsellor?'

Suarez looked like he had just been pummeled. He was wide-eyed and genuinely speechless. Then he made a bad mistake. He turned to Dwight and said:

'If we might be able to have a calm word alone … ?'

'Why alone?' Dwight asked. 'Because my associate is a woman? Are you also implying because she is a woman she can't be calm, reasoned?'

Suarez realized he'd just blown it. Dwight narrowed him in his sights.

'You've heard my associate's offer. Take it or leave it. I promise you: if you don't take it everything my associate told you will not just happen … it will *very much* happen. As our business is done here, I respectfully ask you to leave.'

Suarez stood up, genuinely shaken. He turned to Jennifer.

'I meant no offense.'

'Yes, you did,' she said.

He was gone moments later. When the door closed behind him Jennifer put her face in her hands and said:

'Fuck, that felt good.'

Suarez left at 12.35 p.m. according to the clock on the wall. He knew he had just under eighteen hours to accept our offer or face Jennifer's considerable wrath. She called me around five that afternoon to inform me:

'It's all over, way before the deadline. Your offer has been accepted.'

'I'm pleased. I had no appetite for a fight. Just one last thing: tell Suarez that if my wife ever wants to meet me the door is open.'

But she never got in touch. And that was fine with me.

Flouton, Greenbaum, McIntyre and Milkavic also did excellent work on Klara's behalf, putting her in contact with a lawyer in Amsterdam who, upon discovering that she had a degree in social work, found her a job working in a shelter for newly arrived refugees. They were even able to get her a temporary Dutch work permit as she applied for residency status. Klara and I spoke almost every day on the phone. She now had a room in a shared apartment in 'a cool, but still mixed area called the Jordaan'. I told her about being left Elise's apartment, the settlement I was making with her mother, and the fact that $200,000 of the money – when the apartment was sold – would be put into a trust for her.

'That's not necessary,' she said.

'Elise would have wanted you to have a share of this. She really rated you. And thought you were insanely brave. Her daughter has plenty. Just as I know she'd approve that I am ensuring your mother continues to have her bills covered and that she has the house.'

'With Momma getting all that I'm insisting you keep the rest for yourself.'

'And I am insisting otherwise.'

'My Poppa the Philanthropist. But it won't leave much for you to live on.'

'It's more than enough money to get me out of LA – which is what I want to do now. To get out of here forever.'

'I can understand that. You get your passport yet?'

'Another four weeks. As soon as it is in my hand I'm on the next flight over to see you. Meanwhile I'm doing a road trip.'

'Anywhere interesting?'

'Flagstaff, Arizona.'

'You're kidding me. What got you thinking about that place?'

'Was googling interesting, inexpensive places to live out west. Flagstaff came up. A real change of scene. Maybe even cool.'

'You don't do cool, Poppa.'

'But maybe I can do Flagstaff.'

Snow. That was a surprise. Arizona – the desert state. Red sand. Cactuses. And yet in Flagstaff – altitude 6,900 feet – once winter hit the snow hit as well. My first winter there was a deeply white one. A blizzard slammed down on the town just a few days after I got there. I checked into an old-school downtown hotel; a place that looked like it belonged in the 1950s and had rooms that were small and a bit on the old-fashioned side, but which had a decent bed and a little kitchenette. I did a deal with the guy on the front desk. Four hundred a week – including parking – for the first two weeks. Even though I had some money now I was not going to be stupid with it. Property was not cheap here. You could buy a small 700-square-foot condo for around $250K. Beyond my budget. I was going to find something for under a thousand a month. Already furnished with the bed and sofa and easy chairs in place. A place I could rent on a six-month basis. I didn't want to put down roots. I didn't want to buy into anything for the moment. I wanted to be able to cut and run when the mood took me.

Downtown Flagstaff was indeed hip. An old western town, all renovated. Cool shops. Cool bars. Cool coffee places. A bookstore. An old movie theater turned rock-and-roll concert hall. I kept thinking: this is Klara's scene, not mine. Then I also started wondering: but why shouldn't it be mine?

I slept well at the Hotel Monte Vista. I liked the old-school decor; the view of the hills in the distance. I liked waking up one morning and discovering that almost half a foot of snow had fallen overnight. I had arrived in Flagstaff dressed for Southern California and the heat of Phoenix. Now I had to go out and buy a down jacket and gloves and snow boots and heavy socks and a scarf and a knit hat. Once in footwear that kept me warm and a parka buttoned up against the freezing temperatures I wandered around Flagstaff, dazzled by the way the town had been turned white. I even lost my way in residential back streets, liking the Old West neighborhood feel of it all.

Around an hour into my walk the snow started again. I stared up, noticing the way clouds were shifting across the winter sky, how light broke through only to then be snuffed out. At that very moment Elise came back into my thoughts – as she did most hours. How she talked about people who think they've 'found the light' yet often follow the worst among us into darkness. How her coming into my life had changed it for the good. How she was, for me and so many others, an actual source of decency and possibility in a very bleak world. And then ... that very American need to settle arguments with guns. Now ... *now* ... all I could wonder: was she my one chance at light within all the terrible darkness of now?

I blinked up at the swirling snow. I felt tears. Snow. My first time seeing it since all those years back high up on an electrical pole among tall trees. What a wonder snow was. A real sense of purity, of bleaching away the mess of life. It muffled the noise of the world. It seemed infinite. For a moment or two anyway.

A sudden wind made the snow do somersaults in the sky. A year from now I would find myself – a man twenty-seven pounds lighter than he was when he arrived here – on the same street corner, having just knocked off work as an electrician in the Flagstaff school system. It was a job I found my second week here; a job I took to have something to fill my days ... along with the three nights a week I was handing out meals as a volunteer at a shelter for the homeless. As the snow came down that winter afternoon I would hear a *bing* on my phone. A text from Klara – still in Amsterdam, where I visited her every six months. She was continuing to work with refugees, getting more fluent in Dutch, dating a guitarist in a local rock band named Pieter. To Klara, Amsterdam was now home. But she was still an Angeleno at heart – and on that snowy morning I had a message from her. Telling me:

Go to the LA TIMES website now!!!

I did as instructed. And read a flash at the top of their page:

'*Breaking news – a well-known Beverly Hills Catholic priest, Father Todor Kieuchikov, was gunned down early this morning as he left his residence to visit a parishioner. According to LAPD Homicide Detective Michael Moran: "This murder bears all the markings of a contract hit. As our investigations are ongoing, we cannot say anything further at the moment.*"'

I reeled as I absorbed this news. I messaged Klara back:

My God …

Her message in return:

God had nothing to do with it. Nor did He want to intervene. But I am pretty damn sure that the CEO did. Which is why I will not be coming back to LA anytime soon. And why you mustn't show your face again there for a very long time. That asshole priest should have vanished immediately with all the money offered to him.

I texted back:

He probably thought: disappearing right after all that went down might have raised suspicions. And he believed that, having told the world the story his people told him to tell, he was safe.

Klara's response:

He thought wrong. The man with the money has had the last word.

But that 'last word' moment would be twelve months from now in that mystery we can never truly see; that mystery called the future. For now … this here and now … I was just a sad, still-shaken man in a town not his own, watching the snow do cartwheels in the sky. And suddenly having the urge to get into the car I inherited

– the car that belonged to her – and race out of town. Why this need to drive somewhere, anywhere? Especially on a day when driving was not a smart idea? Grief has its own strange logic; its own way of sending you down roads you never knew existed before.

Like this two-lane blacktop heading north through a deep forest. It opened out into a wide expanse of prairie, whitened by still tumbling snow. I found myself fighting back more tears, pushing the accelerator right down to the floor and thinking: *if I hit black ice and go into a fatal skid, so be it.* Just as I also knew that to accept that fate would be to give my daughter a sorrow that she would never shake and that she did not deserve.

I slowed down.

But my reduction in speed – from almost 90 mph to 60 – did not come soon enough. Because suddenly, pulling out from behind a cluster of trees, there was a highway patrolman on my tail. With his blue lights flashing and his siren now blaring.

I pushed down on the brake. I signaled and pulled over. I was going to turn off the ignition but feared losing heat. I shifted into park.

In the rearview mirror I saw him walk toward me. White. Chunky. Young. He knocked on the window. I hit the button. It rolled down.

'License and registration,' he said.

I handed them over.

'From Los Angeles?'

I nodded.

'You're a long way from home. What brings you out here?'

'Having a break from the world.'

'Carrying any weapons?'

The question threw me – especially as it was delivered in such an offhand way … and deliberately designed to unsettle me. Which it did.

'I own no weapons, sir.'

'Then why were you driving fast?'

'Wasn't thinking.'

'Because you're on the run from something?'

Again the tone was light, almost jokey. I knew that he was playing head games with me. Perhaps because he had nothing better to do out here.

I looked up. I met his cool gaze.

'I was driving fast because … because a friend died. And I was upset. And not paying attention.'

'How did your friend die?'

'She died … of natural causes.'

'And that gives you the right to go twenty miles over the speed limit?'

'I made a mistake, sir.'

'Indeed you did. Nice car.'

I stared right at him, looking directly at the number on his badge, taking it down in my head, committing it to memory, ready to call Dwight or Jennifer tomorrow and have them proceed with an official complaint. The cop saw what I was doing.

'Eyes forward,' he said, his voice still quiet.

'Yes, sir.'

But I still had his number in my head.

Silence. I could see that he was sizing up the situation.

'What do you do back in LA?'

I kept my eyes focused straight ahead. And said:

'I'm a philanthropist.'

'What's that?'

'Someone with enough money to help those without money.'

I could see him taking that in. I could also see him thinking: *if what this guy says is true – if he is a money guy – I am well and truly fucked.*

'You wait here,' he said.

'Yes, sir.'

I watched him in the rearview walk back to the car. I saw him pick up his phone and lift up my license and registration documents and call in the details. I saw him waiting for a response. I saw a bully becoming increasingly anxious that he might have veered into 'end of career' territory. I saw him reach behind him in the car and fish around for something in the back seat. In that instant I reached for my phone and punched in his remembered badge number. Then I tossed the phone onto the passenger seat. The cop came back up into a proper sitting position, a can of Coke now in his hand. I could see him checking if I was still looking ahead. I could see him reach for his phone. He had a brief exchange with whoever was on the other end of the line. His lips tightened. He ended the call. He sat behind the wheel, tapping my documents against his hand, trying to figure out his next move. Then he got out of the car and came walking back towards me. He knocked on the window. I rolled it down. He handed me my documents.

'Next time, sir, don't drive so fast.'

'Understood, sir.'

He regarded me for a very long time.

'You're free to go … even though I know you're hiding something.'

I kept my hands on the wheel, but still turned my head and met his now troubled eyes.

'I'm hiding nothing,' I said. 'I'm just like everyone today. I'm scared.'